GEMINI KEEPS CAPRICORN

Signs of Love #3

ANYTA SUNDAY

First published in 2017 by Anyta Sunday,
Contact at Bürogemeinschaft ATP24, Am Treptower Park 24, 12435 Berlin, Germany

An Anyta Sunday publication
http://www.anytasunday.com

Copyright 2017 Anyta Sunday

Cover Design: Natasha Snow
Gemini and Capricorn Art Design: Maria Gandolfo (Renflowergrapx)

Content Editor: Devil in the Details Editing
Alpha reader: Teresa Crawford
Line Editor: HJS Editing
Proof reader: Labyrinth Bound Edits

All rights reserved. This publication may not be reproduced without prior permission of the copyright owner of this book.

All the characters in this book are fictional and any resemblance to actual persons living or dead is purely coincidental.

Warning: This book contains sexual contact and a main character who takes cluelessness to a whole new level.

For Morry,
my beautiful Gemini cat.
I didn't know this would be your last story.

I need to espresso love by whatever beans necessary.

Chapter One

A long, heavy groan filled his single dorm room. It sounded like a heated sexual encounter, and Wesley Hidaka wished it were. At least *that* burrowing cry yielded orgasm, unlike the groan he'd expelled against page 335 of the never-ending *Civil Law Throughout the Ages*.

In the light of his desk lamp, Wesley banged his pulsing head against the coffee-stained pages, the edges of the book cutting against his forehead.

Apparently, papercuts trumped the eternal suffering of studying civil law.

Excited murmurs of his fellow residents about to head into town and fake-ID their way into Glitter or Dash floated through the bottom gap of his door.

He wanted to snag Suzy and join them on the dance floor.

He thumped his head a couple more times and let out another groan.

Someone flushed in the bathroom next to his room. Five minutes later, the water still gurgled through the pipes.

Page 336.

Page 336, second paragraph.

Page 336, fourth paragraph.

Wesley pulled out a container of chocolate chip cookies he'd baked a few days ago. Crumbs landed atop the fifth paragraph, carpeting the swimming text.

Unable to focus on anything but the threat of fetid flooding, he restlessly pushed himself away from the desk and left his dorm room. Bright light glared off wooden floors and framed motivational posters. Even brighter light flooded the bathroom, making the giant vanity a treat to peer into.

Wesley stuffed his black wristband into his jeans pocket. Setting a determined jaw, he shoved up his sleeves and entered the corner cubicle. Face pinching, he opened the toilet tank and dunked his arm inside. He'd watched his resident assistant—RA—do this before. A quick fiddle and done.

Like a game of Operation.

Except instead of avoiding the guts, you prodded them until the toilet was fixed.

He tweaked a chain, and voila—

His fingers caught on something and stuck. HIS FINGERS CAUGHT ON SOMETHING AND STUCK.

Fixing the toilet by hand was bad enough. Getting eaten by one in the process?

Not the way he cared to go.

He wrenched his arm back so fast, he flew against the cubicle door, spraying water in a nice arc over himself and the dividing wall.

He'd given it a fair shot.

Time to find Lloyd.

If law had legs, it walked in the shape of their RA, Lloyd Alexander Reynolds.

He oversaw the third floor of Williamson Hall. Frankly, he was the only law-related topic that Wesley enjoyed studying.

Wesley leaned against Lloyd's open door.

Hunched over the computer desk, Lloyd pounded the laptop keys, pinching a celery stick between his lips. Unbuttoned shirt-sleeve cuffs flapped around his wrists. Hazel eyes tracked the lines he typed, and he stopped typing a beat to run his hand over his well-shaped head.

He dropped his fingers like he'd forgotten he had spontaneously and abruptly shaved the thick, sandy crop he'd sported yesterday.

Lloyd fiddled open a third button on his wine-red shirt. A slight depression kinked his brow—a badge of concentration and endearing grumpiness.

It always deepened whenever Wesley paid a visit.

"Wesley?" he said, staring at his laptop screen. "How long are you going to stand there?"

Wesley stepped inside the cozy single room. He paused next to Lloyd's desk at a framed "Persuasive Openers" poster. *I believe, I know, I'm certain.* "It is vital that you fix the toilet."

Lloyd stopped typing and used two fingers to remove his celery like a cigar.

Wesley continued, "How do you always know I'm watching you?"

"The smell."

"My excellent aftershave? It's oakmoss and citrus. Tonight, with a splash of eau de *toilet*."

Wesley sat on the corner of Lloyd's desk. "The flusher doesn't pop back up. It sounds like something out of my nightmares. You have to fix it."

"Wesley?"

"Yeah?"

Lloyd pointed the celery stick at him. "'Hey, Lloyd. How're

you doing tonight?' is a nice way to segue into a request from your RA."

Wesley batted his eyes and playfully swung his feet. "Hey, Lloyd."

"Wesley!" Lloyd said cheerily, making eye contact. "What can I do for my favorite third-year resident?"

"I'm your *only* third-year resident."

Lloyd stamped the celery end into a bowl of peanut butter and waited.

Wesley threw his hands up and sighed. "Fine. The toilet. It needs fixing."

"I'll look."

Lloyd popped open the last button of his shirt and shrugged out of it, exposing insanely toned abs in a tight tank top. With a nod, Lloyd left Wesley and checked the bathroom sandwiched between the storage closet and Wesley's dorm room.

Wesley followed him to the problem cubicle and lounged against the sink.

Lloyd side-eyed him. "What do you want?"

Wesley flicked a finger toward the malfunctioning toilet. "It splutters like the first time I tried to give head. I don't need to relive that tender, embarrassing memory on repeat."

Lloyd cocked a disbelieving brow. "The flusher has stuck since before you and I became dorm neighbors. At least two-and-a-half years."

"Fine. I'm trying to avoid my mother's wrath when she realizes I have to wear plastic bags on my feet."

Lloyd paused, observing Wesley's socked feet. "Why would you have to wear plastic bags?"

"Because it's winter, I can't afford my rent, and my landlord won't let me pay him in favors."

"In what parallel world is this?" Lloyd continued staring at Wesley's feet.

Wesley scrunched his toes. Black was a bad color for socks.

They made his feet appear small, but they were exceptionally average. He shifted against the sink, hoping to draw Lloyd's attention upward. "The one where I fail my law quiz tomorrow."

"Well, we can't have that." Focused on the man-eating toilet, Lloyd paid no attention to Wesley's hip thrusting. "But it'll only stay quiet until the next person flushes."

"You're the best."

"Yeah, yeah," Lloyd said, waving him off. "Go study."

Wesley slumped toward the delightful reading awaiting him. At the bathroom door, he changed his mind, pivoted, and leaned against the tiled wall.

Lloyd pulled out a tool kit from under the sink, jerking when he caught Wesley staring. "What are you still doing here? Thought you had law to study."

"Maybe I should study you instead. So I can fix it myself next time."

Lloyd drew out a wrench. "I'd like to see you try."

Wesley narrowed his eyes. "Because guys with pretty faces break more objects than they fix?"

"That's not what I meant."

"Sure about that?"

Lloyd leveled him a look of exasperation. "Very sure. You don't have a pretty face. And I've seen you stab yourself with a cake fork."

"I was expecting a teaspoon. People should make announcements when handing others excruciatingly sharp mini-tridents." Wesley sulked back to his room, only to back up three steps. "Wait. What do you mean I don't have a pretty face?"

Lloyd turned from the toilet and rolled his eyes. "That's what concerns you?"

"This face pulls, I'll have you know." *Pulls girls I mostly turn down.*

"Your modesty also draws them in, I'm sure."

Wesley choked on amused outrage. Lloyd always knew what buttons to press. "I could charm the pants off any guy."

"I wonder how I ever manage to keep mine on," Lloyd said dryly.

Wesley scowled at Lloyd's back. Maybe the toilet would eat him. "I'm leaving to study law now, you shaven-headed, statistic-munching giraffe."

Lloyd slowly turned, his gaze landing on Wesley, and yanked on something in the toilet tank. The gurgling water ceased. "Feel better now?"

"Like I've been reborn."

Lloyd moved to the sink, appraising Wesley in the mirror. "Still without a pretty face."

Wesley guffawed and hoofed back to his law readings. An entire paragraph later, he checked his favorite astrology sites.

He eagerly read his monthly horoscope. Since it was already November, he checked how accurate his yearly one had been—

"Yeah, that looks like a lot of hard law."

Lloyd's voice close behind him made Wesley jump. "I was taking a five-minute break."

"From all that hard work ogling me in the bathroom?"

His chair shifted as Lloyd rested his hands on the back of it. Wesley tipped his head back and looked at him upside-down. "You wish it was hard work. Though I suppose that shirt looks particularly good on you."

"What shirt?"

"Exactly."

"Get back to law."

Wesley swiveled his chair around and scowled at Lloyd, who was blatantly reading his email. "See, this is why we would never work out. Other than RA-student relationships being forbidden and you having an aversion to breaking rules."

"And that I'm seeing someone," Lloyd tossed in.

"I give that another week, tops. We wouldn't work because

7

you're a grumpy, know-it-all Capricorn. We have one of the worst compatibility matches."

A raised brow. "That so?"

"All the sites say we are not relationship material. That our sex would suck."

"It amuses me how thoroughly you've researched this."

"It saddens me I couldn't find a ray of hope." Wesley winked at him. "You're a few rooms down, which greatly appeals to my lazy streak."

"Even if I were single and you weren't my resident, I'd never be one of your flirty flings."

Wesley groaned. "Never say never, Lloyd. I want to prove you wrong—even at the expense of terrible sex."

Lloyd's gaze moved from Wesley back to his email. "Gemini," Lloyd read aloud. "Here is restlessness at its finest."

Wesley pointed a paragraph lower. "I prefer this description."

"Charming, optimistic, and full of irresistible exuberance? I think 'Your dual personality makes figuring you out a challenge' is the most apt." Lloyd folded his arms. "Another week, eh? Think my guy will get sick of me that soon?"

"No, you'll come to your stellar Capricorny senses and ditch him. You might preemptively shave your head, but you deserve better."

Lloyd ran a hand over his head. "I told you. All the men on my mother's side went bald by thirty."

"Are you thirty?"

"Twenty-four."

Wesley flicked a floppy bang out of his eyes. "And I thought I was the difficult one to understand."

"I want to get used to it."

"Your head's so shiny I can see my reflection." It wasn't really, but Wesley loved to tease.

"Sorry to break it to you, but there's a high chance you'll also end up bald."

Wesley leaned forward and whispered conspiratorially. "I have a plan. Shall I enlighten you?"

Lloyd whispered back. "Entertain me."

Wesley tossed all his thick black hair. "I'll use all this lusciousness to lure a Sagittarius, who will realize he loves me more for my playful personality. Then, when my hair falls out, it won't matter that I have a wonky head shape."

Lloyd snorted and stepped toward the door. "I fixed the toilet and put an out-of-order sign on the door until you're done studying." He tapped the Elvis Presley poster hanging on his door.

"How many posters of him do you own?"

"I have a legitimate crush on anything rock 'n' roll. If I could go back in time, I'd slip into twenty-four-year-old Elvis's bed."

"I suppose there's no accounting for taste."

When Lloyd left, Wesley refocused on his law text. He flipped the page, delighted that a diagram took up half the space.

After studying the diagram, he snuck down the hall to Lloyd's room. Hovering in the doorway, he hopped from foot to foot.

Lloyd set down the celery stick he had just tapped against his lips and sighed. "Let me guess. It's too quiet?"

Wesley gave him a sheepish smile. "Law is boring."

"Why do you study it then?"

"Doesn't look boring on my resume."

Lloyd shut his laptop, tucked it under one arm, and stepped into the hall. He locked his door and steered Wesley to his room. "I'll camp out in the hall and growl at you when you try to sneak away from your studies."

Wesley fiddled with his room key card. "You do have a good growly voice."

"Get back to your books."

"But your laptop is so shiny. It competes with your head."

"*Now.*"

Wesley backed into his room, fanning his face. "Yes, sir."

"Only half a year left," Lloyd muttered as he shut Wesley in.

Wesley sank into his chair, full of bright bubbly energy for . . . studying. As he turned pages, hallway conversations welled and ebbed as students approached Lloyd for advice. The gentle rhythm of Lloyd's typing lulled Wesley deeper into his work.

He had just finished a chapter when a conversation outside his door took a turn for the grumpy.

A familiar male voice spoke. Gavin from the fourth floor, the RA that loved micromanaging the other RAs in Williamson Hall. "Being a successful RA requires creativity."

"You mean like playing Guess the Secret Ingredient with your freshmen?" Lloyd said. "I hear anaphylactic shock is all the rage."

"It was a light reaction to strawberries."

"He moved home."

Gavin didn't seem deterred. "My students love the game nights I organize."

"I'm not hosting a shindig with you."

"Why not? It'll be a great way for students to show their friends and family all the fun they're having here in Williamson."

"Boy, oh boy."

"It's not a request, Lloyd. Our coordinator thinks it's a brilliant idea. Nicely showcases dorm life to prospective students during Open Week."

"Get Gemma to help."

"Our coordinator agrees that you need to participate more."

"I hate you."

"The basement should be big enough. We'll need a killer theme. And streamers and balloons, of course."

"Oh look, one of your students is waving for you."

"Where?"

"He popped around the corner to the stairwell."

Gavin's voice trailed off in the distance. "Email me a theme and a plan."

Wesley waited a few more seconds to be sure Gavin had left, then he tiptoed to his door and cracked it open.

Lloyd was hunched in front of Wesley's room, head bowed over his laptop. He paused his typing, waiting.

"Did I hear something about streamers?" Wesley asked.

Lloyd continued hacking at the keyboard. "Get back to your books. There'll be no streamers."

I think of you a latte.

Chapter Two

Wesley loved greeting his regular customers as he waltzed into Me Gusta Robusta. The delightful mix of personalities and backgrounds shared one commonality: they loved coffee.

Weaving through students and staff hunched over laptops, he high-fived Surfer Dude. "Hey, Americano."

"Afternoon, Wes."

"Cappuccino With Almond Milk!"

"Heya."

"Latte," Wesley said as he passed Mr. Preppy.

"*Skinny* latte."

Lippy Latte, is more like it.

Wesley waved off Rachel, whose shift had ended.

He rounded the wooden counter and poked into the kitchen. His close friend Suzy stood at the stove, a burst of flame searing off her eyebrows. She slammed a lid over the pan, cursing.

He propped a shoulder against the archway, crossed a foot over his ankle, and let out a delighted sigh. "Ah, the taste of burned bread and frustration. Now I'm home."

"Work, Wes," Suzy said, wiping her singed eyebrows with the back of her hand. "Agonizing work."

"That would be the law quiz I had today." That one hour had felt like five."

Suzy pulled a black apron from the hooks behind her and threw it at him. "I've faked my way through this job for two months. Tell me I can fake it until graduation."

Wesley tied the apron around his waist. "Has Hazelnut Latte with a side of talking-smack come in yet?"

"Your brother slipped outside to make a call."

Wesley slipped a pad and pen into the apron pocket. "I heard MacDonald's back?"

A dry female voice came from behind him. "And swore off sex for good."

"MacDonald!" Wesley spun around.

MacDonald—*Molly* MacDonald, but no one ever called her by her first name—limped around the counter gripping crutches. A bright pink cast stretched from her ankle, disappearing under a jean skirt. The pink clashed with her wavy red hair, and he was sure she'd chosen it on purpose.

He would normally crush her into a hug.

Today was no different.

One of her crutches fell and smacked against the checkered tiles.

"You'll wrinkle my shirt," she said.

"Good to see you, too." Wesley picked up her crutch and handed it to her.

"Has Avocado Ciabatta missed me?" she asked without inflection.

"He's taking a call."

"I'll sit in his favorite booth."

Wesley cracked her a grin as MacDonald click-clacked toward the corner window booth.

Suzy snuck out of the kitchen with an inspired wave of her

hand—the hand boasting an unfurling flower tattoo peeking out from her sleeve. "Thinking of a menu change. What do you think: orange pesto pasta or mushroom risotto?"

Wesley took a customer's order, then focused on Suzy as he frothed milk. "Which one better complements a seared eyebrow?"

She flipped him the bird.

"Orange pesto," he called after her as she retreated.

A familiar male voice cut over the din of the café. "What the hell are you doing in my booth, MacD?"

His brother Caleb stared down at MacDonald, arms folded. Like always, he wore a checkered shirt open over a plain T-shirt, jeans, and brown cowboy boots. His hair was much shorter than Wesley's mop, but they shared the same dark eyes and pouty mouth. Seeing them sometimes gave people pause; their grandparents were Japanese, and it showed.

MacDonald's lips didn't even twitch. "I like the view."

Caleb gestured to the empty window booth one over. "It's just as good there."

"I like watching the clouds shroud over you. Your eyebrows squish together like a long caterpillar. Makes my day truly special."

Caleb snorted and plunked into the opposite seat. "What happened to your leg?"

"That's not age appropriate," she said.

"I'm almost eighteen."

"You're in high school."

He rubbed non-existent stubble. "You're barely a year older."

"But infinitely smarter."

"Wes!" Caleb yelled across the room.

Wesley set two drinks on a tray, delivered a macchiato, and strolled over to his little brother. "What's the problem?"

Caleb dimpled. "This mature woman is harassing a kid."

"You love it, don't lie to yourself." MacDonald pulled herself up and Caleb steadied one of her crutches before it toppled to the ground.

MacDonald clip-clopped to the counter, calling over her shoulder. "Take five, Wesley. I'll indulge waiting customers in delightful conversation." She yelled out to Suzy. "Avocado ciabatta, pronto."

Wesley set down Caleb's hazelnut latte and took the warmed vinyl seat.

"I've only known her a month," Caleb said, "but she really gets under my skin."

"I see that. Just a sec." He caught retreating MacDonald's attention. "Tell Suzy I change my mind. Go with the mushroom risotto." Wesley's focus skipped to a guy walking into the café. For a second, he thought Lloyd was coming in for his usual dark roast, but it was just a regular hot guy.

Caleb leaned on his elbows and stage-whispered. "When you've taken your fill of man-ass, I'll be here."

Wesley rolled his eyes. "I was checking if he was—"

"Hot?"

"Lloyd."

Caleb glimpsed over at Not-Lloyd. "Aren't you searching for a new man in your life?"

Wesley sighed. "Not just any man. Not anymore."

"The One?"

"I have a dream of saying the words 'I love you.'"

Caleb snorted. "You haven't pulled out that line yet?"

"It's not a line. It's meaningful, and I'm saving it for someone special. Probably a Sagittarius."

"Good luck finding him."

Wesley leaned back against the sticky seat. "What's up at home? How's mom?"

"Same as always. Reads scripture like it's candy. Flirts with the pastor after Sunday service."

"Hates my guts?"

"Holds out hope for you yet."

She would be forever disappointed. Wesley steered Caleb's latte across the table and sipped. "Could have a touch less syrup."

"You'll have to talk to mom eventually. Gimme back my drink."

"How's school?" Wesley pivoted.

"She wants you to visit again."

"Ah, look. Your food."

A plate with ciabatta and avocado landed between them. Caleb dug in like he hadn't eaten in a week. "You're the best, Suzy." Through a mouthful, he said to Wesley, "How well is avoiding Mommie-dearest working out?"

"Beautifully," Wesley said, fidgeting with his wristband. When Caleb opened his mouth to reply, Wesley skirted off the bench and hurried back to Suzy and a bored MacDonald.

"Are we going dancing tonight?" Wesley asked, itching to release the tension hugging his muscles.

"Please," MacDonald said as Wesley changed the tunes on the iPad. "Watch you two go at it like frenetic dancing mimes? I'd rather be dead."

"Suzy?"

"If you count rock 'n' rolling with econ," Suzy called after him. "Professor Cooper is the best, but he won't let you half-ass an assignment."

"Professor Cooper?" Elvis's *Lawdy, Miss Clawdy* came on and Wesley moved to the beat. "First name Jamie? I think Lloyd is friendly with him."

He triple-stepped and pulled Suzy into a quick twirl. She laughed. "I gotta start lunch."

"Orange pesto pasta!"

Suzy smacked him with her dishtowel and headed into the kitchen. "How many times are you going to change your mind?"

MacDonald drawled. "Just as well we write our menu in chalk."

～

After eating a plateful of mushroom risotto and locking up Me Gusta Robusta, Wesley walked MacDonald and Suzy to the library. He wasted a few hours trying to concentrate on his own studies before giving up and heading back to the dorm.

He knocked on Lloyd's door, watching the man pound at his laptop keyboard. He wore beige chinos, a dark belt, and an unbuttoned navy shirt over a black tank top. A buzz of hair growth gave the RA a military facade.

At an acknowledging grunt, Wesley strode in, sank into a cushioned corner chair, and waited patiently for Lloyd to finish his sentence.

Lloyd swiveled to face him, and Wesley waggled his brows and rubbed his fingers together. Lloyd knew what he wanted. It was Friday night, after all.

Lloyd stared at him blankly. "How many this week?"

"Three."

"And still no boyfriend?"

Wesley sighed. "I have a problem."

"You do."

Lloyd pointed at the wicker basket of condoms. It sat atop a small bookshelf crammed with literary classics and books on personal management, motivation, and mathematics. Wesley slowly stood up, drifting a hand over Lloyd's collection of Rubik's cubes and twisty puzzles.

Wesley plucked a condom from the basket. "Glow in the dark. We're getting fancy."

Lloyd replied dryly, "Fancy is a suit and tie, and taking a guy on some dates first."

"I'm still searching for my Sagittarius. Or Aquarius. Or Leo—Leos work. Aries are great, too."

Lloyd peeled his eyes away from his laptop and shook his head. "Horoscopes aren't conclusive. They're touchy-feely mumbo-jumbo."

"Said by a true Capricorn."

"Don't forget to fill in the guest book."

Wesley unhooked the guest book from the wall, wrote in it, and slipped it back in place.

When he left the room, Lloyd breathed out audibly.

Wesley turned back around, tossing the condom up and down. "You'll have to tell me your birthdate eventually."

Lloyd approached the door, his desk chair swiveling behind him. "Is that why you're always eyeing my wallet?"

"Well, I'm not about robbing paupers."

Lloyd bored into him with intense hazel orbs. "You know I'm Capricorn. Why do you continue to hound me for my birthdate?"

"I want to know your precise level of stubbornness and pessimism. Maybe your moon sign gives you redeeming qualities." Air whiffed into his face and Wesley was staring at a closed door. "Or not."

He waited a few moments, grinning like the social lunatic he was starting to suspect he was.

A couple of first years chattered their way past him and into the stairwell.

Wesley knocked again.

Lloyd inched the door open a half-foot. "I'm only available to students with legitimate issues."

"I'm full of issues. I need another condom."

The door drifted open as Lloyd left to grab the basket. He tossed it at Wesley. "Go at it, Romeo."

Wesley fondled the condoms, stirring them around as he grinned broadly. "With vigor."

"Congratulate tonight's Juliet, would you?"

"On pulling all this thick-haired beauty?"

Lloyd shook his head. "On standing it long enough to get naked."

Wesley slipped the condoms into his pockets, thrusting his hips out and biting his bottom lip. "It'll be epic, off-the-charts sex."

"Because he's a Sagittarius?"

"Because he's not uncreative and afraid of sex anywhere other than the bed." Wesley waggled his eyebrows suggestively.

"It's what beds are for. I intend to use my back the next sixty years."

Wesley swallowed a laugh. "I pity the fool—oh look, here he comes."

Lloyd's boyfriend-of-the-month strode through the stairwell door. Wesley winked at Lloyd and backed down the hall, mouthing, "One week."

Inside his room, he threw the condoms into the top drawer along with dozens of others.

Thumping and groaning sounded from the next room. It wasn't Lloyd and his boyfriend, but it made Wesley think of them. What would Lloyd be like in bed?

Grumpy and demanding, probably.

Wesley strapped on some headphones and tossed himself onto the bed. Elvis's deep, sexy voice sang in his ears while his right hand popped open the buttons on his pants.

He studied the young, hot Elvis, who had one eyebrow lifted.

"I know you were a Capricorn," Wesley said, fisting his hard cock. "But I bet you were hot as hell between the sheets." He closed his eyes and jerked his dick, failing to get a good Capricorn hammering out of his head.

"No, no, never," he said through gritted teeth as he quickened his stroke. "Fuck."

His orgasm pulsed long and hard through his denial. He

threw an arm over his mouth and swore. "Never going to happen. My next guy will be Sagittarius. That's a promise."

SMOKE DETECTORS WAILED AT TWO A.M.

Wesley groaned, flipped onto his side, and covered his ears with his pillow.

"What Einstein left the stove on again?" came Lloyd's booming voice. "Right, people, you know the drill, everyone descend to the quad in an orderly manner. Do not use the elevators."

Wesley heard Lloyd banging on doors and ushering students outside. Most went quietly. A few complained Lloyd was being uptight.

"All residents evacuate. No exceptions. Period." A bang met Wesley's door and Lloyd jerked it open. "That means you and"—he glanced at the guestbook in his hand—"Glow-in-the-Dark too."

Wesley reluctantly swiveled out of bed. "He left already, forgot to sign him out. Where's your boy?"

"He only popped by to drop off my car keys. Then went dancing."

"So you didn't get lucky. That explains the mood."

"I'm on duty. Now up."

Yawning, he slumped toward Lloyd's silhouette in his boxers. Lloyd reached for the wall-hook beside the door and thrust a coat at him.

"You'll need it."

Wesley caught it and sank his feet into his shitkickers. "If I catch a cold over someone's crispy burrito, you're nursing me back to health."

Lloyd planted a firm, warm hand on Wesley's neck and

steered him toward the stairwell. "This stinks of Randy's rice. I'm gonna kill him. After following protocol."

PROTOCOL TOOK UNTIL THREE IN THE MORNING.

All one hundred residents over the four floors huddled in the wet quad "at least three hundred feet from the building." Suzy and an unimpressed MacDonald flanked Wesley under his trench coat they held over their heads.

"Remind me to wear sexy underwear to bed," Suzy said, lifting the sagging arm of his coat, her flower tattoo almost smacking Wesley in the face. "I've been caught twice in my cotton undies."

MacDonald hummed. "Great place to score. You could go at it in the puddle over there."

Thank God for his friends. They made the hour bearable. He winked at MacDonald. "How did anyone get close enough for you to have a sexual misadventure?"

After security officers found the blackened pot of Uncle Ben's rice—watch out, Randy!—the RAs were given the all clear.

MacDonald was the first to crutch her way back in, Suzy chasing after her roommate.

Lloyd took a beating in the rain. His soaking-wet boxers and T-shirt clung to him, but he stood gesturing his residents inside first.

Wesley splashed his way over to him.

Gavin got there first, bowling through his fourth-floor residents. "Seriously, one burned pot? Did you have to overreact?"

"Fire is not funny. There is no such thing as overreacting."

"It's the second time Randy's sent us to the quad. He's a disaster waiting to happen—you should send him packing."

"He's a good kid."

"I'm writing a report on Williamson and its RAs. You'd better get a grip on your residents."

Gavin stormed inside.

Lloyd sighed as Wesley walked up to him and held the trench coat over their heads. "That ditzy-assed doofus is officially banned from using the kitchen without supervision."

"Maybe I should talk to him," Wesley said.

"You wouldn't say the same thing?"

"Not to his face."

Lloyd side-eyed him. "Only shaven-headed, statistic-munching giraffes earn that privilege?"

Wesley held the door open. "How do you feel about warm cocoa?"

"Better if it comes with marshmallows."

It's depresso without you, sugar.

Chapter Three

Back in his dorm after Wednesday morning classes, Wesley halted outside the communal lounge. MacDonald slammed into his back, crutches flailing. He gripped the steel bar, steadying her.

"Why, yes," she said blandly. "Do break my other leg. This cast needs a companion."

"Do you hear that?" He poked his head into the lounge, searching for the origin of Lloyd's voice. "It sounds grumpy."

"You have the ears of a dog when it comes to our RA." MacDonald clipped past him and reached her dorm room. "I have studying to do. See you at work."

Another grumbling growl sounded from down the hall. Wesley rushed to the kitchen.

Lloyd jerked his head up from where he leaned against the counter, overlooking Randy frying up his lunch.

"Every day?" Wesley asked Lloyd.

"Every meal."

Randy flashed them an embarrassed grin. "Want any? I made enough."

Wesley grabbed three bowls. "Sure we do." No one said no to

25

a free, hot meal in a dorm. Even if there was a fifty-percent chance it tasted like charcoal.

Randy dished up, and they ate. In silence.

Lloyd prodded at his pasta, lips in a grim line. Curious, Wesley scored a glass of ice chips and began munching on them. Something that usually drove Lloyd insane.

"What's going on?" Wesley asked the moment Randy left. Leaving his dirty dishes behind, of course.

Lloyd sighed. "You were right."

"I like being right." Wesley set his emptied plate on top of Randy's. "What am I right about?"

Lloyd's phone rang, and a wake of air hit Wesley. When he blinked, he was alone in the kitchen.

He didn't mean to overhear the fight, but his feet had a mind of their own. And dammit, they wanted a stroll past Lloyd's room. Multiple times.

Also, it wasn't his fault the anger in Lloyd's voice carried. "Are you lying to me?"

"Maybe alternative fact-ing you?" boy-of-the-month said.

A dry laugh. "If you think Kellyanne Conway-ing me will make this better, you're one of sixty-two million idiots."

"Fuck you. Good luck replacing all this."

"I don't want someone who stepped out of *Vogue*. I want personality and principles."

At the sound of approaching footsteps, Wesley hightailed it back to the kitchen. He grabbed his glass of ice and his palm slipped over the condensation. He caught it a second before it fell and a half-second before Lloyd reappeared.

Lloyd eyed him as he picked up his pasta and heaped a forkful into his mouth. He watched Wesley swirl the ice in his glass and took another bite.

Wesley tipped the cool glass to his lips, and Lloyd spoke. "How much did you catch through my door?"

Ice slid down his chin. One punishing piece slid down his

throat and weaseled under his T-shirt. "What? I'd never." His breath deflated as he glared at Lloyd. "I don't have *any* principles. How'd you know?"

"You're blushing."

"Could be because it's a hot day."

"Or that I know you."

Wesley chewed on a piece of ice. "You do. You were also right about me being right."

A nod. "He only lasted another week."

"Not that, Lloyd. I'm right about you deserving better."

Lloyd paused, pasta teetering on his fork. He popped it into his mouth and chewed. "I want a nice guy who doesn't cheat and likes to go to bed early on a Saturday. Is that too much to ask for?"

"I'm going clubbing this weekend, you can come along and hunt for him if you want."

"Unless you mean book-clubbing, I dislike my chances."

Violet, a freshman girl in a study of green, flurried into the kitchen swiping at tears.

Lloyd pushed off the counter. "Violet, what's the matter?"

"She called me a slutty bitch. How was I supposed to know he was her boyfriend?"

Wesley shoveled ice into his mouth like popcorn. "What happened?"

Lloyd shook his head at him as he handed her a paper towel.

She swiped her face with it. "I can't share a room with her. I can't."

"Let's sit down and discuss this all together. And for the love of God," he said, whirling to Wesley, "stop crunching ice."

Wesley chomped down on the cube, grinning as Lloyd herded Violet toward reconciliation.

He followed, knocking on MacDonald's door so she didn't miss out.

"Why do I let you drag me to this idle gossip?"

27

"Because under it all, you love this stuff."

She didn't deny it but positioned herself on the other side of the lounge door, mirroring him. They peered inside, where Lloyd stood before two pouting girls sitting on the couch.

"We've been dating three weeks! She's seen me with him."

Violet sobbed. "Hanging out. Not humping."

Lloyd ran a hand over the millimeter of hair that had grown back. "Guys, let's search for common ground."

"Girls," one of them said.

"A figure of speech, excuse me."

Gavin purposefully trotted down the hall, a smug smile pulling at his lips.

This was about to get interesting.

Of course, Wesley's phone had to ring.

He reached for it as Gavin butted them out of the way.

Lloyd leaped off his seat and swiveled toward Gavin slinking into the room. "What do you want?"

"To be involved in this discussion."

"Go back upstairs. This isn't any of your business."

"It is my business when your girls fight on my floor. Jeremy is upset."

Lloyd groaned and cast a tired look at the two girls. "How many times do we have to say it? It's unwise to score the floor or screw the crew."

RA Gavin said, "The dorm is best off limits."

"Thank you, Polly. How about you grab yourself a cracker."

Wesley's phone was still ringing in his hand, and he slunk two steps down the hall and answered. "Wes, here."

"Mr. Hidaka. Why, it must be three years since I've had the pleasure of talking to you."

His spine prickled. He knew that voice from years of detention. "Principal Bontempo?"

"Calling from Sandalwood School regarding your brother."

"Caleb?"

"I'm unaware of any other Hidaka sibling. Caleb has too many unexcused absences. Your mother requested we ask you how your family can support Caleb. Can you be here in an hour?"

"Yes, but, what do you mean unexcused absences?"

"Truancy, Mr. Hidaka. You are familiar with the concept as I recall. Come in, and I'm sure we'll find a workable solution."

"What do you mean—"

"See you in an hour."

"But what—" His words were met with a dial tone.

He tried to call his brother but no one answered. On the second try, Caleb clearly declined the call. "What the hell?"

MacDonald snapped her head up at his raised voice. Even Lloyd and Gavin stopped bickering.

Wesley gawked at his phone like it was an alien. No way Caleb ditched school. He was the smart one who'd worked his ass off hoping the elite Treble School of Music would accept him. This had to be a mistake.

Lloyd planted steadying hands on his shoulders. Wesley gazed into concerned hazel eyes.

Someone murmured and Lloyd turned his head. "Cut that shit out, Gavin." He refocused on Wesley, thumbs rubbing warm circles under his collarbone. "Are you all right?"

"They've called me into the office."

"What happened?"

"I need to be across town within the hour. That's like, fifty minutes away by car, but I don't have a car. That leaves me the bus. Because the bus will surely be faster than the car." He absently searched his pockets for his wallet, but he'd left it in his room, hadn't he? "I should take an Uber. If it gets here quick enough, I'll get there in time."

"Hey, Wesley, deep breath there."

"I need to find my wallet. And grab an Uber—would you do

it for me?" Wesley pressed his phone against Lloyd's chest. "Tell them I need them here five minutes ago."

"I'd offer my car, but it's in the shop until the afternoon."

"You can use mine," MacDonald said quietly.

Lloyd snapped up her offer. "Thank you. I'll drive him."

Wesley spoke over the lump in his throat. "But you have a girl crisis on your hands. And Gavin."

The comforting anchor of Lloyd's hands slid off his shoulders. "Gavin, your wish came true. Reconcile the situation without me. Call Gemma to step in for me for the afternoon, would you?"

"Lloyd?" Wesley croaked. "Why did the school call *me*?"

Lloyd steered him to his room and found Wesley's wallet. He slipped it into his pocket. "Come on, let's find out."

WESLEY THREW HIS ARMS UP IN FRUSTRATION, GLARING through the windshield at His Almighty's supposed residence. "Of course!"

Lloyd turned the ignition a third time, and it stuttered again. "She'll warm up in a minute."

"She better go from 0 to 180 in ten."

"We'll get there on time." Lloyd patted the steering wheel, coaxing her to life.

Lloyd followed the directions of his phone's navigation. Wesley dialed his brother's number, ignoring Lloyd's concern and sympathy. So what, he'd called ten times and left three voice messages? Maybe Caleb would pick up his phone on the eleventh go.

Out of luck.

Wesley dropped his phone onto his lap. "We always talk. He tells me everything. Tells me *too much*."

"He'll be fine. He probably feels too guilty to face the music."

"There'll be a lot of music to face. He'll wish he were deaf."

Lloyd glanced at him, voice calm and controlled. "I'm sure he'll never pull a stunt like this again."

"That's the thing, though. It *has* happened before. Unexcused *absences.*"

At the red light, Lloyd patted his thigh. "We'll get there on time."

Warmth seeped through Wesley's jeans and his pulse stuttered. Then *he* stuttered. "Wh—what if he got a girl pregnant?"

"He hasn't," Lloyd said with frustrating assurance.

"How can you be sure the ditching isn't him being responsible?"

"You have a rather active imagination."

"What if he's taking time off school running around with this girl to doctor visits."

"Wesley."

"I'm serious."

Wesley stared out the passenger window as the streets slid by with aching slowness. He palmed his head. "That's why Mom asked the principal to deal with me. She knows about the illegitimate baby and has cut him out of her life."

"I'm sure your mom wouldn't do that."

"You've never met my mom. She's as private, conservative, and high-maintenance as the school we're inching toward." He looked at Lloyd. "What if Caleb, under all his outward snark, is alone? Worried? Desperate?"

The simmering warmth of Lloyd's hand left his knee as he changed gears. "He's got you. You're there for him."

Wesley sighed, thumping his head against the headrest. He lowered his voice. "He pissed me off growing up. Always mom's favorite. He's straight and therefore could do no wrong. I used to wish mom would get mad at him. What if I willed that into existence?"

He squinted skyward out the windshield, clamping his hands

together like he used to during school mass. "I take it back. He's a good kid. He's too young to lose his mom and become a dad." To Lloyd he said, "I'm a terrible person."

"You did what siblings do."

"Is that what you did to yours?"

"No."

"Which is it? Are you noble or I am I terrible?"

"I don't have siblings."

What? Wesley blinked at Lloyd. They had known each other for years. How did he not know this basic piece of information? And if he didn't know *that*, what else didn't he know?

"Not right now, because I'm in a state of panic, but there are some things we need to rectify."

Lloyd looked at him out of the corner of his eye, then shifted gears. "There are *a lot* of things we need to rectify, Wesley."

The approaching light turned yellow, and Lloyd—Mr. Capricorn-follow-the-rules Lloyd—stepped on the gas.

"On time. We're on time." Wesley caught his breath outside Principal Bontempo's office. With its polished bronze plaque and doorknob, the dark wooden door opened.

"A first for you, Mr. Hidaka," Principal Bontempo stood before him, shrew-eyed and gangly in his vacuum-tight suit. He shook Wesley's hand. "Perhaps you've learned how to tell time with the passing years?"

Such a delight was his former principal.

Principal Bontempo's hand stiffened around his, and Wesley followed his narrowed gaze to Lloyd a half step behind him. He dropped Wesley's hand.

"Come inside my office, Mr. Hidaka. Your friend may wait in the hall."

Wesley's neck prickled with angry heat. He glared at Principal Bontempo. God, he'd hated this school.

Just as well he'd grown a few more balls with the passing years.

"Actually, I would like him to join us."

"This is a family matter, Mr. Hidaka. I'm sure your mother wouldn't want your pals involved."

Okay. No, it was fine. He'd handle this. He wasn't sixteen anymore.

This wasn't him being sent to the principal's office for hooking up with Trevor Crace behind the chapel.

"He practically is family." He flattened his stare at the uptight principal. "We're engaged."

Lloyd gave a sharp intake of air, followed by a rough cough.

Wesley reached for Lloyd's arm and wrapped it around the front of his waist. He leaned back against a warm, solid chest. Breath stirred the back of his hair with a whisper that was along the lines of, "Boy, oh boy."

Wesley trailed his fingers over Lloyd's forearm to the back of his hand. Their fingers slotted together, and Wesley almost choked when Lloyd spoke, words sliding down his neck. "Principal Bontempo was simply being delicate about this private matter, honey."

Honey? Wesley's body trembled with the snort he suppressed.

"Now that he's aware of my faithful, undying support for my fiancé," Lloyd continued with a squeeze to his abdomen, "he's sure to invite us both in. We could tell him that funny story about my lawyer cousin suing his florist for a six-figure sum for discrimination."

Wesley stared the principal right in the eye, and Principal Bontempo cleared his throat. "Of course, you're welcome into my office, Mister—?"

"Alexander Reynolds."

Principal Bontempo's eyes lit up. "I do have to ask," he said delightedly toward Lloyd. "Are you related to Tabitha Alexander Reynolds?"

Lloyd hesitated. "That would be my aunt."

"Such a fine woman, from a fine family."

With a bounce in his step, he ushered them toward the plush seats at his massive Victorian desk. He sat in the larger, higher leather chair across from them.

Wesley hunched, resting his arms against the desk. "What is happening with Caleb? Why is he missing classes? Where is he now? Why did you contact me?"

Principal Bontempo opened a file and sorted through sheets of paper. "We contacted you because your mother thinks you'll have more chance getting through to him."

"Through to him? He's a smart kid. If he's missing classes, it's because something's happening at the school." *Or he got a girl pregnant.*

Pray to God, that wasn't it.

"The education received here is of the finest quality. Yes, Caleb was a smart boy with a promising future."

"Was?"

"Over the last two years, his grades have suffered. Solid, but nothing spectacular. The only class he does exceptionally well in is music."

"I don't believe that."

"Believe this: If his behavior doesn't change, he won't receive a letter of recommendation from Sandalwood to the Treble School of Music. Bear in mind, I have countless close contacts on their board of admissions who would accept an applicant based on my judgment."

A dry laugh huffed out of him. "Caleb deserves that letter. Even after our father died, he kept his grades up. He's written essays better than most graduates could come up with."

"His teachers have said he has shown exemplary work in past years. Perhaps that focus was a part of his grieving. Unfortunately, he lacks drive now. He's not good enough for a Sandalwood recommendation. Those are reserved for students who uniformly deliver superior work."

"What does Caleb need to get it?" Wesley said through ground teeth. Lloyd shifted in his chair, and his foot pressed in solid support against Wesley's.

"He might consider applying to another school."

Wesley shot out of his chair. This stupid school where students were only good enough if they molded to Principal Bontempo's vision. "That's not an option."

Principal Bontempo glanced at Lloyd. "I can offer one other alternative. I'll consider the recommendation if he aces all upcoming assignments from this year's core classes and doesn't skip a single class."

Principal Bontempo shut the file and rounded the desk. He opened the door for them.

"That's it?" Wesley said.

"This isn't detention. Leave when you please."

Wesley balled his fists.

Lloyd threw an arm around his neck and pressed firmly against his shoulder as if he sensed Wesley's urgent need to punch something.

"Excuse me, Principal Bontempo," Lloyd said evenly. "May we have a copy of his records and speak to his teachers personally?"

Capricorns were so on top of it like that!

Principal Bontempo peeked at his ridiculous antique pocketwatch. "It's lunch hour. You may try the staff lounge. I'll have a copy of his file by the time you leave."

Wesley stalked past his principal. Lloyd's arm dropped to the small of his back as Lloyd followed close behind.

"Mr. Hidaka?" Principal Bontempo said as they strode toward the staff room. "If he has so much as a sick day, the recommendation is off the table."

Bean thinking of you.

Chapter Four

Lloyd passed Wesley a drink and sat on the opposite booth. They'd spoken little on the drive back, giving Wesley time to scowl out the passenger window.

Instead of legging it to his room, he had beelined for the sports bar across the road from their dorm, returning only to hook Lloyd's arm and drag him over the road with him.

Lloyd leaned back against the buttoned leather, his gaze unnervingly patient.

"Nice school," Lloyd said.

"Isn't it?" Wesley said, unlocking his phone. "Grand Victorian buildings. Award-winning gardens. Pruned sticks up their asses."

Wesley called Caleb. At the dial tone, he grimaced. Then left a message. "Here's how it's going to work, Hazelnut. You're going to stop whatever Highly Important Thing you are doing and get your ass to Me Gusta Robusta in time for my shift. Trust me, you don't want to keep me waiting."

He hung up and tossed the phone onto the pockmarked table.

Lloyd peered at him over his glass.

"What?" Wesley asked.

Lloyd set his drink on a coaster. "It's impossible to imagine you in a shirt, tie, and blazer."

Wesley blew his bangs out of his eyes. "Please."

Lloyd leaned in, lowering his voice. "A fiancé should see these things."

Wesley picked up his drink, hiding a smirk. "This Jack and Coke isn't strong enough."

"That's because there's no Jack in it."

Wesley slid the glass over the table. "There's the problem."

Lloyd swiped the drink and returned to the bar.

Wesley text messaged Caleb's friends asking where his brother was.

Lloyd came back with his drink. "Alcohol can kill you."

"Is that why you never go clubbing? Are you afraid my good friend Alcohol will sneak up and whack you over the head?"

"Good friend?"

"More like acquaintance I see on special occasions and say a fleeting hello to on weekends." Wesley cradled the glass, sighing. "And who becomes my confidante when my brother cuts so much school that Principal Bontempo gives me a talking to."

"What's your plan with Caleb?"

"Find him, first."

His phone dinged. One of Caleb's friends had answered his message.

Why don't you call Mrs. Hidaka?

Wesley groaned. He suspected it was all leading to this, and he dreaded it.

Lloyd looked pointedly at him and his phone, eyebrow lifting.

"That was my cue to do this." Wesley grasped the Jack and Coke and downed it.

"Jesus."

"My mom's favorite word." He dialed home. Three rings and she picked up. "Hey, it's me. Wesley."

A slight beat passed, and then her pinched voice cut down the line. "Thank you for clarifying that. I'd never have recognized the voice of my eldest son."

"Mom, I'm calling—"

"Because you missed talking to me? When was the last time? A year ago?"

"Your fiftieth."

"Right. When you brought that young man around for my birthday dinner. Are you still together?"

"No. I didn't bring him. He was one of your guests. We hit it off." Briefly. In the bathroom.

"Is there any other . . . boyfriend?" his mom asked.

Wesley glanced across the booth at Lloyd, who was watching him. Tiny goosebumps flared over his stomach where Lloyd had squeezed him earlier. "Um, no. Look, Mom—"

"I'm glad to hear it. I'm glad to hear *you*, Wesley."

He closed his eyes. "Why did you ask Sandalwood to call me?"

"Caleb is going through a phase. Like you did at his age."

Wesley gripped his empty cup, wishing more Jack and Coke minus the Coke would materialize. "That 'phase' was me discovering who I am. And there's no boyfriend because there's a Lloyd. My fiancé. Mr. Bontempo loved him."

Lloyd spat a mouthful of soda across the tabletop. Wesley gave him a sheepish grin and threw some napkins over Lloyd's puddle of surprise.

His mom remained quiet, absorbing the information. Wesley shifted in his seat, waiting for her response and avoiding Lloyd's gaze. "You're still young, Wesley. Don't rush into anything."

God, she knew how to make him feel on top of the world. His voice cracked. "Where's Caleb?"

"He doesn't come home anymore."

Wesley almost dropped the phone. He jerked his shoulder to pin it against his ear. "He *what*?"

Lloyd mouthed, "Are you okay?"

Wesley jerked a finger at his empty glass and then the bar. Lloyd set his partially empty soda in front of Wesley.

"I thought he was staying with you?" Mom said.

"What did you do?"

"Now, Wesley, that's unfair."

Unfair? This was coming from experience. "What happened last time he was living at home?"

"We had a ridiculous conversation about him studying music at Treble. Like no other college would be good enough. Sometimes I regret buying him a flute. If your dad were still alive . . ."

If Dad were still alive, he'd have gone to every damn flute lesson. Every impromptu performance. He'd have convinced Principal Bontempo to write that recommendation. "How long hasn't he been home?"

"A month."

"And you never contacted me?" Why hadn't Caleb told him?

"You've made it clear how you feel about that."

She had a point. Still.

"At least he answered my texts," she continued. "He says he's not ready to come home yet."

"How do you know he's safe? Shit. I need to find him."

His mother's voice dropped to a desperate whisper. "Wesley? Please, I want at least one of my sons to come home."

～

Wesley drove *a touch* over the speed limit. A pale-looking Lloyd white-knuckled the overhead handle, wondering aloud why he suggested Wesley drop him off at his car on his way to meet Caleb.

His brother hadn't shown up at Me Gusta Robusta for his shift, and Wesley had roped Suzy into covering for him.

He careened around a corner, speaking loudly in the direction of his phone that flew off the dashboard onto Lloyd's lap.

Lloyd clasped it against his groin, stopping it from sliding between his legs. He lifted it up between them.

"Caleb . . . Hazelnut . . . Avocado Ciabatta. I'm not just a pretty face." Wesley glanced over the top of the phone at Lloyd, who gave an exasperated shake of his head. "I logged into your Google account and tracked you. I'm on my way, and I am *not* thrilled about our next conversation."

Caleb had the teenage balls to sound indignant. "You hacked into my account?"

"I used the password you gave me in case aliens kidnapped you."

"When did I ever—"

"Halloween. We ate questionable lollipops and spent the night spilling our deepest darkest secrets."

"Right." He heard his brother grinning. "The night you told me you wanted to be taken by a teacher or your—"

"Stop talking! I did not mean what I said." Wesley didn't need to look up to see the hefty lift of Lloyd's eyebrow. Heat throttled his neck and he shifted gears, overtaking a granny. "Nothing we said that night was true."

"Which makes it a real mystery how you logged into my Google account."

His brother was too smart for his own good. "I have more important questions."

Stuck behind a tractor, Wesley checked his mirrors, then swerved to the right.

Lloyd balked, lowering the phone to his thigh. Wesley leaned toward it but kept his eyes on the road. You know, safety and all that.

"Have you knocked up some poor girl?"

A snort came down the line. "Not unless the condoms I steal from the stash in your dorm room are past their use-by date."

Lloyd cupped the speaker. "Stash, Wesley?"

"Leftovers. Some boys tire easily. I have too much stamina." Lloyd croaked, then removed his hand. Wesley continued chatting with Caleb, "Please tell me this has nothing to do with girl troubles."

"No girl troubles. Unless you count Mom."

"Watch out for the cyclist!" Lloyd dropped the phone to steer the wheel.

Wesley calmed him with a wink, jerking the car left. "You'll have to speak up, Hazelnut," he called toward the console where his phone had landed.

Lloyd's flat look made Wesley gulp. "Actually, my fiancé is wielding daggers with his eyes. I'll see you in twenty."

∼

AFTER DROPPING LLOYD AT HIS CAR, WESLEY DROVE TO A sketchy area downtown and puttered past rundown warehouses used for weekend markets.

His brother sat on the curb in front of an abandoned factory, backpack squeezed between his thighs, polishing his flute. Wesley parked in front of him.

Caleb paused, then continued buffing the silver buttons of his instrument.

"What are you doing out here?" Wesley stood in the gutter in front of him, flipping the car keys.

Caleb shrugged and jerked a thumb toward the factory. "Hanging out with some guys."

He clamped a fist around the keys. "Oh, God. You sell drugs."

Caleb stopped cleaning his flute and rolled his eyes. "I don't have anything to do with drugs. Except for those lollipops, which came as a surprise to both of us." He started packing his bag.

"Why didn't you tell me you were having issues at home and Sandalwood?"

"Why didn't you tell me you got yourself a fiancé?"

"You know I don't have a fiancé. I was joking. Sort of. I mean, it's my RA."

Caleb perked up. He dimpled and everything. "Lloyd? Are you two finally a thing?"

"Yes, *Lloyd*. What other RA would it be? It's just . . . Principal Bontempo and Mom both managed to show their disdain for—wait, what do you mean 'finally a thing'?"

Caleb zipped his swollen bag. What did he have in there? Half his wardrobe? "You two hooking up was a matter of time. Practically the entire Williamson Hall waged bets on it. Must be a thousand bucks in the pot now."

"What?"

"Can you loan me thirty? I was positive Lloyd would make you wait until next summer when it wouldn't be against the rules. MacD is gonna milk this."

"This is ludicrous."

"Dude, you flirt with Lloyd all the time."

"Well, I know *that*. But . . . it's harmless fun." Wesley helped his brother to his feet. "Besides, he's made it clear he doesn't want a fling with me, and I'm on board with this decision, because we'd be bad in bed."

Caleb lifted a brow, then dropped it again. "I don't want to know. You're not taking me back to Mom's, are you?"

Like there was any point in that. Caleb knew how to scale out of his bedroom window. Wesley had taught him. "Let's head back to the dorm for now."

"In that case. Actually, in any case"—Caleb plucked the keys from Wesley's hand—"I'll drive."

"MacDonald won't be happy if I let you drive her car."

43

Caleb snorted. "Trust me. She'd be thrilled."

Wesley clambered into the passenger seat and shoved Caleb's weighty bag into the backseat. "If you love driving so much, you should buy a car. To afford a car, you need a job. To land a job, you need to ace school and earn a Sandalwood recommendation into the Treble School of Music."

Caleb grinned as he checked his rearview and adjusted it. "Wes, you know I love you, right?"

"Especially when you want something. Or are trying to avoid talking about this school drama."

Caleb's grin widened. "I don't love driving so much as I like living."

"You're evading again. I don't drive *that* badly."

Caleb shook his head. "You should never have been given a license."

"Yet I have one. Because I studied the road rules and passed all my tests. It opened so many doors. Doors I want open for you, too."

"I've worked hard on all my assignments, and I'll ace the exams. I practice hours of flute every day. I am good enough for Treble."

"I believe you, but Principal Bontempo—"

"God, I hate his name. I mean, music is beautiful. Bon, nice. Tempo, rhythm. But there is nothing nice or rhythmic about that fool."

Wesley laughed drily. "Mr. Nice Rhythm decides whether the college of your dreams accepts you or not. And, Hazelnut? The forecast isn't great."

∼

Wesley told him.

To his credit, Caleb listened with minimal interruption. "And ditching, Hazelnut? Why?"

Caleb rubbed the steering wheel. "My grades and my music should be enough."

"Make sure you don't miss another class."

Caleb's lips flattened.

"Caleb?"

"Fine. I've been late to class sometimes because I've been going to rehearsals."

"Rehearsals?"

"I'm in the orchestral accompaniment for Charlie Johnson-Brown's newest production."

"Johnson-Brown's? Like, the famous director, Johnson-Brown?" At Caleb's excited nod, Wesley yelped. "That's incredible!"

Caleb's eyes crinkled. "It is, right?"

"Hell, yeah!" He toned down his excitement in favor of a reproving look. "But you need that recommendation."

"Trust me, I'll work my butt off for it. Promise not to tell Mom about the play?"

"Don't miss another class and I won't have to."

They tapped their knuckles in a brotherly pact.

Wesley leaned back in his seat. "He never smiles, you know."

"He totally does. Just not when you're looking."

"Ah, no."

"Ah, yes."

Wesley dug around for his phone. "I'm sorting this out right now." He called Lloyd, picked up on the first ring. Actually, he picked up *before* the first ring. How was that even possible?

Capricorny senses at play, perhaps.

"Tell me you're alive," Lloyd said with a little too much sincerity. Caleb overheard, apparently. His brother laughed.

"Cars are huge metallic beasts. Don't tell me they'll fold at a scratch or three."

Caleb snickered and called into the phone. "He's safe. I'm driving."

Wesley gave him an appropriately dirty look.

Lloyd's voice hit his ear at the same time his seat belt tickled his throat. "What did you call for, Wesley?"

"Do you smile?"

"Most people do."

"But, I mean, do you smile in my general vicinity?"

"Randy, put down the spatula and step away from the pan." Someone squealed, and Lloyd grumbled. "I've got a dreamer to talk to."

"Be nice," Wesley said.

"I'm always nice." Lloyd hung up, and Wesley shook his head.

"I don't like Randy's chances."

Caleb's lips twitched. "I like yours, though."

I want to kiss your steamy grin.

Chapter Five

On the third floor in Williamson, Wesley's dorm neighbors, Danny, Charlie, Steve, and Randy gathered around the pool table in the lounge, doling out colored bands. A giant blow-up die, each side a different color, and a padded ball rolled across the plush green. "We need at least two more players."

Randy was quick to point out that Wesley and his brother had slipped into the lounge.

Wesley dropped Caleb and his bag onto the couch and gestured for Randy to throw over some elastic bands for his made-up dorm game.

MacDonald, sitting in an armchair across from them, skimmed the book she was holding. Her gaze slipped from Wesley to Caleb and back again. It could have been a trick of the fake chandelier light, but Wesley saw a twinkle in her eye.

"Your keys," Wesley tossed them to her and she cleanly snagged them before resuming her reading.

Wesley plopped down on the couch, snapping three orange bands onto his wrist in front of his favorite black wristband. He counted down to one, and right on cue, MacDonald snapped her book shut. "You had us worried, Hazelnut."

"Awww," his brother said. "Here I didn't think you had it in you, MacD."

She pinned Caleb with a scathing look that Wesley felt to the funny bone. He cuffed Caleb's wrist with three blue bands, but Caleb's gaze stayed rooted on MacDonald in a combination of fascination, fondness, and fear for his life.

Smart boy, his brother.

"What's more important than attending classes?" she asked bluntly.

Caleb glanced toward his backpack. "Playing my flute."

"Your flute?"

"I'm pretty good at it, if I say so myself."

She shook her head, hauling herself onto her good leg. "Boys and their ridiculous hormones."

Caleb straightened. "Wait. What?"

MacDonald grabbed her crutches, and Caleb was on his feet. "I mean it. Let me show you."

"Keep that thing zipped up."

"MacD!"

MacDonald hobbled away, and Caleb stumbled after her despite the rogue sponge ball that almost hit him. Randy tackled him for a wristband. When he let go, Caleb went hurtling through the door.

Wesley laughed, toed off his shitkickers, and swung himself lengthwise on the couch. A ball flew across the room, bounced off big Danny's shoulder, and hit a startled Lloyd in the face as he entered the room.

Lloyd caught the ball and the boys froze. His gaze moved to Danny, then skipped over Wesley to narrow on Randy. "You again?"

"Seven bands to win," Randy said, blushing. He slid to Lloyd's side, and Lloyd stared him down as he peeled the ball away.

"Don't break anything," Lloyd warned.

The game unfroze.

Lloyd rested his elbows on the couch and peered down at Wesley. "Why is your brother banging on MacDonald and Suzy's door?"

"Because he's in love."

"With which girl? Because one option seems saner than the other."

"We Hidakas tend to fall for the ones we shouldn't."

A ball hit him against his chest and Wesley grabbed it. Danny slunk to his side and held out his hand for a wristband. Wesley pulled one off and handed it to him. Large dice rolled across the carpet, landing on blue. Wesley could either take a shot at Randy, who wore a blue band, or make for his brother.

"Pull me up," he said, throwing his arm out toward Lloyd.

Lloyd shook his head, then clutched Wesley's hand and drew him into a sitting position.

Wesley kept hold of Lloyd. He had a good-sized hand and a perfect grip.

He let go, swung off the couch, and carried the ball into the hall. Lloyd followed closely, his body radiating warmth.

Caleb leaned against MacDonald's door, a wry smile on his face. "You have to come out sometime."

Wesley tossed the ball and smacked Caleb on the nose. "Yes, stalking her door is your smoothest move."

Lloyd made a deep throaty sound. "Must run in the family."

In a crazy trust-exercise move, Wesley flopped back and Lloyd caught him against his chest with a surprised *hwuff*. "Aww, Lloyd." Wesley nuzzled against Lloyd's neck. "You say that so fondly. I think you like my incessant need to bug you during RA hours."

Lloyd's poker-faced expression begged Wesley to take drastic action. Anything to glimpse Lloyd's thoughts. Like maybe lick the column of his throat.

As if reading his mind, Lloyd steered Wesley upright. "You keep things interesting."

"So, when's the wedding?" Caleb asked, hooking the ball under his arm.

"We were thinking summer. On a lavender farm. Have you messaged Mom that you're okay?"

"You didn't want to tell her the good news yourself?" Caleb was peeking over Wesley's shoulder, eyes bugging, nicking his head for Wesley to turn around.

Wesley whipped around but caught only a twitch of Lloyd's lips before they settled back into a flat line. This was a game now, was it? *Bring it on, Lloyd.*

Wesley kept one eye trained on Lloyd, who moved down the hall toward a beckoning resident.

Wesley missed Lloyd at his side, but he'd find an excuse to chat with him again. He always did. To his brother, he said, "Tell Mom you're safe."

Caleb fiddled with his phone, then shoved it back into his shirt pocket. "Done."

"Which of your friends do you usually crash with?"

Caleb rocked back on his cowboy boots and gave him a guilty shrug. When the ball popped out from under his arm, he swatted it back into his grip. "My friends' parents don't think it's acceptable that I stay over on weekdays."

Wesley's face pinched into a frown. Then it dawned on him why Caleb had asked to be picked up in front of an abandoned warehouse. "You said you were hanging out with some guys!"

"Hanging out. All night long, Sunday through Thursday. Taking turns stoking a barrel of fire."

"Caleb!"

Caleb pouted. "I haven't lost Hazelnut privileges, have I?"

"Where do I even start?" Wesley wanted to run to Lloyd and ask him to fix this. Because Lloyd was magic at fixing things.

Anything. Everything. "Why didn't you come here? Why didn't you tell me?" He stopped and sniffed the air. "Where do you shower?"

"School gym." Caleb slumped against MacDonald's door and tossed the ball up and down. As though he had thought the plan through. As though he was about to stubbornly defend himself. "I didn't want you to blame yourself for always telling me leaving home was the best move you ever made."

Ignorance was bliss. If only he could get it back . . .

"The guilt's worse now, Hazelnut," he murmured.

Caleb used the sole of his boot against MacDonald's door and kicked off. "It's not all your fault."

"Jeez, thanks."

Caleb tossed him a wide, playful grin that mirrored Wesley's. "It's not like you're allowed permanent guests in your room."

"We're allowed visitors until 10:30, and as long as I tell the on-duty RA someone is staying over, it'll be okay."

"Yeah, for overnight visitors not exceeding two nights a week."

"How do you know this?" Wesley eyed him suspiciously. "Have you been engaging in lengthy discussions with Lloyd on rules and regulations?"

Caleb barked a laugh, then stopped. "I wouldn't say engaging."

Wesley glanced toward Lloyd who was telling off a resident. Even if Lloyd liked him, he didn't like him enough to break rules.

"We'll figure out a plan," Wesley said as much to himself as his cocky-runaway brother.

Wesley's phone buzzed as Randy yelled, "Orange!"

Caleb threw the ball, smacking Wesley right against the heart. With a snorting laugh, Caleb stripped Wesley of his last band.

He scowled, miming kicking Caleb's ass. Then he read the message from MacD:

Have your brother and his "flute" left yet?

And one from his mom:

Thank you, Wesley.

You mocha me horny.

Chapter Six

Over the next seven days, Caleb crashed with him in his single bed. He shuttled Caleb to the kitchen and showers when Lloyd wasn't around. Pretending to say goodbye, he signed him out in the evenings before smuggling him back into his room.

After a week of making up excuses, eyes-in-the-back-of-his-head Lloyd had caught them. Wesley said Caleb had stumbled back for the night because he had a drinking problem and had lost his keys.

That had earned Wesley the death stare—from Lloyd *and* his brother.

If Wesley violated house regulations one more time, Lloyd would have to write him up.

He and Caleb couldn't fuck it up again.

They had to be super sneaksters.

They'd managed once, last night. Here was to hitting it out of the park twice in a row . . .

Wesley peered into the hall from the stairwell, Caleb hovering in his shadow. Lloyd was leaving the kitchen after Steve, halfway between them and Wesley's room.

Lloyd clapped a hand on Steve's shoulder, making the boy jump.

"How about cleaning your dishes?"

"But I have a date."

"At ten-thirty? On a Wednesday?"

"A study date?"

Lloyd directed him back into the kitchen.

Wesley snuck into the hall, whispering to Caleb, "He's in full Cap mode tonight. Be twinkle-toed."

"I'll be light as a motherfucking fairy," Caleb said a bit too loud. At Wesley's glare, he lowered his voice. "I'll follow you."

Wesley inched to the kitchen door. "Stay here. I'll laugh when it's safe for you to slink past."

Dishes rattled in the kitchen, and Wesley rounded into the room with a winning smile.

Lloyd was drying Steve's dishes. He glanced at Wesley, then did a double take.

Wesley hurried to the other end of the kitchen. *Let Lloyd's gaze follow me there.* Wesley made a show of grabbing a glass and filling it with ice. He peered around the open freezer door. Lloyd had stopped drying and was eyeing him.

Wesley broadened his smile.

Lloyd set the plate and dishtowel on the counter, and Steve took his opportunity to exit the kitchen. If he noticed Caleb glued to the wall outside, he said nothing.

"What?" Wesley said, senses prickling under Lloyd's watchful eyes.

"You're looking like you need more fiber in your diet."

An aborted snort came from the hall.

Lloyd's brow shot up. "Wesley?"

Wesley donned big innocent eyes and lifted his cup. "Ice chip?"

"I'm suddenly reminded," Lloyd said, "last night, I went to the bathroom—"

"Good story!" He glanced over Lloyd's shoulder and laughed. Ice jiggled against the glass.

Lloyd closed his eyes in exasperation as Caleb slinked past in the background. "I could have sworn I saw your brother stumbling in. But then I distinctly remember telling you that if you got caught sneaking guests in without following protocol, I'd be forced to write you up. He must have been a figment of my sleep-addled mind."

"The addled mind thing. Definitely."

Caleb's head popped into view at the door and he made a swiping motion—

Wesley palmed his pocket. He hadn't given Caleb the damn room key. "Shit!"

Lloyd dropped his chin to his chest. "I don't want to turn around, do I?"

"Could you hold this for a moment?" Wesley pressed the cold glass into Lloyd's hand and slunk past him. "Oh, and wait right here for me?"

Lloyd huffed, but he waited like the patient Capricorn he was.

∽

EARLY SATURDAY, WESLEY RETURNED FROM A SHOWER TO HIS brother stretched out on the bed, reading through sheets of music, a dorky smile plastered on his face.

"It's visiting hours. It's safe for you to whip out your flute," Wesley said. Hearing his words, he shuddered. "MacDonald has ruined everything."

"You can say that again," Caleb muttered over a mouthful of cookie.

"You're putting crumbs in my bed!" There were always crumbs in his bed. Still . . .

"Seriously? I saw you eat a crumb of stale cracker that you picked from between your pillows."

"It was a chip. Sour cream and onion." Wesley shut up, glaring in that brotherly way. "How are your other assignments coming along?"

"You know."

"I don't. That's why I asked."

A pillow hit his face. "It's fine. Everything except one math assignment. But like, hardly anyone in class did well."

"You have to."

In the background, Wesley heard Gemma's voice—she was in charge this weekend since Lloyd had two days off. What he did on his time off, Wesley wasn't sure. Something structured, no doubt. Maybe shave his head again.

Wesley had a light-bulb moment. "I think I can help!"

"You sound so surprised."

Wesley sent his brother a withering look. "Are you staying here again tonight?"

"You're not the only one with plans. Though mine involve rehearsals, not getting busy."

Actually, Wesley wanted one night of decent sleep. His back was killing him. "Yep, real busy. This mattress is going to get broken in real good."

Caleb hooked his ankles and linked his fingers under his head. "I'll head to a friend's. Though I don't know why you don't get busy in Lloyd's room."

Wesley grabbed Caleb's feet and yanked him over the edge of the bed. "Out."

"But you said I could practice my flute—"

"Gah. Stop talking about your flute!"

"Hey, I held back from saying I wanted to put on a show for you. Give me some credit."

"Out, out, out!"

Caleb sank into his cowboy boots, grabbed his bag and music, and trudged to the door. "Are you sure?"

Wesley narrowed his eyes.

Caleb trotted out.

∾

Wesley baked triple chocolate cookies with a hint of cinnamon.

He grabbed a plateful and made for Lloyd's room. He waited out of sight while Diana complained about being written up for having alcohol on premises.

"Not saying you can't have fun. Just don't do it in your room where it becomes my responsibility. Also, it's Monday."

"Sure, but can't you let it slide? Just this once?"

"I can't. It'll set a precedent."

"Other RAs are way more lax."

"Other RAs get fired."

Gripping the plate, he cursed his stowaway-brother situation, which was nearing two weeks.

Two weeks of little sleep, of monitoring Caleb's homework progress, of shadowing him to school.

He did not want another call from Principal Bontempo.

"Wesley?"

Wesley blinked. Diana was sulking down the hall to the common area.

Wesley popped around the corner and into Lloyd's room. "How'd you know I was waiting?"

"Sixth sense."

Wesley inhaled the baked aromas. "You smelled the cookies, didn't you?"

"You're the only one who bakes."

"I brought you some."

Lloyd leaned back in his chair, pen pinched at the corner of his mouth. He withdrew it. "What do you want?"

"Why would you assume I want something?"

"Please."

Wesley set the cookies on the wedge of free space on his desk. "Triple chocolate cookies."

"With a hint of cinnamon?"

"Of course."

Lloyd stood and shut the door.

Wesley stared at Lloyd's swiveling chair, catching his breath at the sudden block of warmth that shifted at his side. His neck prickled.

"How long have we known each other?"

Wesley flicked at a random page of scribbled statistics that drooped over the side of his desk. "I don't know. Two years, three months, and about seven days?"

Lloyd sunk back into his chair with exasperation. "Forget thirty. If I had kept my hair, it'd have fallen out from these conversations."

Wesley's lips twitched. "That's because Capricorns can't stand us Geminis."

Lloyd leaned forward, resting his forearms on parted knees. "How long have we been friends?"

"What does that matter? We're fiancés now."

"Yeah, well, before that. How long were we friends?"

"Would we call it being friends?" Wesley asked.

"That's up for debate."

Wesley made a quick calculation. "Two years, three months, and five days—you yelled at me the first day."

Lloyd huffed. "You dropped a box of law books on my foot."

"You should have worn shoes."

"I came from the shower."

Wesley remembered all that wet flexing muscle like it was

yesterday. "Then blame all that smooth skin and muscle and the clefts in your marble stomach."

Lloyd whispered conspiratorially, "you get that with exercise."

Wesley whispered back, "or are born blessed, like me."

Lloyd squinted at him. "In all the time we've been friends, you've never baked my favorite cookies."

"We're fiancés now. Besides, they're just cookies."

"You hate cinnamon."

Wesley shifted. "If you're gonna get all Sherlock on me . . ."

Lloyd swooped the cookies off the desk and held them away from Wesley's reach. "Tell me what you want. I'm feeling generous." He picked up a cookie.

"Wait." Wesley gasped. "Did you just smile?"

It had disappeared too quickly.

"When have you ever seen me smile?"

Strike him with a defibrillator, because his heart might have stopped.

Lloyd raised a brow and took another bite of cookie. Crumbs trickled over his jaw and landed on his lap. Lloyd brushed them off, and Wesley cleared his throat. "I want you to tutor Caleb through a gruesome math assignment."

"Knew these cookies were too good to be true."

"I'll make you another batch when finals hit."

Lloyd eyed him, then cocked his head. A pondering hum seeped out of him. Didn't that kick Wesley's heart back into gear?

"Why do you care so much? What does it mean to you if your brother doesn't get into Treble?"

Wesley picked at his wristband. "He's wanted to go since he was a kid."

"You're not telling me everything."

Wesley glared at the damn plate of cookies and spoke like an auctioneer. "If he doesn't get in, Principal Bontempo is right:

he's not good enough. If he doesn't get in, it means Mom's right: he'll have to be someone else."

"Be someone else?" Lloyd asked.

"Do something else. He'll have to do something else." Wesley snapped his wristband hard enough to bruise. "Will you help Caleb with math in return for more cookies?"

～

"I have to plan the January Open Week party with him," Wesley told Suzy at his next shift at Me Gusta Robusta.

"Sounds fair to me. His element for your element."

A snort came from MacDonald working the till. "Anything with Lloyd is his element."

Suzy lifted the vegetable she was peeling and pointed at him in amusement. "Yes, when are you going to radish him?"

"Ravish."

Her brow quirked, and she stared at the radish in her hand. "I'm pretty sure it's radish."

MacDonald and Wesley exchanged a mortified glance, then she said bluntly, "It's good you're not here on a humanities scholarship."

"It's ravish," Wesley said, a tiny smirk pulling at his lips. "When am I finally going to *ravish* him?"

"Asking yourself these questions is a step in the right direction, Wes." Caleb slapped a hand on his back, then winked at MacDonald. "Did you like what you walked into last night?"

Wesley shook his head at Suzy. "Avocado Ciabatta. The quicker he eats, the faster he shuts up about his instrument."

He escorted Caleb to a table and served him a hazelnut latte.

"What was the answer? About the radishing of Lloyd?"

"Is it not enough he's a Capricorn?" Wesley slid into the booth and stole a sip of Caleb's sweet coffee. "The Child of the zodiac and the Elder? That's just fucked up right there."

Caleb's face contorted.

Exactly.

Wesley continued, "We make the worst pairing. He's a stickler for rules—you know how much I hate rules. And Capricorns want a relationship of substance."

"I see your conundrum." Caleb took back his coffee. "Surely there are Cap-Gem exceptions?"

"Since when have I ever been anything exceptional?"

"Again. Good point."

Wesley kicked him under the table. "But let's say I hit my head, wake up from a coma, and don't remember how grumpy he is, and then decide I want him to be my boyfriend. He's plainly said he won't go there with me."

"You haven't trained those flirty muscles for nothing."

"As you've seen, I use them all the time around Lloyd, though they don't do much. I might as well be talking to a rock."

Caleb snorted. "Yeah, a rock hard—"

"Your avocado toast!" Suzy chirped, planting it on the table.

"Perfect timing," Wesley said. "Remind me to give you my share of the tips."

Caleb dug into his food and said over a mouthful, "Everyone wonders why you haven't jumped him yet."

"Were you not listening to the Cap-Gem thing?"

"I don't mean marry him," Caleb said with a pointed glance. "I mean hanky-panky. I know you've at least drunkenly imagined doing the dirty with him."

"We were drugged!"

"Whatever. Admit you find him hot."

"He's hot. So is Bluebeard from *Fables*, but would I ever go there with him? Probably not."

Caleb twirled his fork at Wesley. "Who are you fooling?"

"Fine. I'd go there. But only because I have no principles, and Bluebeard is hot."

"Why haven't you jumped Lloyd yet?"

"When we first met he had a boyfriend. Then when he was single again, I had a boyfriend. Then he had a boyfriend. Then I had a fling. Then he had another boyfriend. Then—"

"I get the picture. You both being single at the same time is unfamiliar territory. What other excuse do you have?"

"Our sex is destined to be bad."

"You might have some legit reasons after all. What else?"

"He's my RA. He'd say it's against the rules. And . . ."

"And?"

"I haven't caught him full-on smiling at me yet."

Grind hard.

Chapter Seven

Wesley rolled out of bed for his Friday morning shift at Me Gusta Robusta with Suzy and MacDonald. Morning shifts were the best. Regulars rocked in, but mostly it stayed quiet.

Old songs blasted from the speakers, and Wesley danced with Suzy between bussing coffees.

When the Cats and the Fiddle's *Gangbusters* came on, they cowboy-styled a spot turn behind the café counter. As the song hit the chorus, MacDonald—at the open till—held two fingers to her head and pulled an air trigger in time to the beat.

Wesley and Suzy wrapped up with a tandem flourish and laughed as they parted back to work. Wesley spun once more on his heel and lifted his head to the next customer. Lloyd sat perched on a barstool behind the counter, watching curiously.

Wesley grinned. Must be time for Lloyd's economics class with Professor Cooper. "Your usual coming up."

Lloyd cleared his throat, halting Wesley. "Maybe it's time to try something out of the ordinary. Something that combines the essentials with something sweet. Like chocolate."

Wesley hitched his brow all the way up. "Are you sure?"

"Of course I'm sure. I'm always sure."

Wesley grabbed a glass and prepped his best mochaccino.

Lloyd sipped the creamy, chocolatey foam. His face pinched as he pulled back. "What *is* this?"

Wesley replaced the mochaccino with Lloyd's usual dark roast filter coffee.

Lloyd stared at the dark liquid, sighed, and drank it with a satisfied hum.

Satisfaction morphed into a groan as fourth-floor Gavin slipped onto the bar stool next to him. "Now I remember why I started avoiding this place."

"You didn't answer my email," Gavin said.

"When did you send it?"

"This morning."

Lloyd drank half his coffee in one gulp. "You are aware of the time, aren't you?"

"Yes. It's 8:45 a.m."

"Boy, oh boy."

Wesley snickered, drawing Lloyd's eye. He topped up Lloyd's coffee.

"Look," Gavin said. "I have a few ideas for Open Week that might give you ideas. Take a peek."

"Send me the link."

"I've got it right here." Gavin heaved a black leather binder onto the counter. "Careful of the fabric samples."

Lloyd stared blankly at the binder, then at Gavin. "You carry that thing around with you?"

"I was hoping to run into you."

"Gavin. I just want to enjoy a bit of coffee and conversation in peace."

"What conversation is better than this?"

MacDonald gave a dry snort as she passed Wesley on her way

into the kitchen. "Gavin," Wesley said from the coffee machine, "stop harassing my customers."

"We're simply discussing that a little more creative involvement from your RA is necessary," Gavin said.

Wesley stopped heating milk in favor of writing a new sentence on the daily quote board.

When it was done, he jumped off the stepstool and pointed with his thumb. Lloyd and Gavin read the sign over his head. *No RA business allowed on premises.*

"There you have it in chalk," Lloyd said to Gavin, and Wesley's lips twitched into a smirk.

Gavin persisted. "I want a portfolio of your chosen theme and a budget proposal by Thanksgiving."

"That's next week."

"Use this weekend to figure it out."

"You'll have it, Gavin." Wesley handed Gavin his usual caramel latte in a to-go cup. Gavin bugged the bejesus out of Lloyd, but he also spiced up daily dorm life considerably. And to be fair, his floor hosted the best parties. "That one's on me."

When Gavin and his leather binder left, Wesley replaced Lloyd's empty glass with a paper one he could take to class.

"We're gonna hit Glitter tonight."

"That's that club you like, right?"

"Yeah. It's perfect for swing, and like the name suggests, there'll be glitter. And streamers—your favorite. You should come."

"Do they serve their drinks with cocktail umbrellas?"

"Yes! How did you know?"

"Lucky guess," Lloyd said, dryly.

"So you'll come?"

"Sounds like a ball."

Wesley smirked at the sarcasm. He played with a sharpie, popping off the lid and stealing Lloyd's cup to write on it.

Lloyd read the note. "If I come you'll buy me a—what's a Glitzcini?"

"A sparkling martini. The club specialty."

Lloyd laid cash down for the coffees. "If only I wasn't on duty tonight. Alas, I am."

Wesley snorted and served another regular. He glanced over Cappuccino With Almond Milk's shoulder at Lloyd as he swung his messenger bag over his shoulder on his way out.

"Are you sure you can't get Gemma to take over your shift?" Wesley called out.

Lloyd didn't even turn around. "I'll see you bright and early in the morning."

∽

Wesley saw Lloyd early in the morning, all right. One in the morning.

He stumbled into Lloyd's room after three solid hours of dancing. He was hot and bothered, and his jeans felt shrink-wrapped onto him. "What are you doing up?" Wesley kicked off his shoes, popped open the top button of his jeans, and dove onto Lloyd's bed.

"Studying. You should try it sometime."

Wesley laughed. "Do you usually study in such romantic lighting? And half naked?" Wesley flipped onto his side and leered. "Lloyd, what exactly are you studying?"

Lloyd looked down at his tank top and boxers, then over at the desk lamp, turned in against the wall. He swiveled on his chair to face him. "I assure you it's not as exciting as it should be on a Friday night."

"The night is still young. I won't distract you for too long."

"I doubt that."

Wesley rolled back onto the bed and yawned. "Have I thanked you for helping me with Caleb?"

"More than once."

"I mean *properly* thanked you." He winked and dipped his toes under a puffy pillow. "How did you score such a big bed?"

"RA privilege. Feet generally go at the other end of it."

Wesley burrowed his feet farther. "How can I thank you? For pretending to be my fiancé?"

Lloyd rubbed the arms of his chair, then placed his elbows on his knees. "I am curious about that questionable lollipop. Halloween? The same night I found you curled up in front of my door. I thought you were drunk."

"I thought I'd dreamed that. How did I end up in bed?"

"You're heavier than you look."

Wesley shot him a look of mock horror. "Guess the lollipop added a few pounds."

"How many lollipops did you eat?"

Their gazes connected, and Wesley smirked. "I was at Steve's haunted house with Caleb. Long story short, we ended up hanging out with a few skeletons in the closet—Halloween ones."

"How disappointing."

Wesley delivered a flat look. Damn, Lloyd made him laugh. "The rest is even more disappointing. I'll spare you the details."

"The devil's in the details." Wesley's breath hitched as Lloyd approached the bed. Firm hands cupped Wesley's ankles and Lloyd swiveled his feet toward the correct end of the bed. Wesley grappled at sheets, laughing. Tingles raced up the backs of his knees. Lloyd's hands retreated and the mattress dipped as he sat next to him.

"You want to know about those secrets I spilled," Wesley said.

"Secrets said without inhibition hold certain truths."

"If you want to know so badly, you'll have to be a naughty RA and get me drunk."

"You're not drunk already?" Lloyd asked.

"Only high from dancing." Wesley swung himself beside

Lloyd in a dizzying rush and leaned against Lloyd's shoulder. "But we could go out again. Have a drink."

Lloyd touched Wesley's cheek, a light, fleeting sweep that left his skin buzzing.

Lloyd blew off a speck of glitter from his index finger. "If the truth is important enough, it'll come out on its own."

Wesley's breath skipped out of him, and with startling swiftness, Lloyd lurched off the bed and returned to his desk chair.

Wesley smoothed the sheets where Lloyd had been sitting. "What did you do that night? Halloween, I mean? Why didn't you come out with us?"

"For one, I was on duty. Cleaning vomit off the bathroom floor. It put me off jelly beans for life."

"For two?"

"What?"

"It sounded like there was more than one reason."

"I wasn't invited." A shadow of disappointment flickered through Lloyd's poker face.

Wesley rubbed his palms over his knees. "I would have invited you."

"I'm your RA. And it's not really my scene. Besides, you don't need a fun-sucker at the party."

"One lick of that lollipop and rules wouldn't have stood a chance."

Lloyd frowned. "That could've been dangerous."

"That could've been you stuck in the closet with me."

Their gazes locked.

A loud knock sounded, and a drunken Diana waltzed in singing Lloyd's name. "Lost my key. I should stop tucking shit in my bra."

Lloyd groaned. "Be there in a sec." He turned back to Wesley. "Where were we?"

Wesley moved to the basket of condoms. "That time of the week I pinch one of these."

A twinkle sparkled in Lloyd's eye. "Who is it this time?"

"A strapping guy. Smart. Principled."

"A teacher?"

"No, my . . ." Wesley grinned. "Damn. He must be waiting for me." Wesley pranced out of the room past Diana, Lloyd's dry response following him.

"He must be one hell of a patient man."

I wanna chai my luck with you.

Chapter Eight

A persistent banging struck his door at an ungodly hour of the morning.

"Go away," Wesley whimpered and rolled onto his side. He finally had his bed to himself and he wanted to enjoy the miracle of morning sheets a few more minutes.

"We had a date," Lloyd's voice boomed through the door.

Only Lloyd could pull him from his sleepy haze. He trundled to the door, adjusting his morning wood. "What?"

Lloyd's gaze darted the length of him, then jerked back to Wesley's face. Wesley woke at the stutter of approval coming through Lloyd's usual calm expression. "You were supposed to help me get Gavin off my back this morning."

"At nine."

"It's ten past, and I've already had two emails from him."

Vying for another approving glance, Wesley made a show of stretching, but Lloyd gazed resolutely forward. "You have to give him points for doggedness."

"I'm getting cold looking at you. Put on some clothes."

Wesley backed toward his dresser. "Cold, Lloyd? Really?"

"Make it quick."

Wesley pulled out two T-shirts and held them to his chest. "This one or this one?"

Lloyd whipped out a T-shirt from the open drawer and tossed it at him. "That one." He found a sweater. "That one." His leather jacket. "That one." His jeans and shoes. "Those. Now come."

Wesley caught it all, warring between the urge to laugh and give Lloyd the bird. "Aren't you grumpy this morning."

"I haven't had coffee yet."

Once they were en-route, Lloyd stopping at every yellow light, Wesley dared to ask, "What did Gavin say this morning?"

Lloyd's lips flattened. Clearly, Gavin had struck a nerve.

"He wants to clear the basement and make it a dance floor for the Open Week party."

"And that's bad because?"

"It's not."

"Oh. So you're grumpy because he made a reasonable suggestion for once and you have to reevaluate your hostile feelings toward him."

Lloyd paused. "There might be some truth in that."

"Gemini strikes a chord! What was the other mail about?"

"RA O'Connor from Richardson House got dismissed for sleeping with a resident."

"What?" Wesley shrieked, then tempered his voice momentarily. "What?"

Lloyd sent him a chastising look. "Rules are in place for a reason."

"Just because things get awkward if it doesn't work out?"

"More than that. Whole floors have split alliances after a breakup. People get hurt."

"Yeah, but . . . That sucks."

Lloyd stretched his arms against the wheel, thumping his head against the headrest. "O'Conner must be kicking himself. A

75

dismissal means he forfeits his twelve-thousand-dollar scholarship."

Wesley whistled.

"He shouldn't have given in to his attraction," Lloyd said as they parked outside a café a few blocks from Party Palace.

Wesley clambered out, mumbling, "He shouldn't have gotten caught."

∼

"We can't have coffee. We have to leave. Now."

"What do you mean, we can't have coffee?" Lloyd sounded incredulous, as though Wesley had casually suggested castration as an alternative to daily washing.

Wesley tugged Lloyd out of the line they'd been waiting in for ten minutes. "I'm the one up at nine in the morning with a grumpy RA. If anyone needs coffee, it's me." He glanced across the room at a top-button-collared man weaving his way in their direction. "But it has to wait."

"Wesley? Right now? I legitimately fear for your life."

"I'll get us coffee later. More than one. My treat."

Lloyd gave up resisting, and they almost escaped the bustling café.

"Young Mister Hidaka!"

Wesley swallowed a groan and clutched Lloyd's forearm as he turned them around to face his childhood pastor. Pastor Geoff had a gray beard, rim-free glasses, and a condescending regard—like usual.

"Your mother prays every week that you come back home." Pastor Geoff registered Lloyd's presence, and his face shadowed. "You've lost your way, son."

That was about as much as Wesley would put up with. "I am very sure of my way, and I'll keep walking it. In fact, I'm going to walk it right now. Vigorously. With my fiancé."

Wesley steered Lloyd out the door, leaving the pastor gaping behind them. He didn't stop walking or let go until they were safely ducking down behind Lloyd's car. Well, Wesley was ducking down. Lloyd was staring at him with disbelief and amusement—and something else.

"Has he stopped watching us yet?" Wesley asked, noticing how close his face was to Lloyd's crotch. Lloyd jerked and bumped against the car door.

Wesley took a moment to absorb Lloyd's reaction, and a smile quivered at his lips. He straightened, keeping barely an inch between them.

Lloyd caught his elbow and helped him along, muttering under his breath. "I *really* need coffee."

"Is that what they're calling it these days?"

Lloyd closed his eyes and took a calming breath, then opened the passenger door. "Get in, flirtster."

Wesley smirked and jumped in.

∼

LLOYD PICKED UP A DAGGER FROM THE ROW OF FAKE SWORDS hanging in the Medieval section of Party Palace, an Ikea-like warehouse for parties.

Lloyd had stepped inside dubiously, but Wesley was convinced he was seeing the light. "We'll have your theme and budget proposal in no time."

"How did I not know this place existed?"

"It's a store for creative types. Not your forte of data, black coffee, and fixing your residents' problems."

Lloyd side-eyed him. "Some residents more than others." He moved to the stone table and inspected a fake goblet. "I'm not completely deficient in creativity, you know."

"Uh-huh," Wesley said drily. "Of course you're not." He

leaned against life-size knight armor and caught sight of his reflection. "I look positively awful."

"You look the same as always."

Wesley pulled away from the mirroring metal and battled his unruly hair. He narrowed his eyes at Lloyd. "You're mean when you have no coffee in you."

Lloyd gave him a once-over. "And you're a decided wreck."

"The slight swell in your slacks when we were in the parking lot proves you are a liar." Wesley paused. "Or that decided wrecks turn you on. Oh my God, decided wrecks turn you on. You know, that explains so many of your past boyfriends."

A warning look.

Wesley smirked and wandered out of the medieval section and down an aisle until they entered a fifties-style diner. Black-and-white checkered tiles, giant milkshake props, and small silver tables decorated with diner baskets and centerpieces stuffed with hand-held photo props. Streamers hung from the ceiling in the shape of mini records.

Near the wall was a large peep-through photo board from *Grease*. Sandy and Danny standing in front of a Dodge. Wesley walked behind Sandy and peeked out at Lloyd. "What'cha think?"

Lloyd's expression flickered with humor. "This reminds me of that one summer when . . ."

Lloyd's neck flushed.

Wesley's curiosity fully aroused, he shoved his head farther into the Sandy face hole until his ears were free. "When what?"

Lloyd circled a diner table. "When I slipped a notch on the Kinsey Scale. 'Predominately homosexual, only incidentally heterosexual.'"

Wesley pouted and ran a hand down Sandy's cardboard figure. "Did she do it for you? Did she make you want to 'flog your log'?"

"Thank you for that fun *Grease* quote."

"What can I say? I'm a big fan."

"Of the log flog?"

Wesley snickered. "That too. I meant a fan of rock 'n' roll—though Sandy never did it for me."

"She never did it for me either."

Wesley planted a hand on cardboard Sandy's hip. "Who got you practicing that questionable 'bowling-hand' gesture then? Don't say Principal McGee."

"Rizzo."

"You're one for surprises."

Lloyd's gaze pinged to Wesley. "What can I say? Boisterous energy gets me hot."

Wesley stumbled out from behind the prop, catching himself on a table edge. "Enlightening stuff. You should tell me *more* about yourself. Anything. Everything."

Lloyd struggled to hide a smile and keep his voice steady. "What do you want to know?"

Wesley looped an arm around Lloyd's and leaned in conspiratorially. "Tell me your birthdate, and I'll make sure to throw you the party of your dreams."

Lloyd whispered back in his ear, his breath stirring a stray bang. "No."

"Lloyd! Please?"

"Stop believing this horoscope nonsense, and I might tell you."

"But it all comes true. Two weeks ago, I read that my life was about to take a sharp turn. Voila! My brother is living with me."

"He's what?" Lloyd pulled away, and Wesley cursed his runaway mouth.

"I mean slumming it with friends."

Lloyd's eyes pinched. "You said he was living with you."

"I never said that. If I had, and you believed that it's true, you'd have to write me up."

Lloyd hesitated. "Why is your brother slumming it with friends?"

Wesley winced. "Because I might have made running away sound like a good idea?" They passed into the adjoining room that sported a seventies theme. "At least he's not sleeping in an abandoned factory anymore."

Lloyd drummed his fingers along a table holding disco-ball centerpieces. The look Lloyd was giving him made him nervous. Wesley feigned particular interest in the mounted records on the wall. When he glanced back, Lloyd was still watching him, face torn in indecision.

Wesley must have woken a sensor or something, because John Paul Young's *Love Is in The Air* started playing through the room's speakers, breaking Lloyd's thoughts.

His gaze lifted off Wesley as he quickly shifted into the next room. Sixties theme.

Music came on the moment Wesley stepped in after him. The Beatles' *I Want to Hold Your Hand*.

Lloyd hesitated, then looped back into the fifties-style diner. Wesley lifted a confused brow but followed him inside. Wesley cheered as Elvis Presley started playing.

"Of course." Lloyd stopped under the belly of streamers.

Between the photo props and the display tables, Wesley tapped his foot against checkered flooring to the opening beats of *Blue Suede Shoes*.

Lloyd sighed. "Should I be afraid?"

"Very." Wesley held out his hand. "Dance with me, Lloyd?"

"When I said I'm not completely deficient in creativity?" Lloyd winced. "I lied."

Wesley curled a finger at him. "Just follow along."

Lloyd hesitated and stepped forward. Before he changed his mind, Wesley hooked Lloyd's warm fingers and pulled him in. "Feel the music. Rock, rock, backstep. Do it as we turn. Use a soft grip so we can pivot and swing better."

Lloyd stumbled, and Wesley showed him again. "Slow-slow, quick-quick." He raised their joined hands and walked under it, turning as he went.

Lloyd lost his grip, so Wesley pulled him in and showed him again. Lloyd was a block of uncoordinated heat, stepping off-beat to Elvis. "Relax, let yourself loosen up."

Lloyd rolled his shoulders, but his dancing efforts didn't much improve.

"You're trying too hard to be perfect. Let yourself make mistakes, go with the music."

Wesley did a big kick and pulled himself tight against Lloyd's body, leg sliding deep between his in a tango step. Lloyd's grip on him tripled, and Wesley grinned at the surprise on his face.

"You can"—Lloyd's Adam's apple bobbed as he swallowed—"really dance."

"Been doing it for years." Wesley shifted out of the tango, no longer dancing, their fingers still hooked, pulses pounding. "I met Suzy through dance class five years ago. We've been partners since. Dance partners. We learned the Lindy Hop, jive, rock 'n' roll. Bit of everything."

"Is she the reason you're a third-year still living in a dorm?"

"Hey, don't dis the dorm."

"No dissing here. I'm still there, aren't I?"

"Williamson gave me a bunch of reasons to stay." Wesley squeezed his fingers against Lloyd's as he ticked them off. "A cleaning service, first of all."

A humored grunt.

"It's five minutes to class."

"Practical, I agree," Lloyd said.

"It's a great way to meet characters—my world wouldn't be nearly as colorful without Randy and Gavin. MacDonald."

"Or mine without you."

Wesley stammered as a flutter hit his chest. "I can literally roll out of bed and two minutes later open shop at Me Gusta Robusta."

"Sounds like you'll be in the dorms until you graduate."

Wesley shrugged. "I think this is my last year. Even if I do love the free stuff from you."

"Free stuff?"

"Condoms, Lloyd."

The air thickened between them, then the song ended, and they broke apart abruptly.

Lloyd rubbed his neck. "What do you think of this for the Williamson party?"

Yes. All the yesses. "*Grease* in particular? Or a fifties theme?"

"*Grease?*"

"Sounds good, but hear me out: It'll end up a basement of pink ladies and leather-clad T-birds. It might allow for more costume variety if we went with a fifties theme."

"Costume variety. I'm rethinking this whole idea. How about a wear-whatever-you-want theme?"

Wesley grabbed a coin from his wallet and set it on the back of his thumb. "Heads, we do a fifties theme. Tails, we don't do a wear-whatever theme."

Lloyd stared at the coin and spoke with the barest hint of sarcasm. "My, what great chances I have."

Wesley sexed up his voice and parodied Sandy as he flipped the coin. "Tell me about it, Cap."

You grabbed my heart in an instant.

Chapter Nine

"Can I borrow your car?" Wesley stood in Lloyd's open door, bent over buckling up his shitkickers. He flashed Lloyd a cajoling smile.

"What's wrong with MacDonald's?"

Wesley tugged up the rim and straightened. "She saw me drive last Friday. She won't let me use it."

"Smart girl." Lloyd checked the time. "Where do you need to be?"

"Shadowing my brother. I've been making sure he gets to Sandalwood."

"Is that where you've been sneaking off to weekday mornings?"

Wesley draped himself against the doorframe and purred. "I like that you noticed."

"What about classes? Work?"

Of course that would be Lloyd's follow up. "I miss a bit of Law here and there, and, except Fridays, I've temporarily swapped to closing shifts at Me Gusta Robusta."

Lloyd grabbed his keys.

Wesley grinned. "Is that a yes to borrowing your car?"

Lloyd grabbed his coat. "That's a yes to taking you myself. Come on."

Three minutes later, buckled into Lloyd's car, they left the student parking lot.

"Where does he usually get on the bus?" Lloyd asked.

"Right outside our dorm—I mean our house. In Chatem Valley. Because why would he get on here? When he lives at home. With Mom. In Chatem Valley."

Lloyd grimaced doubtfully.

Wesley flipped a grin and glanced down the road where his brother was climbing into the bus. "He'll be on bus 172, which passes right through here. Oh look. There it is."

"How convenient."

"I know, right?"

Lloyd side-eyed him and drove behind bus 172. "You spent a good deal of time ass-up in my bedroom doorway buckling your boots. Now you're taking them off again?"

Wesley continued weaseling out of his shitkickers and propped his feet up on the dashboard. "I'm not driving. And we've got fifty minutes. Enough time for me to be comfortable and continue our conversation about your life. Who is this Aunt Tabitha?"

Lloyd followed the bus around a corner. "My mom's sister. I'm her nephew. That makes her my aunt."

Wesley punched him lightly on the arm. "Do you get along?"

"She's wealthy, and not really."

"Do tell."

Lloyd flattened his lips. "Mom got cut off for having me at sixteen, and Tabitha inherited everything. She humiliated my mom for losing her job and asking to help pay my school tuition, and then made me earn them by being her personal assistant during the summer."

"That's awful. Actually, awful doesn't describe this angry feeling balling up in my belly right now. How dare she do that to you? I hate her on your behalf."

Lloyd's lip twitched.

"You should feel proud of yourself. You're working your way through college and winning math-y scholarships."

"I like that you noticed." They shared a humored glance.

"Something else I might have noticed. Overheard. Eavesdropped upon . . ."

Lloyd lifted a brow.

"You were on the phone last night. Talking. Sometimes laughing. With . . . ?"

Lloyd's face lit up, and Wesley didn't like it. "I'll tell you, but you have to keep it to yourself."

"I'll try. Very hard. Because it's you. Now who is he?"

"How'd you know it was a he?"

Wesley gave a petulant pout. All exaggerated, of course. "So there is a he."

"Wesley."

"I guess this explains the recent color in your cheeks and the twinkle in your eye—this isn't healthy, Lloyd, jumping from boy to boy. I thought you wanted to find Mr. Goes-To-Bed-Early-on-Saturdays?"

"I might have to change my mind on that one."

"No changing of the mind. Stick to your best Cap trait and stay determined to find Mr. Perfect-For-You. Even if it means staying single for a long, long time."

"Why, you sound a little jealous."

Wesley laughed. "You wish, Cap."

Lloyd made an amused sound. "Should I go on or not?"

Wesley gestured for him to continue.

"I was chatting with Jamie, who I am hoping will supervise my masters' project next year."

"Oh. Your professor friend."

"Sort of. Heading in that direction, I hope. We both love economics and statistics, and we spend our free time analyzing data—"

"Clearly you should marry him."

Lloyd snorted. "His partner Theo wouldn't like that."

Wesley perked up. "Why didn't you lead with that bit of info?"

Lloyd rolled his eyes.

"What? Fiancés don't like hearing about other important men in their lover's life."

"Right. Well, I have to woo him."

"My emotions are yo-yoing here, Lloyd. Woo him?"

"To supervise my masters. Everyone wants him."

"Who *is* this Casanova?" Wesley whipped out his arm, preparing to smack Lloyd, but his focus moved to Caleb getting off the bus way too early. "Little ditcher. Damn, what should I do?" Wesley pointed at Caleb. "That was your cue to tell me what to do, Lloyd."

"Hop out and talk to him."

"That sounds reasonable. Another idea: Let's follow his cowboy-clomping booty."

Lloyd drove into a vacant parking spot. Wesley opened the door, flinging one foot out without taking off his seat belt.

Caleb was walking down the street in their direction but hadn't noticed them yet.

"Shhh," he said to Lloyd, and pulled the door shut, slamming it on his toe. "Holy motherfucker!" Pain lanced up his foot and calf. "Fuck, fuck, *my toe*."

Lloyd rounded to his side and crouched at the door, palming Wesley's knee. "Are you okay? Let's have a look."

Through gritted teeth, Wesley gave a painful laugh. "I can't believe he didn't notice us through all that."

Lloyd gave him a blank expression. "You don't still want to follow him?"

"Help me get my boots on over that swelling beast."

"You're insane."

"And you're crazy about me."

Lloyd shook his head and gingerly helped Wesley get his boots on.

"Hurry, he turned a corner."

∽

WESLEY PULLED LLOYD INTO A CROWDED AUDITORIUM. "Lost him. Damn toe. I would have gotten here faster if I hadn't—"

"Taken your boots off in my car?"

"—needed to use you as a crutch."

Over the crowd, Wesley spotted his brother slinking onto the stage with his flute case. He grimaced and bit his bottom lip. "I should have listened to you."

Someone cleared their throat behind them. "Are you guys moving up there or not?"

Wesley glanced at him and, with a silent plea to Lloyd, said, "Yes we are."

Lloyd started toward the stage, tucking Wesley close to his side. "You were saying something about listening to me?"

A laugh threaded warmly through his veins. Even his toe felt better. "Guess I should have talked to Caleb outside."

A woman in a red wig and clipboard cut their path. "Where are your numbers?"

Wesley gave her a puzzled look before catching sight of a freestanding board behind her. *Auditions. Dancing extras.*

He flashed her a flirty smile. "Actually, we want to go on stage for a second—"

"You need numbers."

Lloyd tapped into his deep, persuasive voice that always

clenched Wesley's gut. "We don't mean to interrupt your auditions, we—"

Red Wig wasn't affected. *How wasn't she affected?* "Only way to get on stage is with a number. Stan," she said to the lackey behind her. "Tag 'em."

A few seconds later, their backs and stomachs had numbered stickers. Wesley, 198 and Lloyd, 199. Stan shoved them into a line. "Clearly Red Wig isn't human," Wesley murmured as the presumed director yelled out numbers and music started playing in the background.

"Wesley," Lloyd asked, glancing toward the exit. "Why are we standing here like we're auditioning?"

"Because I need to talk to Caleb. *Yell* at him."

Lloyd pinned him with a look, and Wesley tried the same flirty smile on him that hadn't worked with Red Wig. Lloyd's expression softened. A little. Unless it was a trick of the stage light. "You heard Principal Bontempo. If he's caught missing class once, no recommendation to Treble."

"And you're prepared to dance your way across the stage to him?"

"Seems the easiest way."

"Easy?" Wesley followed Lloyd's gaze to the stage where numbered couples twirled and gyrated to—was his brother playing the flute to Pharrell Williams' *Happy*?

Damn, Caleb was talented. "Looks like fun!"

Lloyd stared blankly at him. "Do you not remember the last time we tried to dance? Now add a bum toe to that."

He might have a point.

The music stopped, and the director threw dancers offstage. The director yelled in exasperation. "I'm giving you the chance to fulfill your dreams. Can I see some real dancing?" He studied his board and called a bunch of numbers. A group of girl-boy dancers sashayed on stage.

Wesley could dance just as well. If not better. He'd suck up the toe pain. "We'll be fine," he said to Lloyd, who had his phone pressed to his ear. "Who are you calling?"

"Lifeline?" Lloyd said, then swiveled and talked into the phone. "Gemma, Lloyd here. I'm going to be late for work. Could you fill in until I get there? . . . What am I doing?" He glanced at Wesley, as though he knew he was listening in, and held his gaze. "I'm being a good fiancé."

Wesley grinned and mouthed, "The best."

Fifteen minutes later and more cuts called, it was their turn. Lloyd made a tight noise in the back of his throat.

"We'll move right toward Caleb," Wesley said, testing his toe on the steps leading to the stage. Tender but manageable. "We might not even have to dance. If we do, keep it simple."

Music started, and Wesley grabbed Lloyd's hand. Warm, tingly static skipped up his arm. After recovering from the shock, he tugged Lloyd and threaded him through the dancers.

They only made it halfway to Caleb before the director stopped the music. "One-hundred-ninety-eight and ninety-nine. Why aren't you dancing?"

The other dancers and band gawked at them. Caleb's gulp was visible, and he almost dropped his flute.

The spotlight beamed down on Wesley and Lloyd, and Wesley quite liked it. He grinned. "We're better in the background, by the band." He glared at his brother, who at least had the decency to blush. Caleb lifted his hand and mouthed, "Five minutes."

"Your partner is tall," the director agreed, unconvinced.

Wesley nicked his head in Lloyd's direction. "I worry he'll outshine your main actors. You know, because of all the hotness."

Lloyd laughed, and when Wesley whipped his head around to catch him, Lloyd's lips settled into a teasing flat line. He lifted one eyebrow, though, and Wesley drilled him with a playful glare.

The director barked. "No, you're good right there. When the

music starts, we'll pick up at the countdown. Draw close to your partners and it's kissy-kissy time. Hooray, hooray, New Year's is here. You know the drill." He cued the band, who knocked out a beat in time with the crowd joyfully shouting a countdown.

Ten. Nine. Eight.

Lloyd's gaze dropped to Wesley's lips, and Wesley's heart lurched into his throat.

Seven. Six.

Wesley licked his lips and laughed. "Well, this is something."

"It's something all right." Lloyd rubbed a thumb over Wesley's knuckles where Wesley was choking the life out of Lloyd's hand. He lessened his grip with a sheepish grin.

Five. Four. Three.

Wesley shifted his feet around one of Lloyd's and rested his shaky hand on his chest. "Kissy-kissy time."

Lloyd dipped his head. Wesley's stomach dropped to his knees and through his feet. Lloyd spoke into his ear, voice calm and steady. "It's an audition. We shouldn't."

Two. One.

Lloyd shifted away, but Wesley looped his hand around Lloyd's neck, gave him a diabolical grin, and kissed him. His lips met Lloyd's with humored insistence, but he wasn't ready for the warmth of Lloyd's mouth. The taste of maple syrup from breakfast clung to the bow of his lip.

Wesley stilled his roaming hands against Lloyd's shoulder blades, lips grazing off—

Lloyd slid his fingers through Wesley's hair and cradled his head, drawing him closer.

Wesley's veins sang with a surge of electricity. He listed against Lloyd's strong chest, and Lloyd teased Wesley's lips with his tongue.

Heat rocked through Wesley, and he kept kissing Lloyd well after the music had stopped.

When they parted, Wesley blinked, and blinked again. He

only realized he was staring at Lloyd's swollen bottom lip when Lloyd spoke, "Wesley?"

Wesley looked up into his questioning gaze.

The director yelled their numbers. "You two are out. Bye-bye."

Wesley whirled toward the director. "You're casting us out because of that kiss?"

"Yes. Go."

"Are you completely off your rocker? That kiss was incredible."

The director ignored him and rolled his finger at the band to wrap up. "Flute, thanks for coming in on short notice. Violin and trumpet, you're up."

Wesley scowled at the director. "Serious nut-job that needs glasses," he muttered.

"He's wearing glasses."

Wesley threw his hands up. "See. Sight impaired."

Lloyd regarded Wesley with amusement, and his face beamed. Wesley's breath stalled.

The director shouting numbers yanked him out of his fog. Wesley snagged his brother and hurried the hell off stage.

∽

WESLEY AND CALEB GLARED AT EACH OTHER IN LLOYD'S CAR on their way to Sandalwood.

"What?" Caleb mimed from the backseat.

Wesley tried telepathically to answer him. When Caleb played dumb, Wesley took out his phone.

Wesley: I'm so mad at you.

Caleb: I have Mrs. Carr for first-period music. She's cool. She gets it.

Wesley: Still mad.

Caleb: Shouldn't you be grateful? If it weren't for me, there'd have been no tonsil tennis.

Wesley made an indignant sound, then typed back.

Wesley: Exactly. If it weren't for you, there'd have been no tonsil tennis!

Lloyd caught a glimpse of Caleb through the rearview mirror and then trapped those hazel eyes on Wesley. "I have to wonder if you're talking about me."

Wesley's laugh sounded as forced as it felt. "The world doesn't revolve around you, you know."

"Well, *my* world doesn't," Caleb said.

Wesley narrowed his eyes and smiled slyly as Lloyd stopped outside the school. "I hope you get lots of homework for Thanksgiving weekend, Hazelnut."

As soon as Caleb hopped out, Wesley turned to Lloyd, nervously snapping his wristband. "The kiss was your fault, by the way."

Lloyd restarted the car and drove with precision—like everything he did. "Is that right?"

"You said we shouldn't do it."

"Only you can put two and two together and surprise me." Lloyd side-eyed him. "How does saying we shouldn't do it make it my fault?"

"You made it a rule." He tucked his feet onto the seat, wincing when he bumped his toe. "I like to break rules." Lloyd glanced at him, and Wesley's gaze dropped to his lips. "I like to break them over and over. Repeatedly. What are we talking about?"

Lloyd's lips twitched. "Rules."

"Right. I fight against them because"—he pointed to himself—"Gemini. And you are a Capricorn." He shouldn't forget that. That kiss had done sneaky tricks to his mind. "Your fault."

Lloyd glanced at him. "It won't ever happen again."

Lloyd!

You're like caffeine. You keep me up all night.

Chapter Ten

Wesley stared at various pairs of scissors and a nail clipper that Lloyd fanned in front of him.

"Take your pick," Lloyd said.

Wesley shifted on Lloyd's bed, glancing at the black toenail that was hanging on by a stubborn thread of skin. It was the day before Thanksgiving, two days since the audition, and Wesley wasn't sure which bothered him more: his nail falling off or Lloyd being back to his normal, grumpy self.

He hadn't brought up kissing once.

It was like it had never happened.

Which was good.

Exactly what Wesley wished for.

"The nail clipper didn't work." Wesley eyed the other sets of scissors, which all looked dangerously sharp. "What would you use?"

With his desk chair, Lloyd scooched toward him with a small trashcan. He set it on the floor and scrutinized Wesley's foot.

"Oh, Lloyd, stop looking at me like so. You're making my toes curl."

Lloyd handed Wesley the sharpest pair of scissors. He set the others back in the mother-of-all emergency kits, then returned.

Wesley gripped the scissors so hard, the end stabbed his palm. He jerked with the zing of pain. "Are you sure these scissors aren't too big?"

Lloyd grasped Wesley around the ankle. Not before Wesley caught a burgeoning smile kicking up on one side of his lips. It disappeared when Lloyd settled Wesley's foot onto his lap.

"Pass."

Wesley reluctantly handed over the scissors. "If you cut off my toe, I'll sue you."

"Which will be easier if you ace your law papers."

"That sounded like you think I'm a failure."

"It was motivation." Lloyd grasped the neck of his big toe.

"It's painful."

Lloyd paused before clipping and looked at him.

"Not the toe." Wesley grinned.

"If you don't enjoy law, why are you doing it?"

"Why do anything? Because we want someone to notice."

Operation Toenail resumed. One clip and done. Much easier than Wesley had thought.

Lloyd tossed the dead toenail into the trashcan and cleaned the toe. His fingers were gentle, unlike his tone. "Vanity won't make you happy, Wesley."

"Stop ramming my superficialness with your Capricorny horns."

Lloyd hooked his gaze. "We haven't got to the ramming part yet."

Wesley's breath hitched, and he was keenly aware of Lloyd's hot lap cushioning his heel.

It was his cue for flirty nonsense, but nothing came to him.

Lloyd snapped his gaze back to Wesley's foot and dressed it in a bandage. "You should pursue your passion. Thrive on ambition."

"It's not like I can be a barista my whole life."
"Why not?"

~

THAT PESKY LITTLE 'WHY NOT?' FOLLOWED HIM AROUND ALL day. To the cafeteria, where he took advantage of pigging out before they closed for the long weekend, and to the library, where he fooled himself that he was studying.

Could he work as a barista the rest of his life?

Wouldn't it be hard to make a living? Who wanted to have a thirty-year-old barista as a boyfriend? What about following in his dad's footsteps? He'd been the first Japanese-American to become a judge in their town. He'd been respected. Wesley had a foot in the door if he passed his bar exam.

The day flew by, and the campus emptied as students headed home for the holiday weekend. Dark clouds spilled rain, and Wesley hoofed back toward Williamson.

In the middle of the courtyard outside the dorm, he spotted Lloyd opening an umbrella over his gray shirt, killer pants, and fuck-me belt. Wesley crossed to him and cleared his throat.

A slash of rain hit Wesley's forehead as Lloyd and his umbrella twisted.

Wesley blinked through the droplets. "Where are you off to, Mary Poppins?"

"Calling me that every time it rains is getting ridiculous."

"Not as ridiculous as that ungodly umbrella you always carry around."

Lloyd sheltered Wesley with it and doubled-back to the dorm. "Don't see you complaining now."

Thankfulness prickled Wesley. "I was never complaining. I love portable tents." They stopped outside the main door and Wesley couldn't keep the smile off his face. "Where are you off to? Got a hot date tonight?"

Lloyd's gaze flickered away from his. "I'm meeting someone."

"Oh." Wesley nodded. Of course. "Have fun."

He yanked on the dorm door. It didn't budge.

Lloyd raised a brow. "Your key-card?"

While Wesley fumbled, Lloyd swiped his key and opened the door with his polished dress shoe. "Have you thought about what you are doing this weekend?"

Wesley stepped inside and faced Lloyd from the shelter of the entranceway. "I'll probably lounge in my bed, listening to your voice in my head."

Lloyd's gaze hit his. "My voice?"

"Your 'why not?' Your 'pursue your passion.'"

"Right. That."

Wesley leaned against the door to keep it open. "I mean, the whole day I thought about what you said, and it's true. I love going to work. It's heartwarming serving my regulars: Mr. Muffin. Cappuccino With Almond Milk. Skinny Latte." He sighed. "I crave mornings. Coming into work and breathing in the heavenly scent of coffee. By the end of a shift, I swear I sweat the nutty scent of your favorite dark roast."

Lloyd's tongue darted over his bottom lip as though Wesley was making him thirst for the good stuff. "The dark roast. It is exceptional."

Wesley ground his heel against the door. "Anyway. You have somewhere to be."

"And you?" Lloyd asked.

"Gotta fight a few chapters of law while listening to Caleb try to lure MacDonald out of her room with music."

"I'm not sure who I should wish more luck."

Wesley kicked off the door with a wink. "Sometimes neither am I."

~

That night, Wesley woke with a start from a terrible dream. His gaze bounced around his dark room, where his snoring brother shifted onto his side away from Wesley.

Dream sticking to him like gum on the bottom of a shoe, he shuffled down the dimly lit hall. He couldn't shake the part of the dream where Lloyd had stared him down and said, "You're fun and games but nothing of substance."

He stopped outside Lloyd's room. The door was shut and his light was off.

That had never stopped him in the past.

He knocked. "Lloyd?"

A moment passed.

He was about to turn back when Lloyd's muffled "sec" sounded from behind the door.

Lloyd opened the door, exceptionally naked in his boxers and ankle socks. He blinked, adjusting to the light. Lines crisscrossed one side of his torso where he'd presumably been pressed against rumpled sheets.

When their eyes connected, Lloyd seemed to wake up fast. Straightening, he folded his arms across his chest like he was suddenly aware of his state of undress.

He stepped back into the shadows of his room, gesturing Wesley inside. "What's the matter?" he said, pulling a tank top from his drawers.

"Don't cover up on my behalf."

Lloyd paused with his arms in his sleeves. He stared at Wesley, but the dark room veiled his expression.

Wesley flicked the light switch.

Grunting in protest, Lloyd popped the tank top over his head. "I assume you didn't wake me up at five in the morning for fun—although . . ." He slanted Wesley a look that said it was entirely possible.

Wesley sighed and tossed himself onto Lloyd's bed, which still radiated Lloyd's heat.

Lloyd cautiously approached. "Did your bed give out?"

"I had a kind of dream."

Lloyd's gaze sleepily flickered to Wesley's crotch. "A good one?"

"A bad one."

"That's what I meant. What happened in the dream?"

You hated me. "Mom had a goat. It hurt."

"Did the goat kick you?"

"The goat was the best thing that had ever happened to the family. I liked it more than I care to admit."

Lloyd rubbed his eyes. "Am I dreaming? I don't get it."

"She replaced me. With a goat."

Lloyd twisted sharply, back to Wesley. His shoulders jerked like he might be containing a laugh. But this wasn't a joke. Wesley was being downright serious.

"Not quite the comfort I thought my RA would give me."

Lloyd's dimple made a rare appearance. "Sorry. Can I make you a cup of tea and we talk through this?"

"Tea? Do you know me at all?"

"Coffee, then. Regular milk or goat—"

"Oh my God. *Now* you bring out the playfulness? Come here." Wesley patted the bed. "Comfort me."

Lloyd's eyes glittered momentarily before the room drowned in shadows as he turned off the light. The floor creaked as he made his way to bed. The mattress dipped, and Lloyd rolled onto his side. One of them gulped. Probably Wesley.

Lloyd propped his head on his arm, angling himself to ensure space between them.

Wesley cut through that bullshit right away, curling onto his side against Lloyd's chest. "Better," he said, lips practically pressed against a smooth, toned pec. "Now ask me again if I'm okay."

Lloyd set a warm hand on his side. "Are you okay?"

Wesley gulped in a lungful of Lloyd's earthy scent. "Yes. I mean, no."

Lloyd's fingers slid to his back, running up the side of his spine. "Tell me about it."

"Dream Caleb said the goat made a better driver than I did."

Lloyd's chest shuddered.

"Am I really fun and games but nothing of substance?"

Lloyd's suppressed laughter stopped. He pulled back and looked at Wesley. "Who said that?"

"It was in my dream."

Lloyd rubbed small circles over the curve of Wesley's shoulder. "Dreams aren't real life. Nothing about them has to be true."

"But maybe it's a sign. Maybe there's some truth?"

Fingers stilled. "Fine. Sometimes you are fun and games—"

"See!"

Lloyd slid his hand to Wesley's neck and clasped it. He leaned in closer, speaking firmly. "You're also caring and thoughtful, and you shine such a light wherever you go."

"You don't think I'm a terrible brother?"

"I don't."

"Okay, thanks."

"That's it?"

"Hearing that helped. Yes. Now, shhh. Your bed is cozy and I'm tired."

Wesley snuggled against Lloyd again.

"Wesley?"

"You feel"—Wesley breathed Lloyd in again, pressing his lips against Lloyd's chest— "incredibly good."

"Did you just kiss me?"

"Don't worry, it's not *that* type of kiss."

After a pause: "What type was it?"

"The 'I like being gathered in my friend's arms' type."

"'You like being gathered in your friend's arms' type?'" Caleb said to Wesley, who sat in the backseat of MacDonald's car. "You see how it sounds like you're *more* than friends, right?"

Wesley flicked the back of the seat. "I'm a natural flirt. This stuff comes out while half asleep."

"Do you kiss Suzy on the breast too?"

Wesley choked on the preposterous thought.

"Admit it," MacDonald said wryly. "You want him to screw you up against a wall."

Wesley flicked some more. "That's the point. He'd never do that. He likes his back too much."

"If you don't want to screw the RA, why did we follow him to his home on Thanksgiving?"

Wesley peered through the backseat window at the modest two-story house settled at the edge of a creepy neighborhood. He had always bypassed this route when driving to Sandalwood, but now he was camped outside Lloyd's house with Caleb and MacDonald—and a pressing need for the bathroom.

Wesley glared at the gallon Coke cup he'd finished. MacDonald was shaking her head at him. "I told you what a great idea drinking that Coke was. It's as if you've never stalked anyone before."

Caleb, sitting in the driver's seat, swung his head toward her. His lips said he thought she was hilarious. His eyes, however, showed that he questioned his own sanity.

"We're not stalking," Wesley said, squinting when he spotted Lloyd's figure passing the ground-floor window. "We're fleshing out our picture of him."

Caleb stage-whispered to MacDonald. "He's slowly figuring out what Lloyd means to him."

"I am not." He was.

"Very slowly," Caleb amended.

"I like the status quo," Wesley murmured, and there was

truth to it. The more he got to know Lloyd, the more he liked him. He didn't want to ruin this flirty-friend gig.

"Why did I ever agree to this?" MacDonald drawled.

"The front door's opening!" Wesley and Caleb slunk down until their heads were out of sight.

MacDonald snorted.

Fifteen seconds later, Lloyd appeared at the side of the car. His eyes skimmed the front seats, and Wesley swallowed as they landed on him in the back.

Wesley wiggled his fingers in a guilty wave.

Lloyd gestured for him to hop out.

Caleb groaned. "Busted."

"Amateurs," MacDonald said.

Wesley opened the door and peeled himself out of the car. He stretched and gave Lloyd his best yes-I'm-naughty-but-you-love-me look. "Can I use your bathroom?"

Lloyd stared at him as though he wanted to simultaneously bust out a laugh and shake him. Thoroughly. A few times. "You've only been parked out here twenty minutes."

"You shouldn't have gone through the Subway drive-through," Wesley complained.

"You shouldn't have bought the gallon Coke."

Wesley gaped. "How do you know that?"

"You were literally the car behind me."

"Trust you to use your rearview mirror."

Caleb and MacDonald got out of the car. Lloyd spared them with a plea. "Never let him drive anywhere on his own."

Wesley delightedly slung an arm around Lloyd, gluing himself to his side. "There's my Capricorn."

Lloyd wrapped an arm around his neck and crushed him close, whispering grumpily in his ear, "You could have just accepted my Thanksgiving invitation."

"The one that you extended to all your residents who didn't

have plans?" Despite Lloyd's warm arm, there was a surprising chill in the air. "Hardly a personal invitation."

Lloyd groaned in frustration. "You were the *only* resident without plans." He paused. "At least until MacDonald's parents decided they'd prefer a trip to Vegas over celebrating Thanksgiving."

A warm thrum pulsed in Wesley's stomach. On the tiny porch outside Lloyd's door, Lloyd pulled out his keys.

"Wait. You *wanted me* to come. I never struck you as too shy to ask outright."

"Oh, Wesley, I'm trying to keep Gavin off my back." Lloyd sank his key into the keyhole and looked at him. "Trust me, I am not shy."

I just want to taste your earthy scent.

Chapter Eleven

Lloyd introduced Wesley to his mom, Cathy, a tiny woman with big hair and a huge smile. Lloyd's opposite, though they shared the same bright hazel eyes and dark lashes.

Wesley's insides went haywire when Lloyd slipped into an apron stamped with pictures of playful kittens. Lloyd caught the oven mitt his mom tossed him. They shifted in sync, clearly well-practiced at making family meals together.

Cathy's eyes darted from Wesley to Caleb. "Which is the boy I have to worry about?"

Lloyd jerked a finger in Wesley's direction. "The one who's exceptionally quiet."

Wesley met Lloyd's gaze. "No exceptional stuff here."

"Another trait you need to know about him, Mom? He lies."

Cathy's smile brightened. "I'm starting to see how he's trouble."

"Trouble? Me?" Wesley blew his bangs out of his eyes, then grinned mischievously. "Where do I sign up?"

Cathy laughed, and Lloyd handed him a platter with a tan lump of something from the oven.

"Follow me to the dining room," Lloyd said, grabbing two bowls of vegetables.

Wesley eased the platter onto a long table set for five. "When did you set the table?"

"I didn't. Mom did."

"When did she do that?"

Lloyd set the bowls on the table and turned to him. "When I called her from the road. How do you feel about Tofurky?"

Wesley laughed, gaping at the tan lump he'd carried in. Oh, that wasn't a joke. "Yeah. Sure."

"Wesley," Lloyd warned.

"No, I mean, I don't care about the food. I like your home. Like that you invited us in."

Lloyd's gaze bore into him. His expression warred between amused and frustrated. Lloyd stepped forward. The gentle whiff of him prickled Wesley's senses, and his heart stuttered.

Caleb and MacDonald barged into the room, and Lloyd got bossy. "You two on that side of the table. Wesley sits next to me."

∼

"Stop slipping Tofurky onto my plate," Lloyd said under his breath while Caleb laughed trying to poke a bean into a glaring MacDonald's mouth.

Wesley snuck one last forkful of Tofurky onto Lloyd's plate. "But you are enjoying it so much."

"I was, but now I'm full. You got seconds."

"Your mom offered. It would've been rude to say no." Wesley stabbed a roasted potato and brought it to his lips. "Love these baked vegetables, though."

Caleb waggled his eyebrows at him. "Tried the radishes yet? If you haven't, you should."

Wesley kicked him under the table.

MacDonald jumped. "Really, Wesley? That's all you plan on giving him?"

"Sorry," he said with a chuckle. "Mind passing it on?"

MacDonald brightened. "Gladly."

Caleb scooted his chair toward Cathy. "Great food. Fun turkey."

Cathy grinned at her son. "How do you handle all this energy on a daily basis?"

Lloyd nodded somberly. "It's a challenge."

"Which he loves," Wesley said. "It's in his Cappy nature. Cathy, you must tell me all there is to know about your son. From the beginning. The year he was born. The specific day and time."

"You don't give up." Lloyd leaned back in his chair and crossed his arms.

Cathy winked conspiratorially at Lloyd, automatically making Wesley suspicious. "He was such a squishy wee thing. You'd never believe he'd grow into such a handsome man."

"And the date this handsome man came to be?"

She leaned over her plate and said in hushed tones. "He's told me not to tell you."

Wesley laughed and slapped a hand on Lloyd's thigh, squeezing extra hard. "Why do you thwart my every attempt to know you?"

"Tell me that zodiac signs don't mean anything, and I'll tell you."

"God, you're such a Capricorn!"

Lloyd sighed. "He never learns." The doorbell rang. Lloyd's thigh stiffened under Wesley's hold, reminding him he still hadn't removed his hand. He pulled back, reaching for his water.

Lloyd's brow furrowed. "She wouldn't."

"She would." Cathy sighed and answered the door. She came back half a minute later introducing Aunt Tabitha.

Aunt Tabitha gave them a cursory glance, lips turning down.

She flicked a finger in their direction. "Don't they have their own family to visit?"

"And that, Wesley," Lloyd said wiping his hands on a napkin and standing up, "about sums up my aunt."

"Lloyd," Tabitha said, shocked. "Where are your manners?"

"Excuse me." Lloyd moved past her and disappeared.

Wesley threw a dirty look at the woman, then chased after Lloyd. He found him standing at the open back door, taking in deep, slow breaths.

"Got to hate it when people show up uninvited," he said, slipping next to him on the threshold.

Leaning against the doorframe, Lloyd said, "Sorry she was rude to you."

"Nah, it's fine. She has a point. I kept thinking over dinner how this was what I always envisioned Thanksgiving could be, and then I thought of my mom sitting at our table. Alone."

Lloyd tapped the toes of Wesley's good foot. Wesley continued, "I think I might . . . I mean, after helping clean up."

Lloyd nodded. "How long has it been since you've been home?"

"The gestation period of a baby horse."

Wesley shrugged, studying the floor. As Lloyd shifted, a wall of warmth blocked a chill breeze. "I'll clean up. Do what you have to do. Say what you have to say."

"*I love you.*"

Wesley and Lloyd swung toward the approaching MacDonald and Caleb. Caleb was staring at the back of MacDonald's head, a wry grin on his face. "I want you to have all my babies. Imagine. Lots of little MacDonalds."

Wesley and Lloyd blinked at Caleb as though he'd gone mad. MacDonald *was* mad.

His brother caught their expressions and mouthed, "What?"

"You're crazy," Wesley said.

"Oh, certifiably." Caleb snuck an arm around MacDonald

and said in her ear, loud enough for everyone to hear. "That's why we'd work so well together."

MacDonald almost laughed, but then she thought better of it and met Wesley's eye. "We need to leave. Now."

Wesley searched her face, then searched his brother's face for an answer.

"She's right. We need to leave. Possibly never return." Caleb glanced over his shoulder as though expecting half the town to arrive bearing pitchforks. "Tabitha will never recover from that burn."

MacDonald focused on Lloyd. "I suppose I should apologize for offending that miserable old woman. But I don't want to. Thank you for dinner and goodbye."

Wesley followed their hasty retreat, waving at Lloyd over his shoulder. "Thank you and goodbye, apparently."

∽

WESLEY STUFFED LEFTOVER MILK DUDS INTO HIS MOUTH AND chewed hard as he eyed their front door from the car. The setting sun glinted off the windows of the Victorian façade.

Caleb gripped the steering wheel. They had dropped MacDonald at the dorms and borrowed her car. "This was your idea. You make the first move."

"You seemed pretty eager when I suggested swinging by. Maybe *you* should."

"Rock, paper, scissors?"

Wesley lost. "Best of three?"

"Out you go. I'll hover right behind you."

At the front door, Wesley hauled in a breath and pressed the buzzer. Almost immediately, the door opened.

Their mom stood dressed in a pantsuit. The thick, silver streak running through her piled black hair gave the impression a skunk sat atop her head. Her brows lifted in surprise, and she stepped back, gesturing them inside. "I prayed as much might happen."

"We wanted to talk."

"Well, he did," Caleb murmured. Unable to help himself, he kissed her on the cheek. "I'm still mad."

She rubbed Caleb's upper arm, relief and weariness playing in her eyes. "I made dinner."

Stretched across the dining room table were all their Thanksgiving favorites: mashed potatoes, creamy peas, pumpkin pie, cranberry sauce, and a turkey with a small slice carved out of it.

The lump in Wesley's throat swelled.

"Wow, Mom, were you expecting half the congregation?" Caleb dragged out a chair and dug into the potatoes.

Wesley took a seat, but he didn't think he could eat.

His mom frowned at Caleb. "You don't even say grace anymore?"

Caleb paused, chewing on a turkey leg. "Grace."

Mom sat at the head of the table where a glass of wine awaited her. "How's your law degree coming along, Wesley?"

Wesley's gaze flickered to the spot where their dad once sat. He'd always made his dad smile growing up. He had hoped following in his footsteps and completing a law degree would have made the great Judge Hidaka proud.

He winced apologetically. "Not great. I'll finish my undergraduate, but then I'm quitting college."

He surprised himself with that admission.

His mom sipped her wine. "Don't rush and do anything you'll regret. Maybe things will pick up. Maybe it's a phase."

His mom's second favorite word. "It's not," he said, quietly but firmly. "It never has been. I hate law, and I love men. If we are ever going to have a relationship, you need to accept that. Accept me."

His mom twisted her wine glass, staring at the long-cold food on the table. "Pastor Geoff said he saw you with someone. Was it your . . . fiancé?"

Caleb stopped eating, his gaze ping-ponging between them.

"His name is Lloyd."

The hurt that creased her face was palpable. Wesley tensed, preparing for the barrage of pleas to consider whether a guy was worth breaking their family over.

Caleb cut over her. "I landed a part in the musical accompaniment of a huge production."

Mom shifted her focus to Caleb. "Is your flute the reason you've been failing to show up to class?"

"Yes. But Wes has been helping—"

"It's great that you like to play, Caleb, but music doesn't make money."

Five minutes at home and already Wesley felt like a teenager. Frustrated and angry, he wished Mom would open her eyes. "You should have heard him play, Mom," Wesley said. "He was incredible. Beyond talented. I think he has the passion to make it."

Caleb's throat jutted as he swallowed, a sheen coating his eyes. "Think so?"

"Hell yeah, I hated dragging you out of that auditorium. I mean, I'd do it all over again, but I wish I didn't have to."

"If I didn't say it, thank you. For dropping me off at school. For all the nights you risk your RA's wrath."

They smirked at each other. "We should do something for Lloyd to say thanks," Caleb said.

The idea warmed Wesley, and a cheeky thought compounded his good feelings. "Help me wrangle a few key details from him, and we'll throw a surprise party."

"I want to meet him," Mom said quietly.

Wesley swung his head in her direction. She'd slumped into her chair, cradling her glass.

"I want to understand why this gaying is so important to you, Wesley." She looked at Caleb. "I know you're not running away because of my feelings about your music. You're doing it because you miss your brother."

Caleb shifted on his seat. "I'm doing it because you miss him too."

Tears prickled Wesley's eyes.

Caleb stood up. "I gotta . . . allergies." He fled from the room.

A plea strained her voice. "Let me meet your fiancé?"

∽

That might have been the best time to admit that there wasn't a fiancé.

But Wesley hadn't wanted to ruin the tender, emotional moment.

Which was why he should tell Lloyd his predicament.

He handed Caleb his dorm key and bounded out of the car at a ten-minute walk from Lloyd's house.

It was approaching midnight by the time he padded over Lloyd's lawn. He cursed under his breath when he remembered he'd left his phone in MacDonald's car.

Remembering that Lloyd had mentioned the view from his desk overlooking the street, Wesley hunted for bits of gravel and tossed them against Lloyd's upstairs window. It clinked and clattered, and he grinned. He'd always wanted to do this.

Someone cleared their throat, and Wesley jerked toward Lloyd, shuffling across the grass in slippers and a robe. Lloyd pointed to the window next to the one Wesley had been pelting. "That's my room. Mom kindly asks that you move a few feet to your right, or better yet, come inside."

Wesley cupped his mouth and called out, "Sorry, Cathy!"

"See you in the morning, Wesley!" came a wall-filtered reply.

Wesley headed for the front door. "How does she know I'm staying over?"

"It's midnight. You're play-acting Romeo on my front lawn. She's a smart woman." Lloyd shut the door behind them, and after removing his shoes and jacket, Wesley followed him upstairs.

"Love the look, by the way," Wesley whispered, tugging Lloyd's robe belt. "It's like a flash-forward into the future. You're the grumpy old codger who loves telling off kids for making too much noise—oh wait." Wesley eyed Lloyd up and down by the dim light of the hall. "Maybe it isn't a flash-forward."

"You're right. I won't be like this in sixty years."

"What will you be like?"

"Grumpier."

Lloyd flicked a light on and gestured Wesley inside his surprisingly cluttered childhood room. Shelves lined an entire wall stuffed with books, board games, and more than one Rubik's cube.

Then there was the bed.

"A twin, Lloyd? We'll sure be cozy tonight."

Without looking away from him, Lloyd pulled out a rollaway mattress from under the bed using his foot. "Top or bottom?"

"I'm happy with either," he said with a leer, "but I'd prefer to bottom."

Lloyd shut his eyes. "Boy, oh boy."

Wesley smirked and peeled off his clothes until he was down to his boxers and undershirt. Avoiding eye contact, Lloyd grabbed him a blanket, then unrobed to a similar state of undress and flicked off the light. "I assume you didn't come here to sleep."

"Not quite the proposition I imagined from you, Lloyd."

A pillow smacked Wesley in the face. He laughed as he settled onto the rollaway and stuffed Lloyd's pillow under his head.

Glow-in-the-dark stars covered the ceiling, possibly arranged in constellations. "Guess I'm not the only one obsessed with stars."

Lloyd rolled onto his side and peered down at Wesley. "Why are you here at midnight?"

"Hoping you might sleep-divulge your date of birth?"

"Wesley."

"I told my mom I'm quitting college once I get my undergrad."

"Because of our conversation?"

"It didn't come out of thin air."

"How did you feel when you said it?"

"Guilty, then relieved. Now nervous." Wesley bit his lip. "As my RA, do you think I'm doing the right thing?"

At the mention of RA, Lloyd folded back an inch. "Let's arrange a date and work through some options for you."

"I'm not good at making decisions. I'm inconsistent and terribly indecisive."

"I've noticed."

"I'm pretty screwbally."

"Yet I like you all the same."

Wesley sighed. "I'm thrilled to hear you say that, because I might have told my mom you'd come for dinner on Christmas Eve. As my fiancé?"

Silence.

Wesley's heart thumped as he tried to read Lloyd's expression in the dark. "Please?"

Finally, Lloyd grunted and rolled out of sight on his bed. "The things I do for you."

Can't wait to cream you.

Chapter Twelve

"Thank you so much for breakfast," Wesley said to Cathy. It was just the two of them clearing away the morning dishes.

Cathy flashed that warm, motherly smile. "Anytime, I mean it. It's nice that Lloyd is inviting his friends home."

"He usually doesn't?"

"This is the first time since he started college."

Wesley almost dropped the glasses he was holding.

"Well, expect me here a lot. Invitation or not. Lloyd is the best and he's my friend." A sudden explosion of butterflies writhed through his veins. He blinked and spoke again, quietly. "He's my best friend."

Cathy smiled. "He cares about you, too."

Lloyd picked that moment to waltz into the dining room. "Need me for anything?"

Wesley swallowed, then nodded vigorously. "I need you to go turbo Cap on me."

Cathy left the room, and Lloyd neared him, lifting an eyebrow. "What?"

"I'm having confusing feelings," Wesley said.

Lloyd took the glasses from him and set them on the table. "Explain these feelings?"

"You're my best friend."

Lloyd's lips turned up into a wide smile, cheek dimpling. His glowing, twinkling eyes made Wesley nervous. "That's a good start."

Wesley pinched his wristband, paralyzed by Lloyd's breathtaking smile. The smile he had been waiting to see for so long.

He'd been wrong, though. The smile didn't make him want to jump Lloyd. It made his chest swell.

"If you could say something grumpy right now," Wesley said. "It would help ground me."

Lloyd laughed, and the deep vibrations caused static to zip from Wesley's head to his toes. He narrowed his eyes. "That's not helping."

Lloyd settled warm palms on his shoulders, thumbs pressing against his collarbone. "Believe it or not, I'm not always grumpy. At least ten percent of the time, I'm shamefully cheerful."

"I say we're fiancés all the time. Why does saying we're best friends make me feel weirdly vulnerable?"

"Because you mean it, and that changes things."

Wesley shifted his weight from foot to foot. "Do you feel the same way?"

"I can't go turbo Cap on you right now," he pulled Wesley against his chest and held him warmly. "But I can go turbo best friend."

As part of the best-friend production, Lloyd answered Wesley's nosy questions. Like whether he could scour through all his childhood pictures and what young Lloyd used to do for fun.

Lloyd dragged Wesley across a dewy lawn and ten feet up a sprawling oak into a creaky tree house.

Sunlight trickled in through a roof window. Two stools, a table, and shelves decorated the small interior, and a foliage dream catcher hung against a wall. Wesley sat on the small stool. "So you *did* once have a playful side."

Lloyd wiped cobwebs off a long row of pinecones. "I used to pretend I was a principal. These were my children."

Wesley leaned his elbows on the table and said teasingly, "Do you want to be a school principal when you grow up?"

"Math teacher, then principal. Yes."

"Really?"

Lloyd lifted a fallen pinecone. "Yes."

"In that case, I'm mapping out your future. You'll overthrow Principal Bontempo at Sandalwood, and I won't have to fear sending my kid there."

Lloyd glanced at him, hand stilling on the pinecone. "Planning on having kids?"

"Kid. Singular. I'm gonna helicopter the hell out of him He won't stand a chance with the girls." He leaned back against the wall. "Have you ever thought about it? Having kids?"

"How could I resist? I love shouting at them, remember?"

They shared a smile.

"What's this?" Wesley picked up a contraption made of acorns off the table.

"The abacus I made."

"Of course."

Wesley spent the rest of the day making Lloyd show him all of his childhood haunts. His old school. The grocery store where he stocked up on candy. The track through the woods where he used to jog. He even rifled through his collections of movies and music, noting the sore lack of rock 'n' roll.

After making a right mess of Lloyd's Rubik's cube, Wesley tossed it to him and watched as he methodically set all the sides to their rightful colors.

"There's a light festival at Green Valley Park," Lloyd said, placing the finished cube on a shelf above his bed. "It's walking distance from here." Wesley lifted a nine-by-nine Rubik's cube, and Lloyd protectively lunged for it. "Wanna check it out?"

Twenty minutes later, donned in thick coats and scarves, they were walking through the tea-lit park.

Ten minutes after that, Wesley spotted a hotdog stand.

"Oh, hotdogs. I love hotdogs." Wesley patted his pockets and cursed. "I didn't bring a wallet, and you dumped all your change into the donation bin. Why did you have to be so generous?"

"Yes," Lloyd said drily, "I should have given less to charity on account of your hotdog needs."

Wesley grinned. "So long as you're adequately remorseful. Now come, let's get me a hotdog."

Lloyd gave him a quizzical, almost worried look. "You don't have money."

"I'll barter."

"With what?" Lloyd called out as Wesley skipped ahead to the stand. "And why are you grinning like that?"

Wesley stopped in front of a pretty, twenty-something guy wearing an unfortunate fire-red uniform. He gave him a charmed smile. "Here's the situation," Wesley said the moment Lloyd stepped to his right. "I love hotdogs but am out of cash. I was thinking, you give me a hot one with mustard, hold the onions, and I'll trade you this hunk here."

Hotdog Guy's furrowed brow smoothed out and his lips twitched.

Lloyd murmured under his breath and sighed.

"Your hunk for a hotdog?"

Wesley nodded. "He's very principled. He never breaks the rules, and I'm sure he'd do a great job tending to your meat."

Hotdog Guy grinned, and the lazy roll of his eye over Lloyd did not go unnoticed. Wesley felt Lloyd's body shift as he also recognized the lustful look.

"Oh, you find him hot!" Wesley said, using it to his hotdog-seeking advantage. "He's also an amazing kisser. A little weird about having to do it on a bed, though."

Lloyd groaned, and Wesley almost laughed at the hard squeeze that came to his elbow.

He continued, "But I've read that Capricorns have great stamina and will hold out until they're sure their partner has arrived, if you understand what I'm saying."

"Everyone knows what you're saying," Lloyd said. "The French tourist with no English on the bench behind us knows what you're saying."

Hotdog Guy laughed at Lloyd's dry retort, making Lloyd straighten and shift his attention.

Something about that clawed under Wesley's skin, but it was nothing compared to the sharp pull in his stomach when Hotdog Guy made Lloyd laugh.

Wesley wasn't hungry after all.

"Yeah," Hotdog Guy said, full-on eye-fucking Lloyd, a lingering gaze at his crotch. "I'll give you all the hotdog you want."

With a tight smile, Wesley snatched Lloyd's arm. "I changed my mind. There aren't enough hotdogs in the world good enough for this one."

They made it halfway across the park before Wesley dared to slow down.

"He's not following us," Lloyd said.

"He better not be."

Lloyd gestured Wesley through a narrow arched gate peppered with tea lights. "I'm not sure if I should be offended that you tried to trade me for a hotdog or touched that you didn't."

A noise sounded from the bushes and Wesley halted, causing Lloyd to smack into his back. Wesley stumbled and Lloyd steadied him with firm hands on his hips. "I gotcha," he rumbled in his ear.

Wesley twisted around and gripped Lloyd's shirt. He jerked his head in the direction of the bushes. "I think there's a wild pig or something."

"In town? I doubt—" Lloyd's gaze flickered behind Wesley and filled with horror.

Foliage crunched.

"It's a pig, isn't it?"

"Well, this is awkward," came a male voice.

Lloyd's poker face held firmly in place. "Jamie, hi. I hope you are the man Jamie is always chuckling on the phone with?"

Another male voice. "I'm Theo, and I better be."

Wesley checked out the two men who'd emerged from the bushes. Both tugged at their clothes, cheeks bright from sexy times behind the bushes—and embarrassment.

Wesley recognized the one shoving his sleeve up over a silver watch, but not the guy dimpling wickedly.

Wesley gestured to the guy with the watch and asked Lloyd, "Is this the professor you want supervising you next year?"

Lloyd shifted behind him. "He's the one."

Wesley patted Lloyd's chest and said with a wink, "Public indecency. Looks like you found some leverage."

∽

HALF AN HOUR LATER, LLOYD WAS STOMPING AROUND HIS kitchen while Wesley poured himself a glass of apple juice.

"Leverage, Wesley?"

Wesley jerked. "Gah! You should warn me when the silent treatment ends." He wiped off the juice he'd spilled over his chin and chest.

"Leverage?" Lloyd set a pot of water on the stove and pulled out hotdogs from the fridge.

"Not the most charming way I could have introduced myself," Wesley agreed, twisting the glass in his hand.

Lloyd hardened his gaze. "He's my professor and potentially a friend."

"I was aiming for cute."

"You misfired. Made it look like I was trying to manipulate him."

"I didn't mean it maliciously." Wesley risked a cutesy grin. "How much longer are you gonna be grumpy with me?"

"A little while."

Guess he deserved that. Wesley opened drawers and found a pair of tongs. He handed them over and Lloyd used them to place the hotdogs into the bubbling water.

Wesley read the empty hotdog wrapper before throwing it into the trash. "One hundred percent vegetarian."

He eyed the contents of the pot suspiciously.

Lloyd caught his expression and sighed. "Bit of ketchup and mustard and you won't taste the difference."

"I don't do vegetarian."

"You are very absolute in your statements. Have you even tried?"

"A bite. Years ago. It put me off for life."

Lloyd tonged the fake meat in the pot. "Maybe you tried the wrong vegetarian sausage."

"Tofu is tofu."

"This is seitan."

"They changed the name? Satan. Fits."

"*Seitan*. It's made from wheat gluten. Tofu, from soybeans."

"You're telling me this hotdog will be an explosion of joy to my taste buds?"

"I'm telling you to get over your preconceived notions that it won't work for you, and try it."

Wesley yanked open the fridge, scowling as he pulled out the ketchup and mustard. "Fine. I'll try it."

Five minutes later, Wesley was staring at a ketchup-smeared hotdog in a bun.

Lloyd sat across from him, half his Satan-hotdog devoured.

Wesley moaned. "Do I have to?"

Disappointment flashed over Lloyd's face. "You don't have to do anything."

Wesley picked up the hotdog. After an apprehensive sniff, he bit into it. The seitan was still warm and filled with melted cheese. He crammed more into his mouth. It was delicious. Better than all other hotdogs.

Wesley finished, then said to Lloyd's expectant face, "Could be worse. Are you planning on finishing yours?"

Lloyd's lips curved into an almost grin as he handed over his half hotdog. "You love it."

"Don't get ahead of yourself." He grinned before diving in for another bite. He swallowed it with a moan of enjoyment. "I'll admit, I'm glad I tried. Now what are we doing for the rest of the night?"

"It's late. I should drop you off at the dorm and get some sleep."

"A good idea, yes. Here's a better one . . ."

∞

THEY WATCHED A MOVIE ON LLOYD'S BED, THE LAPTOP resting between their calves. By the end of it, they were yawning in symphony.

"Guess I'll have to crash here again with you," Wesley said with a grin.

"You planned it that way."

"Whatever would make you think that?"

Lloyd's expression said '*Really?*' "You made us watch the 1964 movie *Sleep*."

"Andy Warhol directed it."

"It's three-hundred-and-twenty-one minutes."

"So that's dawn outside? Not a street lamp?"

"Get to bed."

They stumbled about getting ready for bed. Stripped to their boxers and undershirts, they climbed onto their respective mattresses.

Wesley stared at the Capricornus constellation of Lloyd's glow-in-the-dark stars. "Lloyd?" he whispered.

Lloyd dangled one arm over the side of the bed and twitched his fingers to show he was listening.

"I'm sorry for embarrassing you in front of your professor friend."

"It's behind us now," Lloyd said softly.

Wesley would make it up to him, though. He tugged Lloyd's fingers. "I read something. About Capricorns."

A displeased hum. "What's that?"

"Their patience is unmatched."

"True."

"So when you get to the end of it, that's it."

"What's it?"

"You snap."

A deep groan. "I'm afraid that might be true, too."

"Keep being grumpy with me. Fight with me. Tell me when I overstep or say something stupid. Do whatever you have to do. I don't want to be thrown out of your life."

"If I don't get to sleep," Lloyd yawned. "There'll be another fight very soon."

"That's what I'm talking about." Wesley gave Lloyd's fingers another yank, and Lloyd hooked his fingers, knotting them together.

"Hundreds of fights are ahead of us, Wesley. I'll still want you around at the end of them."

I worship the grounds you walk on.

Chapter Thirteen

A week after Thanksgiving weekend, Wesley woke feeling miserable. He groaned and tentatively sat up. The room spun. His arm felt heavy as he swatted at Caleb pathetically. He was still asleep, snoring lightly.

"Hazelnut?" Even his voice sounded croaky.

He prodded his brother's cheek. Nothing.

Fine, he'd search for sympathy elsewhere.

He shuffled to Lloyd's room. His RA hours had just begun. He sat at the desk, tapping away at his laptop.

Wesley groaned and thwumped against the open door.

Lloyd shoved himself out of his chair, scrutinizing him.

Wesley helped him with the diagnosis. "I feel achy and sweaty, and my head's making noise."

Lloyd swiveled toward his first-aid kit and Wesley stumbled into the room after him.

"I'm so hot. Feel my forehead."

"I believe you."

Wesley lunged for Lloyd's hand to press against his burning forehead, missed, and toppled onto Lloyd's bed. "You're my best friend," he moaned as Lloyd picked through the kit. "You should know exactly how hot I am."

"I'm aware of how hot you are."

"What?"

Lloyd paused for a moment before resuming his hunt for a remedy. "How hot you *think* you are."

A momentary grin sliced through Wesley's agony. "You said I'm hot—ouch!"

"Might want to get back to your room, Wesley. Your head is getting too big for you."

That presented a Caleb-sized problem. "My bed won't work for a sick person. Can I crash in here?"

Lloyd straightened. "Is your bro—Never mind. Tuck yourself in. I'll look after you."

True to his word, Lloyd supplied Wesley with an abundance of tissues and painkillers and brought him orange juice that tasted fresh pressed. He checked his temperature and drowned them in darkness when the light started to hurt Wesley's eyes. Then, at the end of the day, he made soup.

Wesley shuffled up in bed, resting against a pillow. The upward-facing desk lamp produced a ring of light against the ceiling. "Lloyd. Nursing me back to health. The sight is enough to make me want to get sick on a semi-regular basis."

Lloyd pressed a spoon of hot broth to his lips. "How can you still talk so much?"

Wesley slurped it down, wincing. "Hearing my own voice. It's worth the pain."

Lloyd's eyes glimmered with a laugh. "Can you take over, or shall I spoon feed you all of this?"

"As much as I love you doing it for me, I fear half the chicken juice is drizzling down my chin and onto your sheets." Wesley took the spoon from Lloyd. "And I don't want sullied sheets being the reason you throw me out."

"I promise you that won't be the reason."

"But you are going to throw me out?"

He wiggled a finger between them. "RA. Resident. You sleeping in here the entire night? Not a good look."

Wesley whimpered. "Even if Hazelnut took the floor, I wouldn't be comfortable."

"I didn't hear any of that. Please don't repeat it." Lloyd planted his hands on his hips and searched the room as though it held an answer. With a sigh, he grabbed a folded blanket from his closet. "I'll take the couch. If anyone asks, your bed broke."

Wesley laughed as Lloyd left the room, then groaned as his head pounded. "Yeah, because there won't be any follow-up questions to *that* excuse."

∽

THE BUG THAT WESLEY CAUGHT TURNED OUT TO BE A RATHER promiscuous one. It fucked with at least half the Williamson residents, confining them to their beds. Poor Lloyd was run off his feet making sure his sick residents made a full and speedy recovery.

Fortunately, it was a 48-hour bug, and Wesley felt better after another day sleeping in Lloyd's bed.

Unfortunately, the bug attacked Lloyd too.

He tried to suck it up like a good Capricorn, but he ended up grunting in bed.

Wesley hated that he had to work most of the morning, but as soon as he was done, he headed for Lloyd. "Finally. I'm all yours."

Lloyd lay on his bed with a freshly fucked aura about him. A sheen to his skin, voice hoarse. "All mine?"

"Nurse Wesley, at your service."

A tight sound escaped Lloyd that might have been a laugh. "Turn off the light?"

Wesley did, then felt his way back to the bed. He smoothed

Lloyd's brow and took his temperature. The small glowing screen of the thermometer showed it was rising.

"I'm taking your first-aid kit to the hall so I can see. You need ibuprofen."

Lloyd curled onto his side, teeth chattering, gaze hooded with fever as he watched Wesley wrestle the large box off Lloyd's shelf.

"Stay right there," Wesley said.

Lloyd's grumbled response followed him out of the room. "Putting a real pin in my plans, there."

Wesley shut the door and jumped at the sight of a massive blanket fort being constructed in the hall. Randy latched onto his ankles and pulled Wesley under the quilt.

"How long was I in Lloyd's room?"

Randy laughed and told him it took up most of the floor.

Awkwardly, with the kit in tow, he crawled toward a lamp set halfway into the fort.

Sheets spanned the hallway, stretched into open dorm rooms.

His room included.

The sound of a flute trailed out of his room and Wesley crawled toward it. Caleb sat under a floral sheet, legs outstretched at the base of his bed. Suzy and MacDonald sat opposite him.

Caleb waggled his brow as he continued to blow into the flute, fingers dancing a mile a minute over its length. MacDonald used the end of her cane to stab him in the foot.

When she caught Wesley staring, she bit out: "He refuses to give back my key."

Wesley didn't point out that she could use Suzy's. Suzy didn't either.

They exchanged a look, and Wesley shuffled back to Lloyd's room, ducking into the kitchen en route.

Water and pill in hand, Wesley shuffled toward Lloyd, blocking his view of the hall. He'd have shut the door, except that he needed light to get his bearings. An exchange of air was a bonus, too.

"What's going on out there?" Lloyd said wearily.

Wesley donned his best innocent expression. "What's going on where?"

Lloyd let out a suspicious groan. "Out there. I smell chaos."

"I'm surprised you can smell *anything*."

Lloyd tried to sit up but Wesley pinned him down, squashing the painkiller against his fever-ridden chest.

"Take this pill, drink this water, and do not look over my shoulder out the door."

"Randy!" Lloyd's yell came out raspy, broken.

"How adorable."

That earned him a dirty look.

Wesley pinched the pill off Lloyd's chest and offered it. "Eat me." He held out the water. "Drink me."

Lloyd stared at the water and pill, then glanced under Wesley's outstretched arm.

"Fine," Wesley relented. Poor Capricorn wouldn't rest without knowing. "Some guys built a giant blanket fort."

Lloyd flung the sheets off and swung his legs off the bed, but he didn't quite make it to his feet. His knees gave out and he steadied himself against Wesley's shoulders, causing Wesley to spill half the water over Lloyd's stomach.

Wesley helped Lloyd struggle out of his T-shirt. He didn't bother with another one, just sagged onto the bed. "Last time the morons knocked over the lamp in the lounge. Glass shattered everywhere."

"That's not gonna happen twice."

"It's Randy. Everything happens twice."

Very true point.

"I'm supposed to be on duty. Gemma doesn't get back until tonight, and there's no way in hell I'll let Gavin manage my residents." Lloyd worked himself up, managing to push back up on his elbows. "Can you ask MacDonald to lend me her crutches?"

Wesley perched next to Lloyd on the bed. "Take the pill. Sleep. Let me handle it for a couple of hours."

Lloyd groaned—and Wesley wasn't sure it was entirely sickness related.

Wesley growled and prodded Lloyd's chest. "You took care of me. Now it's my turn."

Lloyd hummed. "Make sure the kitchen remains out of bounds. No cooking until the fort is put away."

Wesley nodded. "Got it."

"And if they complain—and they will—tell them it's for their own safety."

"Anything else?"

"If the alarm goes off while I'm sick, someone's getting an ass-kicking."

Wesley took the empty glass after Lloyd knocked back his pill. "I almost want it to go off, just to see that."

A cough. "Wesley. Stop."

"Stop what?"

"Making me smile. It hurts."

Wesley drew up the sheets and tucked them around Lloyd's chest. "No promises."

Lloyd reached out and grabbed hold of Wesley's shirt, keeping him close. He let go and pressed the wrinkles out at his shoulder. "Take my phone? Jamie's going to call about meeting up. Can you arrange something for tomorrow?"

"Tomorrow? Try again."

A frustrated sigh morphed into a cough. "Okay. The day after."

"Next week, I got it."

Lloyd wheezed in a deep breath as if to fight him, and let it deflate. "Fine. Visit me later?"

Wesley hit him with two finger guns. "I'll bring hot soup."

"Better be cold if that fort is still up."

~

Wesley arranged the meeting for the following week.

"Are you in the office today?" Wesley asked at the tail end of his conversation with Jamie. "Right now?"

"Yes, why?"

Wesley paid the professor a visit.

His door was open, so Wesley peered inside with a knock to the outside wall. Professor Jamie was eating out of a Tupperware container and he wasn't alone. His boyfriend, Theo, sat near him, socked feet propped up on Jamie's lap.

"Look. Me," Theo sang. "I cooked."

Jamie smirked into his container and twirled spaghetti onto his fork. "Reheated, Theo."

Wesley knocked again.

Theo recognized him immediately. "It's Lloyd's boyfriend. Come in."

Wesley entered, gripping the strap of his messenger bag. "Um, well. I'm here because. Wait, one small clarification. Lloyd isn't my boyfriend."

Theo dropped his feet to the floor and leaned against the corner of Jamie's desk. "You sure?"

"Theo," Jamie said. "You're hardly one to speak."

Theo blew his boyfriend an air kiss. "I've gotten wiser with age."

A bellow exploded in the hall. "What nitwit got tomato sauce all over the microwave?"

Theo jumped up and shut the door. Jamie closed his eyes and laughed. When he reopened, he focused on Wesley. "What brings you here?"

"Apologies. And the hope you might accept them." Wesley rubbed his pinched fingers up and down the strap at his chest. "I was a smartass the first time we met, and it didn't shine a great light on Lloyd. I would almost never—and Lloyd most certainly never—blackmail anyone to get ahead. Lloyd is the most mature, considerate, fair person I know. He is stubbornly good, and I wanted to make that clear."

Theo's gaze pinged from him to Jamie. "Oh, I'm dying to speak."

Jamie shook his head and placed his spaghetti on the desk between piles of student essays. "I like Lloyd. He has passion and drive and he's no nonsense about his work."

"Would you still consider him someone you could do statistical-economical things with?"

Theo snorted. "I like you, Wes."

"I don't have the capacity to supervise another master's project and do it justice," Jamie said. "But Professor Katzenberger is brilliant and I know she's set her sights on Lloyd. She might even give him some research and teaching-assistant work next year."

A wave of disappointment flooded Wesley. He *had* fucked it up for Lloyd after all. "Oh. Okay."

Theo glared at his boyfriend, then turned a chipper smile on Wesley. "Katzenberger is a great professor. And this is a good thing. For dynamics."

He motioned between them.

Jamie nodded. "Lloyd and I get along well, and Theo and I are relatively new in town. It would be nice getting to know you both."

"Not because you're boyfriends and come together in a package or anything!" Theo said. "Just because you're fun. We should all do something together."

Wesley relaxed. Maybe Lloyd would find this better. Friends who turned in early on a Saturday night. "Are you big on the club scene?" Wesley asked.

Theo snorted as Jamie replied, "I hope you mean the math club scene?"

Yep. This couple would fit Wesley and Lloyd perfectly.

Fit *Lloyd* perfectly.

~

"THIS IS WHY IT PAYS NOT TO GET CLOSE TO ANYONE," MacDonald said from the doorway to Wesley's room, where it was Caleb's turn being sick.

Caleb blew her a kiss. "Catch it, sweetheart."

MacDonald swept a red lock off her face with her middle finger, and left. Wesley continued reading Caleb's horoscope. Not that he needed it to know the near future. "It's not looking promising."

"My throat feels like someone's juicing it."

"I told you to go home when I came down with it."

Caleb flattened his lips and changed the conversation. "I have a math assignment I needed to do over the weekend, due tomorrow."

Wesley sank into his chair and groaned. "Why didn't you do it yesterday?"

"I thought I could finish it today."

"You won't be going to school tomorrow anyway."

Caleb rubbed his throat. "I'll be better by then. I have to be. I have rehearsals."

Wesley passed Caleb his half-cup of water. "You're not going to rehearsals either.

~

"YES, I AM. GIMME MY FLU—" CALEB COUGHED VIOLENTLY, struggling out of the bed.

Wesley hugged the flute case to his chest. "Looks like you already got a flu."

"Flu—flu—ugh, I give up." Caleb glowered at Wesley, but not for long, since it seemingly made him dizzy. He steadied himself against the bedside table.

"I'll call the school."

"Hey," Caleb wheezed as Wesley slipped from the room. "Where are you taking that?"

Wesley put his brother's flute on top of the fridge. If Caleb managed to get it, he'd be healthy enough to have it.

He dialed the school.

"Mr. Hidaka," the school secretary said as though afraid of being overheard. "Principal Bontempo will notice if Caleb's not at school assembly."

"He's sick. He can't come in."

A pompous male voice trembled down the line. "I'll take this," Principal Bontempo said. "Wesley Hidaka? Am I overhearing this correctly?"

"Just like the old days," Wesley said with biting sweetness. "Such an uncanny ability to appear everywhere I don't want you to be."

"Let me guess, your brother didn't finish an assignment because he is conveniently sick."

Wesley paced the hall. "He *is* sick."

Principal Bontempo didn't care. "Is there an assignment due? Bear in mind, one visit to the staff room, and I'll know if you lied."

Wesley gripped his phone so hard it popped out of his hand and he had to chase it against his ear again. "Yes, but—"

"Bring in the assignment, and I'll excuse this sick day."

Wesley hung up with a curse. He stormed back into his room. Caleb had drifted back to sleep, one cowboy boot on, the other toppled on the floor by his limp arm.

The unfinished assignment lay on the desk.

Wesley carried the papers to Lloyd's room.

"Oh, bosom friend," he said, striding in when Lloyd opened the door, a towel slung low around his hips. "My kindred spirit! Keeper of secrets!" He flashed Lloyd a sheepish smile and waved the papers. "Doer of math assignments?"

"I was about to shower."

"I put two and two together." He slapped the paper against Lloyd's chest, leaning in with a widening smile and a flutter of his thick eyelashes. "What I can't put together, are these numbers."

Lloyd took the papers, keeping his eyes on Wesley's smile. "Why am I doing this?"

"We have to shove it in Principal Bontempo's face." Wesley was standing so close to Lloyd, he could see the goosebumps on his perked nipple. He lightly pinched it. "Ever think about piercing one?"

Lloyd sucked in a breath and dropped a sheet of paper.

Wesley chased after it, pinning it against Lloyd's upper thigh.

"Wesley," Lloyd groaned with exasperation. "You're driving me mad."

"Two of those words were in my next sentence." Wesley lifted the sheet, the corner dragging up Lloyd's stomach, making his toned abdomen ripple.

Lloyd tucked a finger under Wesley's chin and pushed it up. When Wesley focused on his face, Lloyd smiled with a gentle lift of his eyebrow.

Right. "Driving me." Wesley glanced once more at Lloyd's toned body. "Would you?"

Lloyd's laugh combed through Wesley's sleep-tossed bangs.

Wesley shook his head and tried again. "Would you please drive me to Sandalwood to drop off the math assignment you're doing for Caleb."

"Two things. One: I'm making some mistakes."

Fair enough.

"Two: I'm not doing this for Caleb."

"Yeah," Wesley said with a breezy smile, backing out of the room. "You're doing it for me. Your kindred spirit. Keeper of secrets."

Lloyd followed him. "Doer of—?"

Wesley winked and turned down the hall. "That remains to be seen."

You have a cute mug.

Chapter Fourteen

Elvis's *Jailhouse Rock* pounded from Suzy's room into the hall. Wesley spun and tandem stepped with Suzy in time to the beat. They stopped mid-step to emphasize a musical pause and then completed their swing. "We need to hit Glitter again," she said on the tail end of a laugh.

"New Year's?" Wesley tossed out. Glitter would have all the rock 'n' roll classics playing. Why not?

"You gonna crash at my place after?"

The music died, and MacDonald poked her head out of the room. "My parents will be losing cash in Vegas again. You can all stay at my place."

Wesley's ears bugged. "Did you just invite us to spend time with you?"

"This place is locked up over Christmas," MacDonald said. "I'll be bored with nobody to pick on."

"Better make sure your brother tags along," Suzy said as she disappeared into her room to study.

A cloud of grumpiness had students fleeing the hall as Lloyd trudged through the stairwell door. Lloyd was the reason Wesley had been loitering in the hall to begin with.

Lloyd's gaze snagged on him, and Wesley met him halfway. "Gavin wants to speak to you," Wesley said.

A grunt. "Just what I wanted to hear after an intense five-hour study session."

"He *needs* to speak to you."

"If you see him, tell him I'll have my door open during RA hours."

Wesley followed Lloyd into the communal kitchen. "You know how impatient Gavin is."

Lloyd grabbed a mug and snatched the instant coffee. "What does he want now?"

Wesley glared at the instant coffee, affronted. "I start work in fifteen minutes." He wrestled the glass jar away from Lloyd. In the struggle, Wesley ended up jammed between Lloyd and the counter. "You can wait that long."

Their lengths meshed as Lloyd reached for the jar Wesley held up high behind him. Lloyd's brow creased in frustration. "Maybe today I'm tired of waiting."

"Come on, Cap. You know you can hold out."

"Just a small drink."

"Hmm, no. By the time we finish this argument, it'll be time to start my shift. I'll make your favorite roast."

"You sure know how to tempt me."

"I try."

Lloyd peeled himself away from Wesley. "Better make it a large. I'll need it to face Gavin."

"I'm pretty sure he's here to finalize a date for the Open Week party. Though, fair warning, he was carrying around his leather binder."

Lloyd grumbled. "Maybe I should leave a note on my door. All resident emergencies can find me at Me Gusta Robusta."

"Gonna hide behind me?"

"No," Lloyd said, walking toward his room. "I will sit at the coffee bar and point to the *No RA business allowed on premises* sign when he comes in."

Wesley padded down the hall next to him, smirking.

Lloyd continued, "I'm a good RA with enough grump to strike the right amount of fear into my residents. Gavin doesn't scare me."

"Right," Wesley said as Lloyd opened his door.

Lloyd gave a startled bark.

Gavin was sitting on his desk chair, leather binder spread open on his knees to a glittery page. "About time."

Wesley grinned widely when Lloyd, stiff in the doorway, turned a fiery gaze on him. "You knew he was in here."

"Uh-huh."

"Why didn't you say that from the beginning?"

"I warned you how impatient he was."

Lloyd huffed, the glint in his eye telling Wesley he'd pay later for this joke. He turned to Gavin. "How did you even get in here?"

Gavin waved a key. "In case an RA loses their room key."

"Now I have to worry about you popping up in my room at any hour."

"That shouldn't be a problem. Unless you're hiding something?" Gavin's gaze flickered to Wesley's.

Wesley snorted. "Do you think we're fucking or something? We're not. How many times do I have to say it? He's a Cap. The sex would be bad."

"How do you explain how close you two are then?" Gavin asked.

"We're best friends. Duh."

Gavin lifted a brow. Lloyd kept quiet. Calm.

"O'Conner got fired for slipping into his resident's pants," Gavin said. "You wouldn't want our coordinator to hear any rumors, would you?"

"As Wesley unnecessarily exaggerated, we are not sleeping together, and we won't be anytime soon."

"I heard that you're pretending to be his fiancé? You can see how I might have misunderstood your level of commitment to him."

"I don't like the way you said that," Wesley said. "Lloyd might hate streamers and dancing, but he's not completely void of creativity. He plays the fiancé part to perfection, with warmth and humor, and the right touch of playfulness."

"I'm sure his acting is flawless," Gavin said sarcastically. Wesley fought against flipping him the bird.

Lloyd's jaw tightened as he continued to glare at Gavin.

"I go out of my way to abide house rules," Lloyd said, "and I wish you would go out of yours to respect my space."

Gavin snapped his binder shut and gave a curt nod. "Fine. Would we like to discuss plans for the Open Week party in the lounge?"

Lloyd grunted, then steeled his gaze on Wesley. "How about over an extra-large coffee at Me Gusta Robusta?"

∼

WESLEY SERVED BOTH RAS EXTRA-LARGE COFFEES, AND LET them go at it.

Caleb moped in, ripping his school tie away from his throat. He jerked his thumb at Lloyd and Gavin. "Thought no RA business was allowed on the premises."

Lloyd leaned back on the stool, interrupting his heated conversation with Gavin. "And I thought younger brothers lived at home."

"Keep up the awesome work, guys," Caleb said and hurried to Wesley.

Wesley finished his brother's hazelnut latte and handed it to him stealthily. "Fifties bash. Dress-up optional but recommended. January fifteenth."

"The week of dress rehearsals," Caleb said, humming. "I'll make it work. Where's MacD?"

Caleb scuttled off to his favorite girl in the world, and Wesley busied himself in a rush of orders. When he was through, Lloyd was also. They waved off Gavin.

Lloyd gave Wesley a twinkle of satisfaction, and a similar twinkle mirrored in Wesley's belly.

Lloyd reached into his back pocket for his wallet. "It's close to Christmas."

"Oh yeah? I thought everyone was just crushing on an old dude with a stellar beard."

Lloyd didn't even dignify that with an eye roll. "I'd like to buy fifty gift certificates for a coffee of choice."

"It was *you* who did that last year?"

"Keep it down. I don't want anyone to know."

"Who served you last year? MacDonald, huh?" Wesley shook his head, watching her banter with Caleb. "She never said."

"At least someone can keep a secret." Lloyd handed over a wad of cash. "Can you give the gift certificates to me later? I have a meeting with Jamie."

Wesley's stomach churned. He hadn't yet told Lloyd about Jamie not having time to guide his masters.

"You've gone quiet," Lloyd said, brow creasing. "Are you okay?"

"Me? I'm fine. I just . . . your meeting . . ."

"Yes?"

His breath deflated. "I'm thinking of you."

Lloyd delivered him a smile Wesley didn't deserve and strode out of the café.

∽

After his shift ended, Wesley took the fifty signed gift certificates to Lloyd's room. Lloyd slouched on his bed and stared blankly at the ceiling. Moisture filmed Lloyd's eyes.

"Are you sad?" Wesley asked, because he was an idiot.

Lloyd's voice pinched as he tried to control it. "Why would I be?"

"No reason."

Lloyd forced himself to sit, making as if to spring into RA action.

Wesley touched his shoulder, stilling him. "If you were—"

"I'm not."

"Just checking." Wesley dropped his hand.

"I'm feeling thoroughly checked." A sigh escaped Lloyd's control, and he fell back against the mattress.

Wesley wanted to ease Lloyd's disappointment. He spotted a basket of unfolded laundry, so he knelt beside it and, determining it clean, started the arduous task of matching socks.

Lloyd peered at him over the edge of the bed. "What are you doing?"

"Something nice for you."

Lloyd dwelled in his thoughts, half-watching Wesley. When Wesley was done, he stood before his wallowing friend with his hands on his hips. "Do you have a paper you want me to look over?"

Lloyd blinked. "A paper?"

A slow smirk ticked at the corner of his lips. Lloyd rolled off the bed and rifled through folders on his desk. He handed Wesley what looked like twenty pages of numbers analysis.

"Know what?" Wesley said. "You don't look sad anymore."

Lloyd dropped the pages onto his laptop. He hauled Wesley into a hug, almost toppling Wesley in surprise.

A long exhale washed through Wesley's hair. "Thank you for talking me up to Jamie."

"I'm sorry he's too busy." Wesley lowered his voice. "I should have told you. I didn't know how."

Lloyd's grip tightened against Wesley's shoulder blades and the small of his back, bringing him snug against Lloyd's front. "It would have been hard for me to accept coming from you, and frustrating if I couldn't speak with Jamie immediately."

"He likes you. He wants to be friends." Wesley pulled back and looked at him. "Which is good, right?"

Lloyd nodded a little too insistently. "Of course."

"But you wanted more."

He didn't reply for a long moment, then dropped his arms. "Professor Katzenberger is dedicated. She's a great choice. I'm not sad."

"But maybe just a little?"

"I'll get over it."

"You're mature like that. But . . ." Wesley reached into his pocket.

"But?"

Wesley waved his phone. "Perhaps it would be a waste if you got over it too fast."

Lloyd tucked his thumbs into his belt. "Why's that?"

Wesley swiped and clicked the screen. *Heartbreak Hotel* blasted from the phone's speakers. "Have you never dwelled in melodrama? Purged your hurt through dance? Cried until you were exhausted?"

"Can't say I have."

"Then we have catching up to do." Wesley set the phone on the bookshelf, jumped onto Lloyd's bed, and jumped to the beat. "Dance with me."

Lloyd hesitated, then inched forward. He took Wesley's outstretched hand with a joltingly soft slide of their palms. Wesley had just pulled him onto the bed when urgent knocks pounded the door.

They burst apart. Outside Lloyd's door, Randy was bleeding buckets from his nose.

Lloyd shifted into RA mode, control dwarfing his sadness. "What happened?"

Randy groaned. "I didn't see the door."

"Wesley, get me the first aid—thanks."

∾

WESLEY SCANNED THE SHELVES OF A QUIRKY KNICK-KNACK store. He held up a stainless-steel coffee mug over the neck-high shelf to Caleb, browsing the other side. "And?"

"And what?" Caleb said.

"Will Lloyd like it?"

"I thought you bought him a Christmas present already?"

"That was for his birthday."

"Which you still don't know."

"I'll make one up for him. Do you think he'll like this?"

"It's a coffee cup."

Wesley liked the brushed feel of the steel. Muted gray, understated, solid. "I'll engrave it."

Caleb leaned his elbows on the top shelf. "Why don't you go right to the engagement rings?"

Wesley clasped the coffee mug and searched for other options. "When will you guys give up? Lloyd and I are gonna date."

Caleb leered. "I know you are."

"Aren't. That was meant to be aren't gonna date."

"I don't think you could find a better one."

"Coffee cup?"

"Date."

Wesley found a shinier version of the coffee mug and compared the two. "If I were born a Cancer or he a Sagittarius, maybe."

Gemini Keeps Capricorn

Caleb picked up a silver pendant from a plush box. "Why the hell do you have such an aversion to Capricorns?"

"My horoscopes are almost always spot on and—" Wesley cut himself off.

Caleb didn't let him off the hook. "And?"

"Nothing."

"Come on. I'm your brother. You can tell me anything, and I'm always on your side. Unless you're wrong."

Wesley pegged him with a look, and Caleb grinned.

"Is that necklace you're fondling intended for MacDonald?" Wesley asked innocently.

"She'd cut off my balls if I tried to give her this."

"Then why are you checking it out so hard?"

"Because it would be nice. To give her it." Caleb set it down. "Your turn."

"I'm surprised you haven't put it together."

"Is it because Mom's a Capricorn?"

Wesley studied the two cups in his hands. "And Principal Bontempo. And our pastor. And my first boyfriend. All relationships in my life that soured have been Caps." He laughed. "Man, that sounded like something only a therapist should hear."

Caleb drummed his fingers together under his chin. "Do go on."

"We are happy being best friends. That's it."

Wesley's phone rang. He set down the two cups. "Lloyd! We were just talking about you."

"All wonderful things, I'm sure."

Wesley pivoted away from Caleb's assessing eyes. "What's up?"

"I explained to mom that I won't be with her for dinner on Christmas Eve."

"The whole fiancé bit?"

"Right. She finds it entertaining. She suggested since we're

149

doing Eve at your place that we do Christmas Day with her. I said I would ask. You can say no."

"Do you want me to say no?"

Lloyd's answer came fast and firm. "No."

Grinning, Wesley decided on the brushed-steel cup. "It's a date then."

Over the shelf, Caleb's brow arched pointedly as Wesley disconnected. "Oh, go away."

∼

Wesley woke with a stiff back. He rolled onto his side and rubbed his sore muscles with a significant glare to Caleb.

Caleb yawned and stretched like a cat. His eyes popped open and he grinned. "Good sleep."

"When are you going home?" Wesley asked.

Caleb blew in his face. "When are you?" At the daggers Wesley was throwing, Caleb raised his brows defensively. "It gets lonely, okay?"

"Does being here make it much better?"

"Apparently I like half-naked cuddles with my brother." He hummed. "I think we both need therapy."

Wesley shoved him out of bed. "Last day before Christmas break. Get your ass to school."

Caleb whipped up his uniform from its heap on the floor. "Turn around while I put fresh boxers on."

Wesley slammed his eyes shut. "Someone shoot me."

When they emerged from the room, they saw Danny and Charlie in the hall battling with blow-up dolls.

An unimpressed Lloyd pushed them apart. "What are you, teenagers?"

Danny hugged his doll. "Actually, yeah."

Lloyd pulled the tabs of both dolls and they began deflating.

"Time to grow up. This kind of behavior won't win you the heart of any self-respecting person."

Charlie complained, and Lloyd grabbed his half-collapsed doll and chased him down the hall.

"I can't *wait* to live in the dorm at Treble," Caleb said, sighing.

Wesley squeezed his neck. "We'll get you that recommendation."

They made their way down the hall. Lloyd gave Caleb a hard stare, then turned to Wesley. "Aren't you even trying to pretend anymore?"

"Pretend what?"

"That your brother isn't strolling out of your bedroom every morning."

"He's not. Mostly he's strutting—"

"Wesley."

Wesley shoved Caleb into the kitchen with a cheeky smirk. "No one's coming out of my room. You should really see someone about that addled mind thing."

Lloyd smacked a palm to his head. "A word in my room?"

In Lloyd's room, Wesley sat on the armchair. Not by choice—he'd have opted for the bed—but Lloyd had steered him sternly to the corner. Lloyd sat in his desk chair leveling a full-Cap look at Wesley.

"You can't keep being my exception. Other students slip, and I write them up." He sighed. "I'm sorry, I have to write you up too."

"What?" Wesley spluttered.

Lloyd lifted a hand. "The first two write-ups are warnings. No one will pay attention to them."

Wesley sank into the chair. This sucked, but he supposed Lloyd couldn't turn a blind eye forever. "If no one pays attention, why bother writing me up at all?"

"Either I break rules with everyone, or I tighten them on you."

"Break rules. Always break rules."

Lloyd's lips quirked. "It's hard to believe you are studying the law."

"Harder if you think I'm the son of the great Judge Hidaka," Wesley added with a light-hearted sigh. "What can I say? Split personality. It's the Gemini in me."

You had no filter, and I fell in love.

Chapter Fifteen

Williamson shut a few days before Christmas.
Suzy offered Caleb and Wesley refuge, which Caleb snapped up. Wesley opted to forgive Lloyd for writing him up, and he crashed on his rollaway bed.

It made sense, since they spent so much time together.

They repainted the interior of the tree house, Wesley giving the pinecone kids their individual flair. They even trudged through low fog to a fitness center where Wesley lounged by the indoor pool while Lloyd did muscly things in the metal jungle a floor above.

It was all very best-friendy.

Then Christmas Eve arrived.

Wesley fidgeted with his wristband as he stared at Lloyd in the driver's seat of his car, dressed in a fine shirt and slim-fit dress pants. And belt. Lloyd was always wearing a fuck-me belt.

"I am unreasonably excited to show you off to my mom. Look"—Wesley held out his hand over the console—"I'm shaking. I don't ever shake. Unless it's shake, rattle, and roll, of course."

"Glad your humor is still intact," Lloyd said, turning onto his street.

"I hope she loves you." Wesley snorted at himself. "Of course she will. Who couldn't?"

Lloyd took hold of his trembling hand, linking their fingers together.

"Good plan," Wesley said as Lloyd reached his home. "We should go in like this. Make our relationship look real."

"It is real."

"That's the spirit."

∽

WESLEY GRIPPED LLOYD'S HAND, SWEATING LIKE NO-ONE'S business. The December wind whipping around them did nothing to cool him down, and Christmas lights beamed down on them like an interrogation.

"Mom! We're here," he blurted as soon as the door opened.

"I see that," she said, eyes jumping between the two of them and their joined hands. She focused on Lloyd. "You're my son's fiancé?"

Lloyd's hand twitched as though his first response would have been to shake her hand. He pumped their palms together instead. "Pleased to meet you."

Mom beckoned them inside, and Wesley reluctantly let Lloyd go so they could take off their jackets.

"So," she said, sizing up Lloyd from shoe to shirt. "You're gay."

"I am."

"You don't look very gay."

"Mom," Wesley warned.

Lloyd assumed the expression he reserved for rule-breaking residents. "I don't look very patient either, but let me assure you I am." His gaze flickered to Wesley.

Wesley owed Lloyd big time. He flashed him an appreciative, somewhat sheepish smile.

"We should get to the dining table," Mom said and moved into the next room. "Ham and eggplant salad doesn't eat itself."

Wesley scrunched his nose. "I wish it would."

"You can sit on that side of the table." Mom pointed Lloyd to the end of the table, far from Wesley's usual spot.

Wesley bristled. "He's sitting next to me, where I can grope him under the table."

"Wesley!" His mom gasped, affronted, while Lloyd gently chuckled.

"Where's Hazelnut?"

"Someone call for deliverance from an uncomfortable situation?" Caleb asked, entering the room in a reindeer hat. "Where do you want me?"

"Between them," his mom murmured.

"Across from us," Wesley said.

Mom picked up a wine bottle and poured two glasses. "Lloyd," she said tightly, "Would you like some red wine?"

"No, thank you."

"Both for me then."

Wesley slipped onto a chair, gesturing Lloyd to do the same. "I'll take one, Mom."

"And have you take off with your guy into the bathroom again? The sparkling water is chilled."

Caleb piped up cheerily, "I wouldn't worry about shenanigans happening. I'm pretty sure Lloyd is waiting."

"Waiting," his mom nodded, impressed. "That's something."

Wesley choked on the horror. Imagine having to *wait*.

"Grace!" Caleb said over a mouthful of ham and eggplant. "Tell us. How did you propose?"

Wesley sent him a scathing glare. Caleb was having far too much fun with this.

Lloyd spoke calmly, "Actually, your brother proposed to me." His mischievous gaze landed on Wesley. "Tell them, honey."

Caleb turned his snicker into a cough.

Their mom drained the last dredge of wine from her first glass.

Wesley spun a tale, imagining how he might have done it. "It was the best coffee I ever made. Rich with chocolaty tones—Lloyd's favorite roast. His every sip fried my nerves. I wondered if he would ever get to the message stamped into the bottom of his cup: 'Marry Me?'" Lloyd opened himself toward Wesley, amusement playing at his lips and dancing in his eyes. Wesley shifted his chair and sank against his warm side, one hand palming his thigh. He playfully nipped Lloyd's neck. "Lloyd, my heart. You tell the rest."

Lloyd's eyes remained firmly on his for a few beats. "I said yes."

Wesley gently elbowed his side.

A puff of air escaped him. "I always say yes to Wesley." He looked fleetingly back at him. "No matter what insane thing he asks me to do. I can't help it. I'm in love with him."

Tingles rushed through Wesley, and then he tensed, waiting for his brother to snort.

Caleb kept it together, managing a half-genuine-looking smile. "I wish you guys the best. And Lloyd, the best of luck."

Wesley gave him the evil eye before glancing at his mom, who was staring at Lloyd over her second glass of wine. "You look familiar. I've been trying to put my finger on it."

Lloyd kept his voice even. He must have felt Wesley seize up with frustration, because he slid his hand up and down the inside of his knee. "Perhaps you saw me the week Wesley moved into the dorm?"

Mom drank more wine. "No, I was never invited to his dorm."

"Can I see you for a minute?" Wesley led his mom into the

157

kitchen. "I thought you wanted to understand why being gay—not gaying, by the way—is so important to me? I thought you wanted to meet Lloyd?"

She closed her eyes, sighing. "I do. I did. It's harder than I thought."

"It shouldn't be," Wesley said sadly. "We'll leave. We can try again when you're ready."

He waited for her to stop him, but she didn't.

⁓

"You know my friend Alcohol I told you about?" Wesley asked, keeping his tone light on their way back to Lloyd's. "We need to pay him a visit."

Lloyd appeared sympathetic. "One drink."

"Three."

"Two."

"They better be giant glasses."

They were a standard tumbler.

Lloyd took out a bottle of vodka from the liquor cabinet and mixed it with ginger ale.

Cathy had left them to it, hiking off early to bed. Lloyd and Wesley had the cozy living room to themselves. A decorated tree sat modestly in the corner, perfuming the room with pine. A small fireplace flickered with warm flames, and thick drapes shut out the cold. Despite that, Lloyd had made him put on an extra pair of socks.

The first drink curbed the edge of his lingering disappointment at his mother's reaction to his fake fiancé. The second curbed it even more.

Wesley had figured out how to work the old dusty stereo, and classics from the fifties, sixties, and seventies pulsed around the room. He gave in to dancing, while Lloyd sat on the couch, nursing his drink.

"Dancing out the pain looks like this," Wesley cried as he jumped up and down, spinning and head bopping.

He belted out the lyrics to The Supremes' *You Can't Hurry Love* to Lloyd's wry grin. Danced to two more songs, then used the last of his energy shaking his limbs to the Kinks' *You Really Got Me*.

He collapsed onto the couch, side jammed against Lloyd's. He rested his head on Lloyd's shoulder as he played with his wristband. "See. Dinner's forgotten."

Lloyd wrapped an arm around Wesley's shoulders. They stayed close like that for an entire song, Lloyd's arm a comforting solid weight. A bit too comfortable. Wesley might fall asleep this way. He whisked out of Lloyd's arms to the bookshelf where he'd seen a deck of cards.

"Let's play!" He dropped them onto the coffee table.

"Play what?"

"Strip poker."

Lloyd withdrew the deck and shuffled. "You can take the socks off if you're too warm."

Wesley poked his tongue out and stripped out of the second pair. "I'll have you know, you missed an opportunity." He ran a seductive hand down his body. "I'm impressively ordinary."

"Let's play for something else." Lloyd shuffled.

"Another drink!"

"Or . . ."

"I doubt your idea can top mine."

"We play for my birthdate," Lloyd said. "You win, I tell you."

Every fiber of Wesley trained in on Lloyd. Lloyd's idea topped and surpassed his. "Are you serious?"

"When am I not?"

Good point. "Okay, I'll put in a date too. Something interesting . . . the day I lost my virginity."

"Why would I want to know that? No, how about you wage a future date. If I win, I get to make you run around as I see fit."

"Your personal minion? Sounds like fun."

Lloyd laughed and dealt. Texas Hold'em. He wrote on a small block of paper and tossed it in the middle. "We'll start with the year."

"I already know that."

"Just go along with me."

Wesley had shitty cards, but he wrote down a year too. Lloyd revealed his cards. Two pairs.

"Wait a sec." Wesley rifled through the deck, found two cards he needed, then resumed the game. "Okay, beat that." He turned them to show a flush of hearts.

Lloyd sighed. "Fine. You win."

Wesley cheered, grabbing the folded paper. "Let's see this birthdate."

Lloyd sighed but didn't seem mad.

"Eighth of January," Wesley read aloud. Yeah, right. "You're fucking with me. When is it?"

Lloyd frowned. He found his wallet and showed Wesley his driver's license. "Ouch, that photo does not do you—oh my God. It's true. The eighth."

"Is there some Capricorn magic you want to tell me?"

Wesley looked at him incredulously. "Do you not know what the eighth is?"

"I take it I should?"

Wesley started showering cards on him. "It's Elvis's birthdate. You have Elvis's birthdate." He flung himself back, sprawling like a starfish over the carpet. "I can't even."

"It's a date. It doesn't mean anything."

Wesley stared at the swinging lightshade and laughed.

To some this might be a funny coincidence, but Wesley thought there was something magical about his best friend sharing a birthdate with his idol.

The Doors' *Light My Fire* came on. Wesley rolled to his feet and danced. It felt great to dance, but it would be better with more space and better speakers. "Hey, what are your New Year's Eve plans?" Wesley asked.

Lloyd finished his drink and collected cards off the floor. "I planned to stay home and prepare for a busy January schedule."

"You're kidding."

Lloyd wasn't laughing.

Wesley frowned. "But Glitter. Dancing. Kissing."

"Was that an invitation?" The flash of hesitation in Lloyd's gaze made Wesley's gut clench. It reminded him of Halloween. Of Lloyd not being invited.

"Would you come? Despite your streamer-phobia? I will hold your hand the entire time."

Lloyd set the cards back in the bookshelf. Wesley moved to his side with begging puppy eyes.

"I'm going to be picking glitter off my clothes for weeks afterward, aren't I?"

"Not just your clothes," Wesley said. "It'll get in all your folds and cracks, if you get what I mean."

"You're a master wordsmith."

"Promise you'll come with me?"

Lloyd pretended that relenting was a difficult decision, but Wesley caught a sneaky sparkle of delight in his eye. "Fine. I'll tag along."

"Great. We can suck on some mind-expanding lollipops and find the nearest closet."

"No sucking on lollipops or mind-expanding anything."

Wesley laughed so hard he knocked a CD case off the shelf and caught it against Lloyd's chest. "No lollipops. No naughty business in the bathrooms. Got it."

A soft shake of Lloyd's head. He popped the CD case back onto the shelf and turned off the music. "What am I going to do with you?"

"Nothing fun, by the sounds of it."

"Let's get you to bed."

Wesley pivoted and headed out of the living room. "Sounding better."

A chuckle drifted behind him. Wesley slowed his step until Lloyd was right behind him. When he slowed even more, Lloyd grabbed his hips and steered Wesley upstairs.

Wesley stripped to boxers and climbed into bed.

Lloyd took a minute longer. When he stepped past Wesley, Wesley cuffed Lloyd's ankle, stilling him. "Thank you for being there tonight." He absently rubbed over the hairs at Lloyd's shin. "Not just at home with my mom, but now. Here."

Their eyes connected. "I'm sorry things didn't work out the way you wanted."

Wesley made light of it. "You told me your birthdate, so something went right."

"Get some sleep, Wesley."

Lights popped off and sheets *churred* as Lloyd slid in bed. Wesley smiled sleepily.

∾

WESLEY WOKE UP WITH A RIDICULOUS SPRING IN HIS STEP. Light and energetic, like a man reborn.

He returned from the bathroom—and tripped over the bottom mattress. He flailed and had two choices: land on the empty mattress or pivot and land on Lloyd.

He fell with enthusiasm against a sleepy Lloyd. A sleepy, *hard* Lloyd.

Lloyd's eyes opened, gaze dark. He grabbed Wesley and rolled them until he was pinned to the mattress, a hard, hot body pressing into him.

"Merry Christmas!" Wesley said.

Lloyd jerked away, muttering. Jaw clenched, he stormed into the bathroom.

Wesley laughed and followed him to the locked door. "You're grumpy."

All he got was a grunt in response.

"Is this the no-coffee-in-your-system situation?"

"No, it's the leave-unless-you-want-to-overhear-me-jack-off situation."

Wesley's breath caught and blood shot to his groin. He was hesitating. He was *hard* and hesitating.

"You know," he said silkily, "sometimes friends help out friends."

"I'm not interested in being your fuck-buddy."

"You sure?" Wesley palmed his hard cock thinking about it. "Because my mouth around your cock would feel amazing. That's the advantage of having hair, Lloyd, you'd have something to grip as you sink down my throat." Wesley stuffed his hand down his boxers, thumb gliding over a bead of pre-come. "A quick blowjob, no strings attached? Best friends helping best friends. I'd work you until you came, yelling—"

"WESLEY!"

"Exactly like that."

A muffled curse broke through the door. "Go make coffee. Gallons of it."

"Your mom is down there."

"And?"

"I'm really fucking hard right now. Toss me some lube and I'll sort myself out in your bedroom."

"You're killing me." A shuffle. A cupboard squealing on hinges.

The bathroom door cracked opened and lube came hurtling out, followed by the snap of the lock.

Wesley laughed. "If you change your mind about the fuck-buddy thing, let me know."

Lloyd groaned. "Not going to happen."

Wesley threw himself on the bottom bed and kicked off his

boxers. He was hard and straining, and he couldn't squeeze lube out fast enough.

Through the thin walls came soft, slick sounds. Familiar sounds that made Wesley imagine Lloyd fucking his hand. Did he pump through his tight fingers fantasizing about pretty-faced guys?

Wesley's lube-covered hand throttled his cock. The thrill blasted through his body, spiraling thoughts of Lloyd.

Having sex.

With Wesley.

Lloyd's eyes would roll back as he pushed inside him, bottom lip parting, then he'd stare right into Wesley's eyes as he pulled back out and slammed back in.

A muffled grunt came through the wall, and Wesley jerked himself faster, gasping. Had Lloyd heard him? Would knowing what Wesley was doing turn him on too?

Wesley threw a leg up onto Lloyd's bed, heel dragging over twisted sheets. He spread his other knee and dipped the tip of his middle finger in his ass as he pumped his dick.

Lloyd would be a demanding lover. In control. He'd move slowly and study every reaction. When the moans intensified, he'd palm Wesley's mouth and fuck faster.

Wesley wished he could get his finger deeper. For a moment, he cast his eyes about Lloyd's room wondering where he might find a dildo. Or a fucking carrot for all he cared right now. Just something thick and hard thrusting in him.

Another moan escaped from the bathroom.

Wesley gave up on his ass and gripped the inside of his knee, pretending the touch was Lloyd's. Pretending Lloyd's gaze burned into him with every thrust.

Lloyd might tell him to touch his nipples and Wesley might smirk at him and say *Make me*. Lloyd would pound him harder for it. Pin his hands above Wesley's head so he'd have to come without touching himself—

Wesley shot ribbons of come over his stomach as his orgasm wrung through him. It hit so hard, he was shaking.

He caught his breath, leg dropping from Lloyd's bed.

"Well, fuck." Aftershocks rumbled deep within him.

Lloyd knocked on the door and Wesley carelessly beckoned him in.

Lloyd froze at the foot of Wesley's bed, where Wesley lazily dragged his finger through the come pooling in his bellybutton. A towel flapped onto his groin. "Bathroom is free."

Wesley grinned and lazily stood, slinging the towel around his waist. "I don't want it to be weird, so I'm just going to tell you that I thought of you. I couldn't help myself."

Lloyd bore that hazel gaze into him, just like he'd imagined in his fantasy. He spoke in a measured tone. "You don't want it to be weird, and *that's* why you're telling me?"

Wesley winked. "Considering the circumstances, our closeness"—to put the thin walls in a kinder light—"I thought we should address the elephant in the room."

Lloyd let out a slow breath and gestured between them. "Considering the circumstances."

"Come on, Lloyd. It was clear we were going to think about each other."

"Okay, good," Lloyd nodded, "we are admitting this."

"Yes!" Wesley said, exasperated. So they thought of each other while jacking off. Big deal. Best friends did that sometimes. More than that sometimes. Lloyd didn't have to worry he'd suddenly want to be his boyfriend.

He heard loud and clear that Lloyd didn't want anything sexual between them. Maybe he wasn't Lloyd's type. Which was fine, just fine, because Lloyd was still a Capricorn.

Totally not his type either.

"You're right," Lloyd said, lips twisting upward. "I thought of you too."

Wesley grinned at him. "Perfect. Get it out in the open. Let's move on with Christmas Day."

"I didn't think you would admit it," Lloyd mussed, brow pinching.

"Well, I did."

"I thought we would dance around this until we moved out of Williamson."

"That would have been awkward and, to be honest, not what I want of us."

"Of us?"

"Despite you being a stickler for rules and me a flirtster, I think we have a special connection. I want it to last. That means no awkward dances."

Lloyd's smile reached deep into his eyes, making Wesley wonder if Lloyd was thinking about their last two actual dances.

A laugh shivered over Lloyd's bottom lip, and his tongue darted out over it.

Wesley lifted his gaze. "Let's be frank with each other."

"Okay."

"My only caveat? Don't mention the no-sex thing again. I get it."

Lloyd sighed, sounding relieved. "I'm sorry. I wish things were different."

Wesley wasn't his type. Got it. "It is what it is."

"I'm glad you understand."

Wesley shook off a thread of disappointment. Best friends was better anyway. That would last way beyond their college years. That was something a Cap and a Gem could have forever. "We can still be close."

"You have no idea how much I want that."

Wesley rubbed Lloyd's chest playfully, his nightshirt soft under his palm. "I can't promise not to flirt, though."

"It wouldn't be the same if you didn't." Lloyd clasped Wesley's hand to his chest. "Wesley?"

"Lloyd?"

"What do you think about going out for dinner and a movie?"

"It's Christmas Day, silly."

"I meant next week, after I get back from my trip with mom."

Wesley ran through the list of work he had to do for his classes. "Okay, but I have to force myself to catch up on law readings first. I'll need until Friday."

"Friday, then. It's a date."

∽

OTHER THAN HIS CRAVING FOR MEAT, CHRISTMAS DAY WAS perfect.

Cathy kept taking photos of them, grinning like she'd indulged in too much eggnog. "It's a special occasion. This'll be the last one, promise. Get closer and say seitan."

Wesley slung an arm around Lloyd's shoulders and Lloyd wrapped an arm around his waist, fingers drumming his side warmly. Wesley grinned, and when asked to pose for a silly shot, he wrapped himself around Lloyd and pretended to go vampire, lightly biting the crook of his neck.

Lloyd bucked, sending Wesley and Cathy into a gut-clenching belly laugh.

"I'd love a copy of one of these," Wesley said, chuckling.

Cathy promised him an album.

After breakfast, Wesley handed out gifts. Chocolates for Cathy. "I decided to play it safe this Christmas until we get to know each other better."

"They're great. You're great. This day is great."

When he and Lloyd were alone in the living room, Wesley sat next to Lloyd on the couch and handed him his gift.

Lloyd unwrapped the coffee mug, and Wesley blurted, "Don't worry, it's not a proposal."

His laugh sounded tinny, and Lloyd stopped it with a warm palm cupping his knee. "It's perfect."

They both eyed the engraving on the brushed steel: *Lloyd Reynolds: shaven-headed, statistic-munching giraffe.* "It's meant endearingly," Wesley said.

"I'd never have guessed."

Wesley playfully shoved him, and Lloyd folded so easily that Wesley toppled onto him. Lloyd's rumbling laugh reached deep inside, vibrations stirring his cock. If only they could have a repeat of earlier.

Lloyd gripped Wesley and rolled them until Lloyd was the heady weight against him. Before he could appreciate all that muscle, Lloyd was off him and across the room. He pulled a fancy envelope from the bookshelf and passed it to him. "Merry Christmas."

Wesley opened, then yelped in surprise. "It's like you know me."

"I like to think so."

"I mean, know me *a latte*."

Lloyd snorted. "Glad you like it."

Wesley glanced at the receipt for an advanced coffee-art course. He'd mentioned once that he wanted to get more into it, and Lloyd had remembered. Fuck, this best-friends thing was underrated. He wanted this forever.

"We should move in together when we finish at Williamson."

A rare 100-watt smile lit Lloyd's face. "It's like *you* really know *me*."

Decant stop me from loving you.

Chapter Sixteen

On Friday evening, Wesley and Lloyd squeezed down the movie aisle to their seats. Two teenagers in front of them were enthusiastically necking each other. Loudly.

"Really?" Lloyd shook his head. "The previews haven't even started."

Wesley settled the popcorn between his thighs and grabbed Lloyd's hand, stopping him from turning up the grump on their horny neighbors. "They are so into it." He steered Lloyd's hand to the popcorn. "We don't want to be those guys telling the lovebirds to shut it."

A guy shushed them from behind.

Lloyd glared back, then leaned into Wesley, his hand bouncing the box against Wesley's groin as he fished for a good handful of popcorn. "You make a good point."

"An excellent one. Why don't you take the popcorn"—*before you pop me a boner*—"and pass my Coke."

Lloyd's lips twitched as they made the swap. "Don't drink it all at once."

Wesley drank it all at once.

Then had to leave halfway through the movie to visit the bathroom.

He returned, pushing through the busy aisle, and plunked himself down.

Lloyd was still shaking his head at him.

"What did I miss?"

The guy in the row behind them, who'd earlier shushed them, cleared his throat pointedly.

Wesley scooched closer to Lloyd and gestured for him to summarize quietly.

Little puffs of breath skittered over the skin under his earlobe, and Wesley wriggled with a shiver, causing Lloyd's lips to bump against the shell of his ear.

"They professed their love," Lloyd told him.

Wesley turned his face and cupped his hands around Lloyd's ear. "I missed the best bit?"

Lloyd shook his head. "That's still coming."

"You know what's going to happen?"

"Some of what's going to happen."

Trailers! They give far too much of the story away. "Don't tell me. I want to be surprised."

~

New Year's Eve rolled around in a wink.

At Glitter, a hive of people swung to rock 'n' roll surrounded by sparkly streamers. A few guys from Williamson had returned early from Christmas break to celebrate. Randy, Diana, Violet, and to Lloyd's chagrin, Gavin.

A couple of hours before midnight, Wesley bought Lloyd his second drink of the evening. Making his way through cheering throngs of students, he watched Suzy try to pull Lloyd to the dance floor. Whatever she said, she managed to make him consider it. A hesitation he hadn't even given Wesley!

Wesley sat in the booth and sipped his drink, then tried Lloyd's beer. He never understood beer drinking. It tasted like dirt and bubbly water.

"Here's your poison," Wesley said, sliding the beer across the table to Lloyd before slinging himself on the opposite seat.

Suzy grabbed Wesley's Jack and Coke and gave it a good gulp. "Your boy won't come out and dance."

Lloyd wavered, glancing at the packed dance floor. "Not tonight."

Wesley tapped Suzy's flower tattoo, and she returned his drink. He gave it a good tasting and slid out of his seat. "Let's show him what he's missing."

Suzy's eyes sparkled. "I got the DJ to put on some Elvis."

"Fuck, yeah."

The first beats of *Hound Dog* pulsed through the room. Wesley slunk backward to the beat, curling his finger for Suzy to follow. A sharp thrill zinged through him at having Lloyd's full attention.

Wesley reached for Suzy and they snapped into a dance worthy of clearing the dance floor. They might have been showing off. A little.

It was New Year's Eve, after all.

They morphed into a dance routine they'd done a couple of years back. Wesley lifted Suzy into the Ferris wheel and, near the end of the song, added a ground flip. They finished, breathing hard and grinning like the dance geeks they were.

Quite a few watched them. MacDonald and Caleb. Even Gavin, whose jaw had noticeably dropped.

Lloyd, however, had stopped watching. He was holding his phone against his ear, nodding.

Wesley and Suzy dorked about, trying new step combinations. Wesley stopped when Lloyd approached, and Suzy scampered off to the bar.

"As much fun as it is watching you dance, I have to bail."

Wesley's stomach knotted in disappointment. "Getting too late for you, old man?"

Lloyd smiled. "No, Mom's feeling sick. I have to take her some ibuprofen. I'll stay with her until the new year."

"Want me to come with you?"

"And have you catch it?"

Someone shoved into Lloyd and he stepped forward. Wesley steadied him with an appreciative squeeze to his guns. "I told you. These things are worth it to have you play nurse."

"You and Suzy are having fun. Dance in the year and I'll see you tomorrow."

Wesley draped himself closer and kissed his cheek. "Pity there'll be no reenacting our audition at midnight."

Lloyd's eyes darkened as Wesley pulled back, and if Wesley didn't know better, he'd call it a lustful gaze. But hadn't Lloyd made it clear Wesley wasn't his type?

Maybe his beer goggles were on.

Lloyd's gaze flickered beyond Wesley's shoulder and his jaw tightened. "Can I ever catch a break?"

Wesley glanced behind. Gavin was threading his way over, gaze settled on Lloyd.

With a frustrated laugh, Wesley shoved Lloyd toward the exit. "Go. I'll stop him from ending your year on a grumpy note."

~

"Sure, we can meet this morning instead." Lloyd grinned and hung up the phone.

"What lucky person will be seeing you this morning?" Wesley asked from his favorite spot at the edge of Lloyd's door.

"Do you always eavesdrop on my conversations?"

"Ten percent of the time I ask Suzy to do it."

Lloyd shoved the phone into his pocket and grabbed his wallet. "Are you here at eleven?"

"Yep. My shift starts at twelve. Who was on the phone? Jamie?"

"Uh . . . yeah," Lloyd murmured. He braced his hands on Wesley and turned him out of his bedroom.

"What? You're pushing me out of your room? You're crushing my feelings."

Lloyd scribbled a note on his door whiteboard. "I have to. If I return to my room one more time to find you draped on my bed . . . A man only has so much willpower."

"A Capricorn losing his patience?" A little shiver shot through Wesley. "What would that look like?"

Lloyd twitched. "I may be late to work. Do you think you could field any resident queries until I return?"

"Really?" Wesley asked, rolling his shoulders back. "You'd want me? Yelling at residents? Hell yeah!" A curl of panic followed. "But what if I can't make my voice grumpy enough? What if the fire alarm goes off?"

Lloyd paused. "I was only talking ten minutes. I'll hoof it and make it two."

"Phew. That was a close one. Randy would've laid siege to Williamson."

Lloyd laughed, striding through to the stairwell. Wesley called after him, "Oh, and don't make any plans tonight."

The door shut, and Wesley snagged Caleb and MacDonald and camped in the lounge to plan the final details of the night.

∿

At seven o'clock, Wesley approached Lloyd's room, playing with the zipper of his baggy windbreaker.

He needed to lure Lloyd out of the dorm.

When Caleb messaged him that everything was ready, Wesley made his move. He grabbed hold of the top of Lloyd's doorframe and drummed it. "There you are."

Gemini Keeps Capricorn

Lloyd tapped twice on his laptop and swiveled. His gaze snapped to Wesley's shaven legs—and lingered.

Thank the Lord. He was human after all.

Lloyd's face contorted, undecided what emotion to settle on. He swallowed and went with disbelief. "Did you shave your entire legs?"

Wesley winked.

"Smooth legs is a new look on you," Lloyd said, clearing his throat and swallowing again. "A good look but a new one."

Wesley sent him a wicked smile. "Ten more minutes and your head will implode."

"What?"

"Hmm?"

Lloyd shook off his confusion, lifting his gaze to Wesley's face. "My mind is swimming with numbers. Are you coming in to prop your feet on my pillow? Or do you prefer to flaunt those thighs?"

"Though I do love to flaunt, I want you to come with me. Outside. It's nice out."

"Is it?" Lloyd peered out the window into the dark, drizzly night.

"Er, atmospheric out. Besides, you shouldn't be hunched over a computer on your evening off."

"It's an evening off my RA duties. I still have other things to do. Give me ten minutes."

"No. You're not working a minute longer."

Lloyd cracked an amused grin and returned to clicking stuff on his laptop. "You think you can tell me what to do?"

"I think I can tell you what not to do."

"Wesley. I have data that needs interpreting. Deal with it for eight more minutes."

"Fine," Wesley bit out, narrowing his eyes.

"Good."

He folded his arms with a huff. "It's such a fresh evening. If I were stuck to my law readings, I'd want you to drag me from them to appreciate the fine outdoors."

Lloyd let out a bark of laughter. "If I ever see you stuck to law readings, I promise I'll drag you anywhere you want."

Wesley sniffed. "I guess I'll go on my own."

Lloyd stood. "This data I'm crunching is for you. Something I hope you'll find interesting." He grabbed his coat and slipped it on. "It's not that I don't like"—he peered out at the milky rain—"romantic evening walks."

Romantic. A much more apt adjective than "atmospheric" to describe the soft rain and full moon.

As they started walking toward the staircase, Wesley winked. "Now tell me all about this interesting data."

Lloyd sighed. "You're going to zone out, aren't you?"

"Already have."

∽

THEY BURST OUT OF WILLIAMSON INTO THE DREARY EVENING. Lloyd kept staring at Wesley's legs. "Aren't you cold?"

Freezing. But it was only for a minute. "I'm fine."

"The goosebumps on your thighs suggest otherwise. What are you wearing under that jacket?"

Wesley swallowed a smirk and led Lloyd to Me Gusta Robusta. The lights inside had been switched off as promised. Excitement had him fumbling with his keys. "I have a niggly feeling I forgot to switch off the filter coffee machine. Can we check real quick?"

"You're as bad as Randy."

"Worse." Wesley slipped the key into the lock and pulled Lloyd inside with him.

Lights popped on, followed by a chorus of "Surprise!" as a *Grease*-inspired party roared to life.

Wesley laughed at the jaw-slackened shock that gripped

Lloyd's face. Lloyd's eyes swept the café interior that Caleb, MacDonald, and Suzy had spent all evening covering with checkered tablecloths and a fuck-ton of vinyl records.

MacDonald sat on a stool at the bar wearing tight black pants and a Sandy-style wig. Caleb leaned at the counter, his hair gelled back, dressed in a leather T-bird jacket.

Suzy stood on the counter behind them in a pink jacket, trying to untangle an even pinker strand of her wig from one of the hundreds of streamers Wesley had strung up.

Theo and Jamie wore red track-and-field T-shirts and hilarious white shorts. Theo was grinning over at Wesley like he was in on a secret.

Everyone, save one guest, had arrived.

Lloyd pulled Wesley against him, crushing him into a hug. The heat of Lloyd's body against his sent a thousand jolts through him. He was close to singing when Lloyd spoke into his ear. "Delightfully unexpected."

"Just the type of surprise we were going for."

Lloyd's breath tickled over the shell of his ear. "I did tell you my birthday was on the eighth, right?"

Wesley pulled back, grinning. "Again. We were going for the element of surprise." He unzipped his windbreaker and caught his brother's attention. "Hazelnut! Throw me my shoes and lipstick."

Wesley tossed his jacket over a hook behind the door, revealing the full extent of his costume. A collared, short-sleeve shirt and mid-thigh black skirt, cinched at the waist with a belt.

Lloyd gulped and muttered under his breath.

Wesley smirked as he sank into bright red heels. He used the reflection in the door to add a swipe of lipstick to his Rizzo costume. He turned to Lloyd. "Does this make you want to"—Wesley glanced down at Lloyd's crotch—"flog?"

"Boy, oh boy."

"Boy on boy? I'll take that as a yes." Wesley swiped Caleb's sunglasses as he strutted past and slipped them on. "Now what do you think?"

"You're crazy."

"Oh! I almost forgot. Your costume is wedged down my skirt."

"I rest my case."

Wesley slipped a hand into the skirt's hidden pocket in the ass, pulling out a nametag. "My windbreaker doesn't have pockets. It was the only place to put it."

Lloyd made a point of casting a glance around the decorated room. "The only place?"

Poking out his tongue, Wesley peeled off the foil and stuck the tag to Lloyd's forehead. "Nicely warmed for your naked head."

Wesley tugged him behind the counter and Lloyd stooped, checking himself out in the reflective side of the coffee machine. His cheek dimpled. "Principal McGee?"

"You do want to be a principal when you grow up. Now. Present time!" Wesley fished under the counter where he'd stowed Lloyd's gift. He caught Lloyd's twinkling eyes and lost himself staring for a moment. Then he cleared his throat and handed over the blue-wrapped gift. "Happy pre-birthday, Lloyd."

Lloyd took it and said softly, "No one has ever thrown me a surprise party before." He swallowed, tenderness filming his eyes. "Thank you. I love it."

Wesley felt like butterflies might burst out of his chest. The feeling was overwhelming, and he didn't know what to say. He was standing too close, yet not close enough.

Lloyd pressed the present against his chest. With a nervous gulp, Wesley said, "Go on then. Open it."

Lloyd picked at the sticky tape.

"It's for the wall next to your bed," Wesley said. "Or if you ever take the Persuasive Openers poster down."

Lloyd's dark, amused gaze hit Wesley right in the gut. Lust flickered through Wesley, making his pulse jump.

Lloyd peeled off the wrapping to a framed picture of him dressed as Rizzo. A gut-tickling laugh pounded out of Lloyd, and Wesley's cock responded. He turned toward the coffee machine and set it up for making a round of coffees.

Lloyd's gaze didn't leave him for a second. "It is a fun look on you."

"Feast your eyes. Because this is the only time you'll see me in heels. How anyone dances in these sole-stabbing slippers is beyond me."

Lloyd eyed his legs. "What about the skirt?"

Caleb snuck to Wesley's side, pulling at the lapels of his leather jacket. "Not that I want to interrupt, but some of us need hazelnut coffee."

Wesley stopped grinding coffee and glared at him.

Caleb backed up a step. "Whoa, the lady looks ready to pounce." He pointed toward Lloyd. "That way. Do it that way."

Wesley flipped him off with a smile.

A shrill yelp came from Suzy as she lost her balance and toppled off the counter. Lloyd stepped in and caught her in his arms damsel style. She clasped her Frenchy wig before it slipped off, rambling gibberish about Lloyd and his improving reflexes.

Once Suzy was upright, Wesley snagged her into helping serve coffees—in milkshake glasses, of course.

Wesley called out for everyone to gather around. One guest was missing, but maybe he'd had second thoughts about showing up. "Let the poker begin."

Warily, Lloyd said, "You are aware our college frowns upon the game."

"In exchange for money." Wesley hooked an arm around his and urged him around the counter, each wobbly step biting the back of his heels. "I read the rules."

Lloyd's step stuttered. "*You* read the rules?"

"Okay, so I asked Gavin about them."

A tight frown etched Lloyd's brow. "Gavin?"

Wesley squeezed his arm. "I could hardly ask you and keep this a surprise."

An almost placated grunt met his reply.

"Also, regarding Gavin . . ."

Lloyd instantly stiffened, which meant Wesley needed to don a shameless smile.

Wesley looked across the room as the café door opened. Lloyd followed Wesley's gaze, then fixed Wesley with a look of horror. "Gavin? You invited Gavin?"

Wesley drew him toward the table. "He's a big part of your life. Like the annoying brother you never had."

Caleb overheard that tidbit and opened his mouth in mock outrage. "How would you know anything about having an annoying brother?"

Lloyd greeted his guests and squirreled himself into conversation while Wesley greeted Gavin.

Gavin pinched a fake cigarette, smoke wafting out the end of it. "I'm not sure coming was such a good idea."

Wesley gestured him to take a seat at the table. "Try to be nice. It'll be fun."

Suzy grabbed Gavin's arm and pulled him to her side. Wesley seated himself on the opposite side next to Lloyd.

"Poker then," Lloyd said, eyeing MacDonald as she planted a deck of cards on the table. "What are we playing for?"

Caleb upturned a bag of lollipops and doled them out. "Candy."

Lloyd eyed the candy and pinned Wesley with a questioning gaze.

Wesley gave a disappointed headshake. "Not enough closet space."

~

Caleb had just finished dealing their hole cards when Gavin balked. He planted his phone on the table and shot Lloyd a disgruntled look. "Lloyd. I am serious."

Lloyd peeked at his cards and drawled, "We're playing for non-hallucinogenic candy. I think we'll be fine."

"Not the game. You never replied to my email about acquiring licenses to play your song list next week."

"You're getting riled up because I haven't emailed?"

Gavin gestured with his cigarette. Smoke tendrils curled over the table. "There's so much to take care of. I'm losing track. I searched your name in my email and it popped up. Unanswered."

Lloyd waved the smoke away.

Wesley settled in to watch them go at it.

"What were you doing searching my name?" Lloyd asked.

"I assumed you'd forgotten to do something, and since I knew I'd be in your company, I thought it prudent to check."

"He got the licenses," Wesley chimed in.

Lloyd batted all the smoke as though miming a bitch-slap against Gavin. "I can think of dozens of ways to say happy pre-birthday. Would it have hurt to start with one?"

Gavin nodded once, sharply. "Happy pre-birthday, Lloyd."

"Was that hard?"

Gavin blew on his cigarette with too much force and smoke spluttered from the end. "Not as hard as it seems to be to reply to an email."

"Gavin," Lloyd said between clenched teeth.

Everyone's attention trained in on the two RAs now. Maybe Wesley shouldn't have invited Gavin?

He gave Lloyd an apologetic pat on the knee.

"I'm saying," Gavin said. "It explains why your floor has the tendency to be, well, a little looser than the rest of Williamson."

"They follow the rules."

"Yes." Gavin's gaze skipped to Wesley and back. "But do you?"

Wesley squeezed a red lollipop, sighing. "I wish I'd broken a few more rules tonight." He unwrapped the lollipop, sidled around the table to Gavin, and popped it into his mouth before he could blow any more smoke. He patted the top of Gavin's head with fond frustration. "It's strawberry. The flavor of occasional fuck-ups. Suck it and move on."

After that, they played a few games. Wesley was always the first player out, while Theo and MacDonald battled it out for the win.

Lloyd seemed relieved when Wesley lost all his lollipops—until Suzy gave him hers to play one last game.

Caleb dealt and they did a round of tossing lollipops onto a pile. Jamie dropped out before the flop. After another round of betting, Wesley was surprised to find he was still in.

Who knew the game could be exciting! He jiggled his leg, impatient to see the turn card.

Lloyd glanced at him, shaking his head. "Don't ever play for money."

Theo threw in a lollipop, a tight stare glued on MacDonald, who did the same.

Jamie rubbed his boyfriend's back and said to Lloyd, "I'm fascinated to know more about this data you've been crunching."

Lloyd gave Wesley a sneaky peek out of his eye, which made Wesley start paying attention.

"It's too small a study to be significantly relevant, but my partial study seems to suggest there are some matches better than others."

"Matches?" Wesley asked, gaze ping-ponging between professor and student.

Lloyd leaned back. "Star-sign compatibility. I've been doing a statistical analysis of it based on birth dates and marriages."

Wesley whooped out a laugh and slapped Lloyd's thigh. "You should have told me!"

"I tried."

"You called it data crunching. It's like how you feel when I go at it with ice. You just can't hear it." Wesley scooted his chair nearer to Lloyd. "Gems and Caps. Give me the statistical lowdown." Wesley groaned, reading the bad news in Lloyd's flickering expression. "We really do suck together?"

"Yes, to reduce complex stats to its most basic point."

"How did you ever think I'd like to hear that?"

"I said you'd find it interesting. Not that you'd like it."

Wesley's gut gave a sad little twist.

Lloyd threw a lollipop onto the pile, and Caleb flipped the turn card. "But we're not the worst pairing."

Gee, that made him feel so much better. He cranked out a hollow laugh. "I told you we'd never work together."

"There are outliers. Some Cap-Gem couples made it work."

"What about Pisces and Virgo?" Caleb asked, with a none-too-subtle glance at MacDonald.

Lloyd had done his research. He kept the table entertained as Wesley glared at the cards.

The conversation turned, and Gavin was asking if Theo and Jamie would come to Williamson's Fifties Bash next week.

"We'd love to recycle these costumes," Jamie started, and Theo excitedly continued for them.

"But we can't. We're going to see a lawyer."

"Wow," Wesley said. "I've never heard anyone so excited by the prospect."

Theo's grin got loopy. "She specializes in surrogacy."

He beamed at Jamie, who curled a palm around his neck and kissed him sweetly. "I love you."

The table bubbled with excited questions and best wishes.

Wesley realized he was rubbing Lloyd's forearm under the

183

table. He pulled away with an unfamiliar flush creeping up his neck.

Lloyd leaned against Wesley, breath tickling his jaw. He hoped his gulp wasn't audible. "Your turn."

Wesley checked his cards again, lips twisting. "Could I . . ." He reached for one of Lloyd's cards. A queen. He'd taken an earlier peek.

Arched eyebrows and unimpressed stares latched onto him. "Fine. I'm out."

You're so nutty, and I love it.

Chapter Seventeen

The next day Lloyd drowned himself in data while Wesley picked the Internet apart for information on zodiacs.

Capricorn, specifically.

Restlessness thrummed in his veins. With a frustrated grunt, he shoved his chair away from the desk. Raking a hand through his hair, he sent a leering Elvis a pinched look.

It wasn't fair that every time he gazed at his fantasy-crush, he was reminded of Lloyd and their shared birthdays.

Wasn't fair that Lloyd had stubbornly taken root in all his sexy fantasies. If Lloyd only knew how many times Wesley had been on the cusp of suggesting—again—they be friends that fuck. Wesley would even cover his face if necessary.

"I'm lying to myself," he muttered. "It's not my face that's putting him off. It's our friendship. He's afraid to lose it."

Elvis continued to leer.

"A lot of help you are."

He sent Caleb a message asking when he'd be back from rehearsals. No response came.

Wesley moped his way down the hall, jumping over a Nerf soccer ball two residents were shooting at each other.

Lloyd's door was open. He seemed to be packing some of his crap in a messenger bag. A delighted butterfly danced in his gut as he snuck in and flopped into Lloyd's vacated desk chair.

Lloyd acknowledged him with a keen smile and whisked to his dresser.

"Do you want to do nothing? With me?" Wesley asked, sitting upright when Lloyd peeled off his T-shirt. "Or something. We could also do something."

"I'm about to meet someone," Lloyd said, changing into a fresh shirt. "We can watch something on Netflix later if you want."

Wesley stilled, searching the room for a clock. "You're meeting someone at five in the evening?"

"I know. Such an inconsiderate time." Lloyd sat on the bed and opened the laces on his polished leather shoes.

Wesley folded his arms. "Who are you meeting?"

"How about you choose a movie. Nothing longer than three hours." A sharp look, belied by a twitch in his cheek. "I have stuff to do tomorrow."

Lloyd's evasion made Wesley's gut cramp.

He was meeting someone.

It shouldn't have been so shocking, considering Lloyd had been flittering off "meeting someone" since before Thanksgiving. He'd convinced himself it was Jamie related, but maybe it wasn't. Maybe Lloyd had met a guy?

Maybe they were dating?

Maybe Lloyd hadn't told him anything about it because Wesley had the tendency to pick apart Lloyd's boyfriends?

Anyone would have picked them apart though. None were good enough for Lloyd. Half of them cheated, and the other half blatantly said they were only in it for the sex.

Lloyd had never *hidden* a boyfriend though. He'd always listened to Wesley's bulleted points why boyfriend-of-the-month wouldn't last. The previous two times, Lloyd had prepared a rebuttal.

Alarm bells rang in Wesley's head.

Maybe Lloyd really liked this mystery guy? Maybe he was afraid of Wesley ruining it for him?

Which would be tempting, considering the annoyingly impractical, possessive feelings Wesley had been having.

But if Lloyd really liked the guy, and the guy really liked Lloyd, he wouldn't pick him apart.

Lloyd was his best friend. Wesley wanted him happy.

"Do these secret meetings spark joy in you?" Wesley asked, trying not to let his throat tighten.

Lloyd slipped his wallet and keys into his pocket and nodded. "A lot of things spark joy in me. Data analysis. Surprise parties."

"Your surprise party comes after data analysis?"

Lloyd rolled his eyes. "Descending order."

"You saved that one. Got more joy sparkage?"

Lloyd sat on his bed and clasped his hands together. "It would spark a crazy amount of joy if—"

Wesley leaned his elbows on his knees, mirroring Lloyd. "If what?"

Lloyd stared into his eyes and swallowed. "If this amazing guy I'm dating would let me call him my boyfriend."

Fuck Wesley dead. It was true. Mystery meeting guy was someone special.

All his self-talk about being a good friend and accepting the boyfriend flew out the window. He jerked back against the chair. "You don't think it's too soon? It's been, what? A month and a half?"

Everything in the room seemed to still. The gentle smile on Lloyd's face disappeared. His expression smoothed, becoming impossible to read. "We've known each other longer than that. In some ways, it feels like we've been boyfriends from day one."

Wesley swallowed hard and snapped his wristband hard. "Sounds like you found Mr. Perfect."

"Mr. More Than Perfect. You think calling each other boyfriend is too soon?"

"Maybe the whole secrecy thing should change first?"

Lloyd sighed. "You're right. It hasn't been ideal." Lloyd stood, patting his pockets. "I guess it will have to wait."

Wesley felt a strange mix of guilt and relief.

He was a terrible person. Fuck.

"Stop," he called out as Lloyd walked out of his bedroom. Lloyd paused but didn't turn around. "I'm wrong." It took all of Wesley's resolve to bite out, "Whoever this guy is, he would be lucky to have you call him your boyfriend."

Lloyd whirled around.

Maybe Wesley had put too much hatred in his tone? He searched inside for an apology, but it was not forthcoming. Jealousy turned him into a bitch, apparently.

Lloyd stared at him, muttering under his breath. He palmed his head as though he'd forgotten he had no hair to rake. "Boy, oh boy. Wesley, I don't even know where to start." He let out a huff and slammed his eyes shut. "I'll be back later."

Wesley pouted as he scurried from the room, turning his back to Lloyd. "Fine."

A tight, disbelieving laugh. "Don't bother with cafeteria food. I'll bring takeout to go with the movie."

"I want meat."

∼

WESLEY SPENT THE NEXT FEW HOURS GLOWERING AT everyone. Suzy. Randy. Elvis.

"Whoa," Caleb said, prancing into his dorm room. "Whatever did the King do to you?"

Wesley jerked his desk chair around. "You're at fault here. You shouldn't have run away from home."

"Dude," Caleb said, setting his flute on the dresser, "what put you in a funk?"

"I'm not in a fuck."

"Watch out, Freud."

Wesley hooked a finger under his band and teased it. "I'm a bad best friend."

Caleb flung himself onto the bed and propped his head. "I'm listening."

Wesley opened his mouth to unload, but Caleb stopped him, sniffing the air. "Did you make those cookies again? The ones with the cinnamon?"

Yes, he had. That's what he'd been doing while scaring off residents with scathing stares.

From his desk drawer, he pulled out a container full of cookies that he had set aside for Lloyd. Lloyd who was meeting his, well, probably boyfriend by now. His throat tightened. "Go nuts."

"Thanks!" Caleb bit into one with a happy sigh. "Continue."

"I've been stupid."

Caleb spoke around a mouthful of cookie, "Ah, Mr. Stupid. Struggles a bit with social cues? Never knows when to piss off? He and I are well acquainted."

Wesley stared at the ceiling. "Maybe if I had some actual principles. If I never eavesdropped. If I drove diligently."

"Then you wouldn't be you." Caleb plunked his booted feet onto Wesley's thighs, drawing his attention. Wesley expected his brother to smirk. Instead, Caleb met his gaze. "And I like you."

"You're my brother, you have to like me."

"No, I don't. That's what I think I've learned from you and Mom."

"What do you mean?"

Caleb sighed. "Just because we're family doesn't mean we

have to like each other. Respect and tolerate for the most part, okay. We don't otherwise have to give a flying fuck about each other. But I do. I want to." Caleb blinked hard. "I would *choose* you to be my brother."

A sob bubbled up Wesley's throat. He swallowed it back down, but a tear slipped and landed on Caleb's boots. Wesley clutched the leather, squeezing Caleb's ankle as he laughed. "Why do you so badly want me home?"

"I've been selfish about that. You and mom should figure things out without any pressure from me. Or not figure things out. Up to you."

"You're freaking me out."

"Why?"

"You sound mature. Might be the first time I've seen this look on you."

Caleb grinned. "It suits me, doesn't it? Come on, say it. I look good."

That was Wesley's cue to dump Caleb's feet back onto the bed. "Give me those cookies back."

They wrestled for the cookies until crumbs carpeted the bed. They both had stitches from laughing so hard.

Wesley turned his head and flicked his brother in the nose. "I'd choose you, too."

∼

Thanks to Caleb, Wesley was in good spirits when Lloyd returned.

Or at least he better disguised his inner bitch.

Lloyd gave him a funny look when they bumped into each other outside Lloyd's room. Possibly because Wesley was lurking around his door.

The nice shirt peeked through Lloyd's open coat. His shoes shined like the knife that was cutting into Wesley's chest. Totally date clothes. "You look good," he said, trying to keep his tone flirty not envious.

Lloyd shifted the Thai takeout while he fished out his dorm key, crowding Wesley.

Wesley's back hit the door and he glued his hands to the paneling to keep from crushing Lloyd against him. Wonderful aromas wafted from the bag. "Grab it," he said.

Wesley's hands shot out and cradled the bag. "So hot," he murmured, staring at Lloyd. Then he cleared his throat. "The food."

With a small smile and shake of his head, Lloyd swiped the key card and turned the handle. He pushed slowly to prevent Wesley tumbling backwards.

Wesley caught his breath once Lloyd took the bag from him and moved to the desk.

"Did you choose a movie?" Lloyd asked.

"Uh, no." That might have been a better use of time than pacing in front of his door like a crazy stalker.

Lloyd pulled containers out of a paper bag. "Chicken cashew stir-fry for you, tofu and veggies for me."

He eyed Lloyd cracking open his salad. Wesley gasped. "You're not vegetarian, are you?"

"How can this be shocking news to you?"

"But. But." Wesley eyed Lloyd's tight, muscular physique. "You look like you eat meat. A lot of it." He scooped a piece of chicken onto his fork. "I thought you only did the veggie at home."

"I do the veggie here, too."

"Now I feel bad for trying to trade you to that hotdog vendor."

"Oh, *now* you feel bad?" Lloyd dug into his veggies.

"I'm learning a lot about you today. You have a mystery boyfriend. You're a vegetarian. Next you'll tell me you've been searching for the guy that knocked up your mom twenty-four years ago."

Lloyd swallowed his mouthful. "Not a mystery I'm interested in. Although, on the topic of fathers, I have wanted to ask about yours."

Wesley speared a piece of chicken. "The great Judge Hidaka was the reason I wanted to be a lawyer. Dad was fair and kind, and I wish I'd come out before he died of heart failure." A wistful smile pulled at his lips. "He would have accepted me. Might have convinced mom, too."

"I'm sorry."

"I'm not going to break down or anything. I did enough of that junior and senior year at Sandalwood. Caleb buried himself in his studies and flute, Mom turned toward the church, and I was a mess. I came out, refused to listen to anyone who told me what to do, and let anyone who showed interest fuck me. It wasn't all this prettiness you see before you today." Wesley winked.

Lloyd didn't laugh. He set his tofu and veggies down and curled a finger under Wesley's chin until Wesley held Lloyd's sympathetic gaze. "That must have been tough."

"Now I focus on the fond memories."

Lloyd's finger skimmed the side of his jaw before retreating. "I'd like to hear one, if you feel like sharing."

Wesley did. He felt like sharing everything with Lloyd. "Dad introduced me to Elvis Presley and rock 'n' roll."

Delight sparked in Lloyd's eye, mirroring Wesley's own. "When I was twelve, Caleb got sick and had a stuck-in-bed movie marathon. *Rock Around the Clock. Jailhouse Rock. Grease.* I told him I wanted to dance like that, and Dad made it happen. Once a week for the next four years he dropped me at lessons and dance-offs." A lump tightened his throat. "Told me I could be whatever I wanted to be."

Lloyd rolled his chair closer and offered him a napkin. Wesley dabbed a traitorous tear.

"You would've made him proud," Lloyd said, rubbing his back. "You're the most you person I've ever met."

Wesley laugh came out strained. "Wow, I'm teary tonight. We'd better watch something light."

"*Grease*, perhaps?"

"Good suggestion. Here's another one: *Jailhouse Rock*."

"And have you mooning all over Elvis?" Lloyd lightly squeezed Wesley's neck and rolled back to his dinner. "Veto."

They settled on *Rock Around The Clock*, the laptop nestled between their feet. Wesley snuck glances at Lloyd during all his favorite parts, happy to see Lloyd absorbed in the film but jealous that he couldn't stop wondering whether the mystery guy was officially Lloyd's boyfriend.

When the movie ended, Wesley procrastinated cleaning the dinner mess by pretending he wanted seconds.

He slouched in Lloyd's chair and prodded at his food.

He gave up, dropping his plastic fork. "How was your date?"

Lloyd looked as though he might detect the green-eyed beast sulking in Wesley's eyes.

Wesley asked again, this time forcing a sweeter smile.

Lloyd pressed his lips in deliberation. "I loved it, and I think he had a good time too, only . . ."

"Only, what?" Wesley bit out.

"I've realized something that is both humorous and painful."

Humorous and painful? Curiosity trumped jealousy any day. "What's that?"

"I don't think he gets that we're dating."

"Oh God. You think you're practically boyfriends but he's mistaking your moves for friendship?"

Lloyd crossed his arms and sighed. "It seems like it."

Wesley tried to bite back a grin but failed. "It's hard being gay sometimes. Too many clueless men."

"Some more than others."

Wesley fidgeted with the band at his wrist. "Are you going to tell him?"

"Not tonight. I need to think about the last few months and laugh, possibly cry. Tomorrow, though."

"Or hear me out," Wesley suggested. "You could take it as a sign not to finagle into his pants."

Lloyd's lip curled and his cheek pitted. "Oh, I am definitely finagling into his pants."

The twist in Wesley's gut hurt. "Have fun with that. Use condoms."

Lloyd leaned over Wesley to clean away the last food container. Eyes trained on Wesley, his voice dripped with frustration. "Part of me wishes I could jump him, but he lives in this building and I don't want to lose my job. But when the timing's right? I'm going to fly through a whole *stash* of condoms."

Wesley pulled his wristband so hard it snapped and broke. "Fuck." He shoved Lloyd away as he jumped to his feet, unable to make eye contact.

"Pass it here, maybe I can fix it."

"You can't. It's fine. It is what it is." Wesley didn't look at him, fearing his face would give him away. He forced a flirty tone on his way out. "I hope he's good enough for you."

Lloyd snagged his elbow, but Wesley shook him off. He ran to his room but wasn't fast enough to avoid hearing Lloyd's: "I hope I'm good enough for him."

Wesley shut his door. Elvis was staring at him like he knew too much. "Oh, shut up."

I perked up the minute I saw you.

Chapter Eighteen

At work, Wesley had a fight with the filter machine. The cold brew slipped off its pad, and in his effort to shove it back into place, the handle hooked his wrist. One ill-timed yank later, coffee splashed over his face and seeped through his white T-shirt.

This literally never happened to him.

He was supposed to be the coffee whisperer.

Maybe it was opposite day. Maybe after his shift, he'd rock up to his law tutorial and spout law stuff like a pro.

At least this mess happened after he'd taken Lloyd's daily order.

"I gave your fiancé his tall black," Suzy said, lifting a brow at the new look Wesley was sporting. "He's sitting outside if you want to take five."

With frustration and eagerness, Wesley moved through the bustling café crowd outside. At the far end of the courtyard, he glimpsed Lloyd's teal shirt and the back of his shaved head.

Wesley threaded his way, wringing coffee out of his T-shirt.

He slowed down when he saw that Lloyd wasn't sitting alone.

An attractive man sat opposite him, his pretty face lighting up in a laugh. Pretty leaned in flirtatiously.

Wesley risked a glance at his unsightly reflection in the café window. He turned away, shoulders dropping as—

Someone grabbed his wrist and he whirled around, donning his game face.

Lloyd. Who was sitting in the shadows of a potted tree. In the same teal shirt.

"Wesley?"

Lloyd looked at him, then across the courtyard at the table Wesley had been walking toward. When he refocused on Wesley, a secret smile quirked his lips.

Wesley blurted. "Hey, yeah, so I was . . ."

"Cursing the American Eagle problem?"

Wesley grinned sheepishly. "Having a weird day."

Lloyd handed him a napkin. "You've got something on your chin."

Of course. Wesley wiped it off with a self-deprecating laugh just as MacDonald walked past. "Wesley. Looking good."

"Smelling better."

She disappeared inside for her shift.

Wesley picked up Lloyd's coffee and hid himself in a long sip.

"Don't worry," Lloyd said, gesturing him to take a seat. "You look good covered in Me Gusta Robusta."

Wesley choked, spraying a mouthful of coffee all over Lloyd and his damn shirt. If only Lloyd meant that in the dirty way his mind wanted him to.

Lloyd blinked, then stood and unbuttoned his shirt. "I agree," he said, shrugging it off. "Too many people with the same shirt."

Wesley gave a strangled chuckle.

"Do you have time to talk?" Lloyd asked, gesturing him to take a seat.

"Depends," Wesley blurted. "Is this about you and your

boyfriend?" A laugh rumbled out of Lloyd, and Wesley bristled. "What's so funny?"

"The fact you're jealous. So tickling and sweet."

Heat shot up his neck. His feelings were that obvious?

"Oh, Wesley. Sit down. Let's talk about this. About us. About what's going on here."

Dammit, Lloyd knew he was jealous. Properly jealous.

He cursed his newly bare wrist.

His whole body burned with the sudden need to find a boulder and hide under it. "You know how much I love talking. But"—he started walking backward toward the café entrance—"I have to get back to the thing. That makes the coffee. Because I have to be a man. I mean, man it."

"Wesley," Lloyd said in amused exasperation. "I want you."

"The coffee machine wants me more."

"Wesley!"

Wesley ducked inside and threw himself into a dozen orders. Lloyd tried to catch him twice more, but both times Wesley weaseled away. He overheard Lloyd telling MacDonald that he had someone to meet and would Wesley be done with his shift by the time he returned?

The last two hours bussing coffees wrung the last bit of energy out of him. He lounged against the counter across from MacDonald wiping the counter. "Want to do something after we close up?"

"I thought you had plans to follow Lloyd around like a puppy?"

Wesley tossed out a melodramatic sigh. "Turns out all I have in life is coffee."

"Is this because Lloyd is meeting up with someone as we speak?"

Why yes. Thank you for mentioning it. "How was I the last person to know he was dating?"

"Because you are clueless. And blind."

"It's not as though I'm surprised he has a life outside of me." Wesley smashed his face into a dishtowel and groaned. "Why does he have a life outside of me?"

"You and your brother. Both idiots." She pinned Wesley with a dozen daggers flying out of her eyes. She opened her mouth to say something biting, then firmly sealed her lips. She grabbed him by his shoulders and shook him. "Stop damn well fooling yourself."

Someone slow-clapped behind the counter and they both jerked to Caleb. "I couldn't have said it better, MacD."

Then it was two against one, and Wesley shifted uncomfortably under their cutting stares.

Wesley slumped against the coffee machine and sighed. "Yeah, yeah. I gotta grow a pair and tell him how I feel."

∽

"How do I grow a pair?"

Elvis was no help.

Wesley cleared his throat and addressed the stand-in Lloyd again. "You're a Capricorn. You're solid and mature, and you go for what you want. You like rules and structure. I like dancing. I like gossip. I like teasing and crunching ice to get a rise out of you. But I can't flirt with you anymore." Wesley notched his voice lower, acting as Lloyd. "Why?" He switched back to his voice. "Because I mean it."

Wesley sighed, then changed into a shirt and the hottest jeans he owned.

He combed a hand through his hair and yanked open his door—

Lloyd stood on the other side, poised to knock. He wore a dashing button-down over a fitted T-shirt and dark jeans with a silver-buckled belt. He looked hot as hell and those hazel eyes sent a lethal voltage of electricity right to Wesley's crotch.

"What are you doing here?" Wesley asked, startled.

Lloyd cast an eye down Wesley's impressively tight outfit. "Where are *you* going?"

Wesley balled Lloyd's shirt, dragged him inside his room, and shut the door. "I was coming for you."

Lloyd looked down where Wesley still gripped him, then into his eyes. "*I* was coming for my *boyfriend*."

Lloyd spun him around and shoved Wesley against the door. Their bodies collided, and Lloyd kissed his speechless lips. Their mouths slid together and locked, unlocked, and refitted. Lloyd was everywhere. A hand roaming from waist to hip, another cupping the back of his head, clenching Wesley's hair.

A moan trembled out of Wesley, and Lloyd kissed him harder, deeper, with a fevered urgency Wesley had only ever dreamed of.

"You beautiful, crushingly clueless man."

Lloyd's mouth parted against Wesley's lips, sending wild tremors down his arms and up his legs to pool in his crotch.

Relief and elation surged warmly through Wesley. He clutched Lloyd against him, demanding an explanation—and that he never stop kissing him.

Wesley canted his hips against Lloyd's equally hard crotch. "Fuck. *Fuck.*" Wesley rested his head back and looked at Lloyd. "Me? You've been dating me?"

"I don't think you can find a more classic date than dinner and a movie. I paid."

"Because they could only take cash and my wallet was empty!"

"We bought the date menu."

"I didn't want you to spend too much. It was cheaper."

"We've been holding hands and squeezing appendages!"

"You're my best friend! And I'm an outrageous flirt."

"Do you squeeze many men's thighs?"

"Not recently." Now that he thought about it, not at all.

"Why'd you say no to us fucking then? You said you didn't want that with me."

Lloyd clasped his face. "I didn't want it to be a fling. Didn't want to be a fuck buddy. I wanted to date you. I want us to be boyfriends."

Boyfriends. His stomach did acrobatics. "What were those meetings about then?"

Lloyd's thumb stroked his cheek. "Studying."

Wesley licked his lip. "So we were dating?"

Lloyd's laugh made his wet lip tingle. "Yes."

"And I missed it?"

"I'm saying yes again, because I have to state the obvious from now on."

Wesley touched their lips together. "You should have kissed me sooner." He abruptly pulled back. "Why didn't you kiss me sooner?"

"The same reason I haven't thrown you on the bed and fucked your brains out like I think about doing three times an hour."

Wesley's cock throbbed.

"Because it's against Williamson RA policy," Lloyd said. "Kissing you has already broken about a dozen rules."

"Please tell me we can break a dozen more."

"I've forced myself not to kiss you the last two weeks because once I taste you"—Lloyd sucked in Wesley's lip with a deep breath—"God, the more I want. I won't be able to stop myself."

Wesley chased his retreating lips and parted them with a swipe of his tongue. "Mmm, don't stop yourself."

"Gavin's already on my balls about you. He can't wait to get me fired."

"I'll keep it a secret."

"When have you ever kept a secret?"

True. "How much do you like this job, anyway?"

Lloyd groaned and dragged an open-mouthed kiss over his

jaw. "Turns out I love this job. I love the challenges and resolving problems."

"Resolve our rather hard problem then," Wesley said, rocking their cocks together.

Lloyd growled and pinned Wesley's hips with his. "I already have a solution." He took a slow breath. "We wait until we wrap up the school year—"

"Wait?"

"I know it's frustrating but it's possible. I've managed the last couple of years, and we only have a few months to go."

"You've wanted to get into my pants for years?"

"Since the first time you crunched ice with a smirk. I hated that you were out-of-bounds. I tried so hard to get over you but it's impossible."

Wesley hauled Lloyd in and attacked his lips, shoving his tongue down his throat and hitching a leg to his hip. "I've been fascinated with you too. You call me a flirtster, but the truth is I only flirt with you." His hands paused against Lloyd's ass. "Wow, I am so fucking oblivious." He ground against Lloyd again. "Let's do some stating of the obvious. On my bed. The floor if your back can handle it."

Lloyd laughed into a kiss and reluctantly pulled back. "My aunt would humiliate my mom if I got fired too. I won't do that to her."

"How about we fuck but you don't get fired? You can gag me. I'll be quiet."

Lloyd palmed his crotch with a grunt. "This is why I haven't kissed you a thousand times already."

"You can't hold out to the end of the year now." Surely?

"I'm Capricorn, remember? Try me."

"I'm Gemini. I'll break you."

∽

203

"And the award for most romantic admission goes to: *I'll break you*, by Wesley Hidaka," Caleb said from his spot at the counter, munching his usual avocado toast.

Suzy snorted from the archway leading to the café kitchen.

"Lloyd has a point," MacDonald said, picking crumbs off the counter and flicking them into the trashcan. "You told us about you and him the moment you walked into work. I think he's right to make you wait."

Wesley poured milk into a cappuccino, making a perfect heart. "I can't stand you right now."

"Because I have a point."

"Oh my God," Suzy shrieked, waving her phone around. "Last night was when you and Lloyd made it official, right?"

Wesley raised a curious brow.

"MacDonald won the bet. She guessed freakishly close to the date."

"I thought it would be tomorrow," she said, glancing at Wesley.

Tomorrow. The eighth of January.

She'd known Lloyd's birthdate all along.

"As treasurer of the monies," Suzy said. "I can say the grand is rightfully yours. We'll keep it quiet so Lloyd doesn't get in trouble."

Wesley ground more coffee. "If it had been your hearts on the line . . ." He paused. "Actually, I would have done the same."

"What will you do with all that cash?" Suzy asked MacDonald. "Spend it? Donate it to a good cause?"

"Yes," MacDonald said, voice dripping with sarcasm. "I'll donate it to the cause that makes my heart melt the most."

Wesley made and delivered two more cappuccinos. Was Lloyd right about making them wait? Sure he'd told Suzy, MacDonald, and Caleb but . . .

"But you guys are like extra limbs," Wesley said pulling paper cups off the top of the coffee machine. "I should be able to share things with you."

"As long as I'm not your right arm or your third leg," Caleb said. "I'm cool with this analogy."

MacDonald shrugged. "I still think Lloyd's right to wait."

Wesley eyed his brother. "What do you think, Hazelnut?"

"The opposite of whatever MacD says."

MacDonald rolled her eyes. "You sure know how to woo a woman."

Caleb leaned over the counter and tucked a stray hair behind her ear. "I sure know how to make sparks fly."

Suzy sighed. "I don't think Gavin would get him fired."

"Thank you!" Wesley said. "He's not gonna rat on him. Deep down Gavin thinks Lloyd is pretty okay."

"Deep, *deep* down," MacDonald said.

"See, this means it's okay to break Lloyd's resolve not to have sex!"

Someone cleared their throat, and the hairs on Wesley's nape prickled. He gulped, and turned a winning smile on his *boyfriend*, who stood, arms crossed, on the other side of the counter.

"Your usual, coming up!" Wesley made Lloyd an extra-large dark roast.

Wesley slid it over the wooden countertop and Lloyd took the paper cup, covering Wesley's hand with a firm press. "You honestly think Gemini can break Capricorn?"

Wesley started at Lloyd's lips and blatantly took in the rest of him. The shirt fit like a glove, his dark chinos, that come-get-me belt seated low on his hips. "I am highly motivated."

Lloyd slid his fingers up and down Wesley's.

"We're boyfriends. We're supposed to be at it like bunnies," Wesley said with a delighted thrill.

"Says who?"

"Says three of the four of us staring at you right now."

Someone waved their hand between them. "Excuse me. Is anyone going to serve me?"

"Want do you want?" Wesley snapped his attention to his regular. "Oh, Latte."

"*Skinny* Latte."

Wesley took Lloyd's drink and handed it to Skinny Latte. "You'll love this. Extra lite."

Lloyd scowled as Skinny Latte walked away with his coffee. "One of the perks of dating you is now walking out the door with that insolent jerk."

Wesley bit his bottom lip suggestively. "Dating me involves more perks than coffee. Give me your room key and I'll surprise you."

Lloyd reached into his pocket. Instead of drawing out his key, he drew out his phone.

"Who are you calling?" Wesley asked.

"Someone to put bars on my door."

"Bars open the possibilities . . ."

Caleb made a yakking sound. "That's my cue to wash my ears out. See you after rehearsals."

Lloyd leaned in and lowered his voice just for Wesley to hear. "How about you and I go out for dinner tonight?"

"Dinner?"

"Seven-thirty."

Butterflies washed through him.

MacDonald planted a fresh coffee in front of Lloyd. He picked it up, acknowledging thanks. Keeping his eyes on Wesley, he backed toward the entrance. "Oh, and Wesley. It's a *date*."

∾

At seven-thirty, Wesley shoved on his coat and left his room. He banged into Lloyd in the hallway, who was wearing his gray coat. A green scarf hung over his shoulder. He looked devastatingly handsome, and the leather gloves were a delightful touch."

Wesley fumbled with the last button on his short trench coat. "Hey."

"Hey," Lloyd said, running his eye appreciatively over Wesley and his soft but clingy jeans. "I was going to do the whole picking-you-up thing."

Wesley gave up on the button. "I was headed to your room, but if you want to get me . . ." He stepped back toward his room.

Lloyd snagged his sleeve with a nervous chuckle. "We don't need a reenactment. This is good, too."

"Wow," Caleb said with Suzy and MacDonald behind their opened door. "They are adorkable."

Wesley and Lloyd glared at them, then refocused on each other. Wesley grinned. He did feel kind of *dork*able.

Because he knew it was a date this time.

His hands were sweating.

They moved to the stairwell and grabbed the door handle at the same time, knocking their heads together.

Wesley laughed uncontrollably.

Once they spilled outside, Lloyd stopped them. He took his scarf and looped it around Wesley's neck. "I like that you're nervous."

"Nervous? That's a joke." He choked on his breath and gave up. "Okay. Maybe a little. Why do you like it?"

Lloyd tapped Wesley's nose, "For one, it's adorable."

"For two?"

"I won't have to worry about you breaking me."

∾

"I LOVE THE LEVEL OF DETAIL THAT WENT INTO PLANNING THIS date," Wesley said as they stopped outside the hotdog stand in the park of lights.

"It gets better." Lloyd caught the vendor's attention—a different guy than the one who'd drooled over Lloyd the last time. Thank God.

The vendor smiled. "Your seitan dogs are steamed and ready."

Wesley blinked at Lloyd. Lloyd had come here and organized this? Wesley gulped.

The vendor caught Wesley's attention. "Are you eating a regular one?"

Wesley darted a look at Lloyd. "How many of yours did you bring?"

"A couple."

Wesley turned back to the vendor. "I'll have one of his."

Once they had their vegetarian hotdogs, Wesley and Lloyd walked through the park. Lights glittered around them, bright in the frosty air, wonderfully romantic.

"So. About us," Wesley said once he'd licked his fingers clean of ketchup. "When did you know I liked you?"

Lloyd stopped under the arch of tea-lights and took Wesley's hands, tugging him close. "I found a few clues. The moment we danced in Party Palace. Our kiss at auditions. You following me home at Thanksgiving. But the best clue?" Lloyd bumped their noses together. "When you realized I was your best friend."

"The day of your first smile."

Lloyd pulled back a fraction, gaze sinking into his. "First? I've been smiling in your general vicinity since day one."

Wesley's breath caught. "Yeah, you looking at me like that is going to be a problem."

Lloyd's brow pinched, and Wesley snuggled against him. "It makes me want to do things with you. To you."

Lloyd reached between them, digging in his coat pocket, which was jammed close to Wesley's hardening cock. "Let's not beat around the bush." Wesley grinned wickedly. "Let's go behind it and beat each other off."

Lloyd produced a flask. "How about a nightcap instead?"

"You brought a flask!" He grabbed it off Lloyd. "You own a flask?"

"The night wouldn't be complete without this."

Wesley uncapped and took a gulp. He spluttered and glowered at Lloyd. "That's not Jack."

"Of course not. I'm your RA." He smirked, the codger. "I funneled my favorite roast into the flask. Prepared by my favorite barista."

"Me?"

"No. MacDonald." Lloyd grinned. "Yes, you. Idiot."

Light and tingly, Wesley walked with Lloyd around the park and then through town back to the dorms. They entered Williamson at midnight.

Wesley followed Lloyd into his bedroom. While Lloyd slipped off his gloves and coat, Wesley pulled two condoms out of the basket. Prelubricated. Studded. "Yes and yes, but—ah, that's better," he said, pulling out a third option. "Start with the basics."

Lloyd was a wall of warmth behind him, and Wesley folded against his chest. Large hands slid over the curve of Wesley's shoulders and turned him around, then Lloyd walked him out of the room.

"I'll make you breakfast in the morning," Lloyd said and shut the door in Wesley's smirking face.

"Fine," Wesley said through the door. "But three guesses what I'm doing next."

Lloyd's laugh filtered through the door, and Wesley grinned as he sent Lloyd a message on his way back to his Caleb-annexed room.

Wesley: Happy birthday, Cap.

Lloyd made breakfast in the dorm kitchen. By the looks of it, Wesley would be lucky to get a second scrumptiously sweet pancake.

Half the floor had sniffed their way into the room, and Lloyd kept doling out pancakes as if to prove he wasn't having a breakfast date with his resident.

Wesley sat on the counter, heels tapping the cupboards. The students eyed him like they knew something was brewing between them.

Caleb trundled in as Lloyd poured the last of the batter into a pan. "Oh, yes please."

Lloyd rolled his eyes. "So much for romance."

Caleb yawned. "I'll give half of it to Wes." He turned to Wesley. "Did you ask him yet?"

Lloyd flipped the pancake. "Ask me what?"

Wesley checked no one was peeking into the kitchen and ran his socked foot up Lloyd's thigh. "Can I borrow your car?"

"Three guesses what my answer is."

Wesley pouted. "Can you drive Caleb and me to his rehearsal and then drop him at Sandalwood?"

Lloyd slid the pancake onto a plate Caleb grabbed. "Another three guesses."

Lloyd's cheek dimpled and Wesley knew it was a yes. This boyfriend gig had some advantages. Wesley tossed him a big, sparkly smile. "Say the word and I'll properly thank you for it."

"Say the word," Caleb grumbled and tore the pancake in half for Wesley, "and I'll vacate the kitchen."

"Leave!" Wesley said at the precise moment Lloyd said, "Stay!"

Your ex was such a drip. You deserve something much bitter.

Chapter Nineteen

Lloyd dropped them off at rehearsals and watched from the back of the auditorium as Wesley confronted the director about their auditioning kiss. "There's no way you wouldn't remember it."

"I remember it."

Wesley tossed his hands up. "Why did you cut us then?"

"Are you that desperate to be in my show?"

"I don't want to be in your show. I'm desperate to hear you admit it."

"Admit what?"

"That the kiss was amazing!"

Caleb stopped blowing into his flute from the stage behind him. "That guy bugging you, sir? He's not related to me."

The director motioned to his assistant and Wesley weaved out of their grasp, speed-walking toward a thoroughly entertained Lloyd, who leaned with folded arms against a brick column, one ankle crossed.

Wesley slowed his gait and eye-fucked every inch of his boyfriend.

"I can tell you why we didn't make the cut," Lloyd said. "But I'm afraid how you'll react."

Wesley stopped in front of him. "What do you think I'm going to do? Curse you?"

"Yes," Lloyd said and lowered his voice, "after trying to jump me."

∽

LLOYD WAS RIGHT. AT 'UNRESOLVED SEXUAL TENSION stealing the spotlight,' Wesley tried to jump him. Then ended up cursing when Lloyd steered them out into a cold drizzle.

He scowled at him the entire drive to Sandalwood, while Lloyd took the higher road of pretending not to notice.

"Shit," Caleb said as they parked in the school lot. "That's my math teacher. I gotta get to class without her seeing how tardy I am."

Wesley glared between the seats at his brother. "The things I do for you. You owe me."

"I promise," he said with a fleeting look toward Lloyd. "I'm working on it."

Wesley unbuckled. "All right. Come on, Lloyd. We've got distracting to do."

Lloyd murmured disapproval under his breath, but walked with Wesley to the entrance steps, catching Mrs. Bailey's attention.

"Mr. Hidaka," she said, surprised. "How lovely to see you again. Are you here for your brother?"

Yes, yes, he was. "How is he doing?"

"Fine. Let's hope it stays that way."

Wesley glared at skedaddling Caleb over her shoulder. "Let's hope."

Mrs. Bailey followed his gaze, turning.

Wesley thought fast, snagging her attention as Caleb skedaddled around the building and out of sight. "The gardens. They are so well pruned. My fiancé and I were hoping to talk to someone about having a wedding ceremony here."

Mrs. Bailey shrieked. "How lovely."

"We were thinking an outdoor afternoon tea? We'll declare our everlasting love for each other and our guests will cheer us over lattes and cappuccinos."

"You must talk to Principal Bontempo right away. His office is on my way to class. Come." She beckoned them into the brick prison, and they had little choice but to follow.

"Sandalwood gardens?" Lloyd asked under his breath. "Really?"

"Hell no. I still want a lavender farm."

"Good. Otherwise it sounded perfect."

Mrs. Bailey dropped them outside Principal Bontempo's office and Wesley faked a cheery wave as if he couldn't wait to approach the bastard.

As soon as she rounded the corner, Wesley grabbed Lloyd and yanked him down the hall.

Principal Bontempo's voice cut around an upcoming corner, and Wesley panicked. He scanned the hall for an escape and latched onto a supply closet. "Quick," he hissed, gesturing Lloyd into the closet.

"We won't both fit in there."

"Yes, we will."

He shoved Lloyd in, squished himself against him like a vertical game of Twister, and shut the door. Darkness swallowed them. Something fell and dug into Wesley's thigh.

Lloyd's chest swelled with a deep breath.

Wesley pressed his mouth against the curve of Lloyd's shoulder to muffle a sudden laugh.

They waited for Principal Bontempo's footsteps to pass before Wesley grappled for the door handle.

He twisted it. The door didn't budge.

Wesley bit the inside of his cheek. "You know how I said I always wanted to be stuck in the closet with you?"

Lloyd's sigh sifted through Wesley's hair. "You're kidding me."

"Not even a little bit." Wesley shifted a bit. "Something's digging into my thigh."

"Most oblivious guy I know."

Wesley laughed. "Something *else* is digging into my thigh. Can you reach and—" Lloyd removed the offending broomstick. "Better. Now reach in between us."

"You're an opportunist."

"I can't help that you feel so good. Maybe you should say something Cappy."

"Why?"

"So I'm reminded why I don't start making out with you right now."

Lloyd groaned. "You're my resident. I'm your—"

"RA. It's against the rules. You do Cappy so well."

"Try the door again."

"You're right. Making out would be a terrible idea. We'll want a quick fuck to go with it."

"I'm not into quick fucks. Not with you. Certainly not our first time."

Wesley was one tingly breath away from grinding his hips against Lloyd in earnest. "Someone please open the door!"

Twenty seconds later, bright light hit them. Wesley and Lloyd tumbled out, crumbling to Principal Bontempo's feet.

"Mr. Hidaka. It's like going back in time."

Lloyd regained his footing first, then helped Wesley up, whispering, "You okay?"

Wesley glanced at Principal Bontempo and hung his head. "Ask me again in an hour."

Principal Bontempo cleared his throat. "May I see you in my office, please?"

Bowed head, Wesley slumped into the principal's office with Lloyd at his side.

They were gestured to seats in front of the massive desk, and Wesley wished the velvet-padded chair would suck him up.

It was junior year all over again, with an impending lecture on how he should control his urges.

He gripped the curve of the seat. He wouldn't stand for it. "I won't stand for it. My fiancé and I will kiss where and when we please." Not that they even got to the kissing.

Principal Bontempo and Lloyd jerked their heads in the direction of his outburst.

Respect and a glimmer of something softer shone in Lloyd's eye.

The principal stood behind his imposing chair, hands braced on the back. "School grounds are hardly appropriate, and I'd have thought you'd find a better place than the supply closet." He sighed. "While you're here, let's talk about your brother."

"He handed in his math assignment. He's acing all his core subjects."

"Mr. Hidaka. While your brother has put in more effort and his attendance has been passable the last six school weeks, his commitment has been sketchy at best. With him trying to excuse himself for another two days—"

"What are you talking about?" Wesley frowned.

"Caleb came into my office yesterday asking me to allow him two more days off. I refused."

"He never mentioned it to me."

"He threw quite the hysterics. Much like you were prone to—"

"This isn't about me!" Wesley exploded out of his seat, the back of his hand accidentally knocking papers off Principal Bontempo's desk. They drifted to the table, and Lloyd stood knotting his and Wesley's hands.

Lloyd looked coolly at the principal. "Mr. Bontempo—"

"Principal Bontempo."

"Mr. Bontempo, get to your point."

Principal Bontempo's gaze hardened to small steel rods. "Perhaps Caleb's role model"—he pointedly glanced at Wesley—"needs to take a hard look at his actions."

Wesley seethed, gripping Lloyd like a vice.

Lloyd responded, voice tight, but delivered with the patience of a Capricorn. "I think we are done here."

Wesley bit down his anger. He wasn't finished fighting for Caleb yet. "Why didn't you excuse him the two days? Caleb came to you directly. The time must be important to him. You could have signed it off as sick leave. Why didn't you?"

Principal Bontempo gazed out his office window that faced one of Sandalwood's courtyards. "If I had known how difficult you Hidakas were, I'd never have admitted you to my school. Four years later, I'm having the same conversation. Of course, back then it was about you. And I was talking to your mother."

Wesley stared at the back of his graying head. "What?"

Principal Bontempo gave them a cursory look over his shoulder. "You were whip smart, but a truant. She pleaded me to write you a recommendation to that fancy private college you're at."

Wesley rocked on his feet. Lloyd's grip shifted to his elbow to keep him from plunking backwards. "You did. You wrote a letter."

"It would've been ungracious of me not to after she donated so generously toward the new music department."

Shock slapped Wesley mute. He struggled to find his voice. When he did, it came out a croak. "How much did she give you?"

"I think you mean how much did she donate to the school."

"How *much*?"

Principal Bontempo turned with a non-too-subtle glint in his eye. "Fifty."

"Moral issues aside, I like that you tried to donate fifty dollars," Lloyd said. They sat in a window booth of a small café across from Sandalwood's parking lot. Raindrops weaved over the glass.

Wesley banged his forehead against his place setting. "Was I the only one who didn't get he meant fifty thousand?"

Lloyd's feet slipped between his under the table. "To be fair, there were only three of us in his office."

Wesley groaned. "Caleb is attending class if I have to drag him by his flute." Hearing that now-tainted word, he shuddered with a curse to MacDonald under his breath.

Their coffee arrived, and Wesley almost spat it out. "Bad. This whole day is bad. Was it just me, or did Bontempo think you might shower the school in donations?"

"It wasn't just you. He looked at me and saw my Aunt Tabitha."

"Promise me something?"

Lloyd squeezed Wesley's ankle.

"One day you'll overthrow that tyrant and become principal of Sandalwood. You'll be a firm but fair leader, and you'll come here on your lunch breaks."

Lloyd sipped the terrible coffee and winced. "Why would I come here?"

"Because I'll own this place. It'll be the best indie café in town."

"It'll swarm with hormonal teenagers."

"Full of drama. It'll be great." Wesley stared outside the window at the imposing school across the road and sank into the seat. "I hate to admit that Principal Bontempo might have a point. But he might have a point."

Lloyd leaned his forearms against the table. "What do you mean?"

"I'm full of drama. Maybe if I hadn't run away from home, if I'd gone home more often, if I had been a better role model, this situation with Caleb wouldn't be happening."

"You don't give yourself enough credit. You've been through a lot too. You'll work this out. I'll help you."

"Got fifty thousand laying around?"

Lloyd laughed drily, then stopped. "I don't." His brow furrowed. "But . . ." He stood abruptly. "Come."

Lloyd herded him through the rain into the car, refusing to tell Wesley his plan. Ten minutes' drive later, Lloyd pulled into the posh side of town and parked outside a gated mansion.

"What are we doing? What's going on?" Wesley's gut churned, fearful he knew the answer.

Lloyd sucked in a breath and exited the car. Wesley lurched after him, forgetting to unbuckle. The seatbelt whipped against his chest. He yanked it off and hurried to Lloyd at the gate buzzer. "Stop. Lloyd. No."

"Some things are more important than pride."

"You'd ask your aunt for money?"

Lloyd swallowed. Wesley noted his shudder. "She donates in much larger sums all the time."

"No." He pulled the keys out of Lloyd's hand and started walking back to the car. When Lloyd didn't follow, Wesley rounded to the driver's side and opened the door. "I will never let you ask that woman for anything."

"She loves putting her stake wherever she can," Lloyd said.

"Get in the car."

"If she donates to Sandalwood, Principal Bontempo might have another stroke of 'graciousness' and get him into Treble."

"If you don't get your ass in the car, I'm driving off without you."

Lloyd snapped into the moment. "Don't even think about sitting behind the—"

Wesley slung himself into the car behind the wheel, shut the door, and started the engine.

Lloyd wasted no time jumping into the passenger seat.

Wesley pulled away from the curb the moment his door shut. Window wipers swung back and forth. "Lloyd, and I say this from the bottom of my heart, what the fuck?"

They whizzed around a corner and Lloyd clenched the overhead handle. "I hate you thinking Caleb missing out on his dream is your fault."

"Your aunt is not the solution."

"You're a bit close to the sidewalk."

Wesley bounced his palm over the wheel to emphasize his point. "You'd be indebted to her for the rest of your life."

"Fire hydrant ahead."

"I'd feel guiltier about that."

"I don't know what to say. I'm touched you hauled me away, but—fire hydrant!"

Wesley swerved into a deep puddle, arcing water over the side of the car. Hydrant avoided.

"Could you call your mom and put her on speaker for me?"

Lloyd stared blankly at him.

Wesley cocked his hips off the seat. "Phone's in my pocket. Reach in."

"Have I mentioned how much you drive me crazy?"

An approaching traffic light turned yellow and Wesley halted to a screeching stop, butt slamming back to the seat. "See. I can follow the rules too."

Lloyd clutched his belt, shaking his head. "What will I do with you?"

"I can think of plenty. But first, the phone. Your mom."

"Why do you want to call my mom?"

"To tell her what a generous, self-sacrificing idiot she raised."

Wesley sat across from Caleb at his usual window booth, cradling Caleb's hazelnut coffee.

Caleb glanced up from the book he was reading. He read Wesley right, because he bookmarked his text and set it to the side. "Fuck. You know I'm losing my chance at Treble."

"Do you have to, Hazelnut?"

"Dress rehearsals got shifted from the weekend to Thursday and Friday."

"This is your future."

"They are both my dream, and I can't bail on Johnson-Brown now."

MacDonald cleared her throat and set avocado toast in front of Caleb. Her eyes narrowed on him. "You'd turn down a chance at Treble just to play flute in one play?"

"If the principal would excuse my absence and write the letter, I could do both." Caleb met Wesley's gaze with a defeated shrug. "But I can't."

"Damn Principal Bontempo and his rigid rules," Wesley said.

"Exactly."

MacDonald still stared at Caleb, her face not betraying a single emotion. Either Caleb read her better or Wesley had gone temporarily insane. Caleb snagged her hand and delivered a small kiss to her fingertips. "Don't worry about me, MacD. I'm going to make something of music."

Wesley searched for ways to change his mind, but who was Wesley to stop Caleb from walking his own path?

He slid the latte over.

The rest of his shift, Wesley struggled to concentrate. Worry mixed with anger and confusing tenderness kept creeping up on him.

Suzy left work in a hurry, saying she was late to meet someone, so he and MacDonald closed up shop.

Walking back to Williamson, Wesley tried to call Lloyd. He

wasn't answering. He also wasn't in his room. "Fuck," he said, throat constricting in frustration and panic. "Fuck."

MacDonald was by his side in a heartbeat. "Stop puffing. What do you need?"

"Fuck. I need to go home."

MacDonald's leg was well enough to drive him home—or so she claimed. "Do you want me to go in with you?" she offered. "I have a particular gift in offending the heartless." She gave the slightest acknowledging nod. "And everyone else."

"How did you ever break your leg?"

MacDonald looked out the side window. "I slipped in the shower."

"Why did you come into work swearing off sex?"

"I was practicing when I slipped."

"Practicing?"

"Practicing." She huffed a short laugh. "If I can't even do it right alone, I don't think I'm made for it. Now get out of the car before I realize how much I regret this conversation."

Wesley leaned over the console and smacked a kiss on her temple. "Thanks for dropping me off."

"I'll wait until you're done."

Wesley thanked her, got out of the car, and faced his mom.

∼

THEY STARED AT EACH OTHER OVER HOT CHOCOLATES. His mom sat on the blue-floral armchair, and Wesley sat across her on a matching sofa.

"Why don't you ever wear shirts anymore? Always these clingy T-shirts and jeans that make your legs look like they got put in the dryer too long."

Wesley looked at the white V-neck he'd worn to work. If she thought this was tight . . . "I haven't worn a button-up shirt since

Gemini Keeps Capricorn

Sandalwood, and I only wore one there because it was the uniform."

"It makes you look mature."

"The clingy T-shirts? Or the uniform?"

Mom gave him parental eyes that said, *You know exactly which.* He did.

"Well," Mom said after a sip of hot chocolate that left a milky mustache on her upper lip, "you didn't surprise me with this visit just to discuss our varying opinions on your outfits."

"Not today."

"Not today?" Hope glimmered in her eyes. "Does our future hold a more frivolous discussion?"

Wesley set his drink on the coffee table. "Why did you pay Principal Bontempo to make sure I got a letter of recommendation?"

Mom hopped off the armchair and moved to the corner cabinet. Wesley's eye was drawn to a dozen of Dad's old CDs. Cases open, as though Mom had been listening to them. She picked up two coasters from a stack. "It was a donation. To the music department, I believe."

Wesley took the coaster she was wielding and slipped it under his cup. She stared at him.

"Is it difficult to believe I've always cared?"

"Mom."

"I know." She set her drink on a coaster. "It doesn't mean anything if I don't accept the gaying."

"I wish you would," Wesley said.

"Your father left enough money to pay for your and Caleb's school and college tuition, and a little extra."

"Fifty extra?"

She shot him a frown. "Fifty thousand, Wesley."

A burst of tenderness filled him. He swallowed back a laugh. "Oh, Mom." He sighed. "We are more alike than I sometimes give us credit for."

"Was that a compliment or an insult?"

"A bit of both."

She blew an escaped strand of black hair off her face. "You're more like your father. He had a cheeky streak that stole my heart."

Soft silence descended on them, and Wesley reluctantly broke it. "Caleb is insanely talented. He would be perfect at Treble, but he's not getting the recommendation he needs." Principal Bontempo could probably even dissuade the admissions board from letting Caleb in on music merit alone.

His mom sagged against the arm of the chair, cupping her chin. "There's no money left. He can always go to another college."

Wesley rubbed the handle of his cup but didn't lift it. "It's his dream, Mom."

Mom pressed her lips together, then nodded with a sigh.

Wesley stood with one more fleeting glance to Dad's beloved CDs. "MacDonald is waiting for me in the car."

His mom walked him outside. Wesley hauled in an uneven breath. "Mom?"

"Wesley?"

"Would you like to come to Williamson's Fifties Bash?"

I want to Joe you just how much I care.

Chapter Twenty

Wesley scrolled through webpage after webpage of law material. He barely heard Caleb come and go, and only paused in his research when Lloyd cleared his throat.

His boyfriend held out a container of curry and stuffed naan. "Eat something."

"I don't have time."

"Two minutes to eat, then I'm out of your hair," Lloyd said.

"How about you feed me as I continue reading?" At Lloyd's stern look, Wesley took the food and bit into the warm naan. He moaned and stuffed more in his mouth.

He leaned back in his chair, swallowing the warm, buttery bread. "Why didn't you force me to eat hours ago?"

Lloyd smirked, looking at the laptop, and his smile settled into a softer line. "Are you doing what I think you're doing?"

Wesley bit his lip and stared at the screen. "Yes."

~

The night of researching brought him to Sandalwood.

He strode through the halls, his speech rolling through his

mind. Turning into the hall leading to the principal's office, he banged into—

"MacDonald?" Surely, he wasn't seeing right. "What are you doing here?"

MacDonald righted herself, then said, "I was never here, okay?"

"What does that mean?"

She moved past him. "Gotta go. Helping prepare the basement for the bash."

Wesley grabbed her elbow. "Did you give the principal a piece of your mind?"

When she spoke, it was quiet. "No, I donated for his reconsideration."

"Donated?"

"My second home growing up was a Vegas casino and some underground clubs. I know how to play, and thanks to you and Lloyd, I had a thousand bucks to work with."

"MacDonald . . ."

"It's just money." She pulled away, and her shoes clapped against the polished floors as she left.

With growing urgency, Wesley found Principal Bontempo just leaving his office.

"Mr. Hidaka. Back so soon."

"I'd like to speak with you, sir."

"I'm booked up with meetings. You'll have to arrange another appointment."

"This won't take five minutes."

Principal Bontempo walked brusquely down the hall and Wesley kept pace. "Talk to me en route to assembly, if you must."

"You're glowing like that young woman who left your office gave the school a sizeable donation."

"I cannot discuss prior private meetings. But a thirty-grand extension to the library catalog might be likely."

Thirty grand? Jesus, MacDonald.

"I bet she happened to mention she knew Caleb."

Shrewd eyes landed on his. "I take it you know Mrs. MacDonald?"

"I do. And I also know the law."

∼

Wesley barely made it back in time for work.

His regulars came in, entertaining as always, but mildly distracting.

Itching to tell Lloyd about Sandalwood, he also wanted to hunt Caleb down and have a chat.

He was nervous about tonight's bash. Particularly showing his mom around the dorm.

Fearful of hoping it would be better than their last visits, he hoped anyway.

As soon as he locked up the café for the evening, he beelined for the Williamson basement.

Cleared of equipment, the large room had plenty of space for a dance floor. Black-and-white helium-filled balloons covered the ceiling. MacDonald was stirring a punch bowl. Suzy and Randy were setting finger food on two adjoining tables.

Precariously perched on a ladder, Lloyd and Gavin were fighting crimson bows and streamers.

"We need to double-up around the windows," Gavin said, holding up the bow above a basement window, then shifting it to the corner. "Give it more accent."

Lloyd looked ready to deck him. "You're doing this on purpose, aren't you?"

Gavin moved the bow back to the middle of the window and cocked his head. "Doing what on purpose?"

"Juicing me of the will to live." Lloyd stole the bow and pinned it before Gavin could change his mind again.

"It's just a dance, Lloyd."

"Exactly. A dance. No one needs so many bows."

"We don't have time to argue," Gavin said. "Guests will be arriving in less than an hour. Now pass another bow."

Wesley scanned the room for his brother and found cowboy boots poking out from under a checkered tablecloth. Wesley nudged the soles, and Caleb backward crawled from underneath the table.

"Wes," Caleb said, dusting the knees of his costume. Suspenders were holding his pants up. "You're here. Is that a hazelnut latte in your hand?"

Wesley lured him into the corner of the room with it.

"Gimmie."

"In a sec. I need to say something."

Caleb's gaze remained trained on the latte. "What's up?"

"First, rehearsals. How'd they go?"

Caleb pulled at the elastic with his thumbs. "Perfect. Weird though, wondering if this show would be the highlight of my fluting future."

"It won't be. Even if Treble doesn't happen, you'll pursue your passion." Wesley glanced at his boyfriend smacking a bow out of Gavin's hand. "You thrive on ambition."

Caleb flushed. "I smell the hazelnut, gimmie—"

"MacDonald," Wesley said, and Caleb's gaze jerked up. "Keep trying."

The elastic snapped hard against his chest. "Keep trying? Where did that come from?"

Wesley twisted the coffee cup in his hand. "She asked me to keep quiet, but I can't. I won't."

He told his brother what she'd done. When he was through, he held out the latte.

Caleb stared at him. He stopped Wesley from speaking again with a raised finger. Ignoring the latte, he turned and strode over to MacDonald who was plunking plastic cups onto the table.

He spun her around and she yelped, ready to drum out an

insult. Caleb stopped her with a kiss. He pulled back and gazed into her bright, wary eyes. Caressing his thumb over her cheek, he kissed her again. "Save me dances, Molly. Save me all of them."

He spun on his heel and came back for his latte.

MacDonald stared at him, blinking, one finger unconsciously touching her lip. She noticed the basement had stilled, all eyes on her, and she snapped her walls back up with a scowl at Wesley.

Wesley mouthed, "Sorry not sorry."

He herded his trembling brother to his room. Caleb set down his barely touched latte and flopped onto the bed. "I'm too young to have fallen this much in love," he said. "But she's it, Wes. That girl is the one I'm marrying."

Wesley believed him.

Caleb sighed, then distracted himself eyeing Wesley up. "What are you wearing tonight?"

Wesley had changed into dance jeans and a fifties-style red-and-white letterman jacket. He'd just zipped it up when his phone dinged. "Mom's here. She's in the parking lot."

Caleb rolled off the bed. "I'll get her."

His brother left as Lloyd arrived and they skirted past each other.

Lloyd languidly took Wesley in from boot to jacket. "You look . . ."

"Sexy as hell?"

Lloyd cupped his neck as if forcing himself not to hurdle the distance between them and manhandle all that sexiness. Wesley shamelessly heeled his chubbing crotch, watching with delight the lust and control warring on Lloyd's face.

Lloyd opened the door wide to limit temptation. Clever Capricorn. "How did it go at Sandalwood?"

Wesley pivoted to the mirror and messed with his hair. "It's amazing how much legal jargon I spouted in the five-minute walk to assembly."

Pride settled into Lloyd's expression. "Even if it didn't work, the fact that you tried counts."

"You should have seen the color drain from Bontempo's face."

"It worked, then?"

"I fed him a hearty bowl of bullshit. It sufficiently scared him." Wesley popped the collar of his jacket with a pose, making Lloyd grin. "He didn't say it outright, but it was there in subtext. He's reconsidering MacDonald's 'donation' and writing a recommendation letter." He gave a self-deprecating laugh. "Law studies came in useful after all. Dad would be proud."

"He would have been more than proud."

Wesley flustered. "No costume tonight?"

Lloyd pulled Wesley toward him, close enough their breaths mingled. "I have something for you. Close your eyes."

Wesley closed his eyes.

Lloyd bunched up his sleeve and pushed something over his hand. Material smacked against the inside of his wrist.

Wesley grinned. "Are you slipping a corsage on me?"

"Call it whatever you want."

Wesley peeked. He opened his eyes wider, pulling his arm up to study the double-wrap leather band.

"Do you like it?" Lloyd asked.

"Like it? I love it. I love you." Wesley's heart skipped at the hit of emotion that stunned Lloyd to silence. Wesley said it again, holding Lloyd's gaze. Drawing closer. "I love you."

It was the first time he'd said the words to a boyfriend. With Lloyd they came light and easy. Felt so good, he wanted to say them again. "I love you—" Wesley caught Gavin waltzing toward his open door, and pushed Lloyd away with a laugh. "Unicorns. I love unicorns."

Lloyd's brow shot up. "Unicorns?" He spotted Gavin and nodded. "Unicorns, yes. I'm not sure I love them as much as Europe or ukuleles, unicycles, or uniforms, but they're amusing."

"Unicorns are way better than any of those other long-u words."

Gavin rapped his knuckles on the doorframe, eyes pinging between them. "Ready to speak to our guests, Lloyd?"

Lloyd held Wesley's gaze a few heart-stopping moments, and then shifted toward Gavin.

Wesley followed at his elbow with a nervous spring in his step. "Unicorns have a magical horn. Though it does make you wonder why they're not called uni*horns*."

"Corn comes from the Latin and means horn."

Wesley paused, and Lloyd continued down the hall with Gavin. "Do you know everything?" he called after him.

Lloyd turned and walked backwards. "Yes."

Gavin wasn't paying attention, and Wesley mouthed, "I love you." Lloyd bloomed with a grin and somehow sounded decidedly in control. "Let's continue this discussion later."

"Looking forward to it. Also, feel free to save me from my mom at any time."

A snicker came from behind. Wesley whirled around to find Caleb and his mom approaching. Of course.

Wesley did a double take. Their mom wore a pleated floral skirt and collared top, and her hair bobbed around her shoulders.

She glanced around the floor and smiled tentatively. "So."

"So," Wesley said, shifting from foot to foot.

Caleb chuckled and hooked an arm around Wesley's neck. "So this is where our Wesley lives."

∽

AFTER WALKING MOM THROUGH THEIR FLOOR, THEY MOVED to the party. Costumed crowds hovered around the snack tables, and a dozen pairs danced in the middle of the room.

Wesley searched fruitlessly for Suzy. His mom had spoken at length to Caleb, and briefly to MacDonald. But now, Caleb was drawing MacDonald onto the dance floor, leaving Wesley alone with his mom.

Lloyd was within earshot, standing at the punch bowl. "It's a family-friendly event," he admonished, plucking a flask from Steve's hand. Randy made a furtive glance at the punchbowl that Lloyd failed to catch. "Shoo. Both of you."

Mom pressed the pleats of her skirt, then gave up and looked at him. "You have an interesting bunch of friends."

This was true. "I love them."

Despite the music, the silence stretched awkwardly. "I'm going to get some punch."

She heeled off, and Wesley sank against the wall and breathed out, yearning to dance. He dug out his phone and texted Suzy to emerge from wherever she was hiding.

He waited two songs for a response, but nothing was forthcoming. Luckily his mom fell into conversation with another mom that had turned up.

Wesley stalked the crowd for Lloyd and bumped into Gavin running a finger down a page in his leather binder. Wesley smirked. "It's running smoothly." He stole the binder and slipped it on the windowsill. "Enjoy yourself. Dance."

Gavin looked at his watch. "The first performance is about to start."

Of course there'd be performances. Gavin was involved. Mr. Creativity extraordinaire.

"Looks like she's ready," Gavin said.

Wesley turned.

Suzy was strolling onto the dance floor in a bright-floral rockabilly dress and big hair.

Sounds of a microphone turning on crackled around the room.

Caleb's voice burst from the speakers. "Is it on? Yep, cool. If we could clear the floor for one song, please."

Wesley grew about two inches in surprise. He slipped to the front of the gathering crowd.

Suzy curled her finger and beckoned someone from the crowd. An Elvis impersonator strode toward her, wearing tight black pants, a big-collared white shirt, and pompadour hair.

From this angle, his young Elvis look was perfect. The sunglasses were a nice touch. Suzy! Who was this hottie?

Elvis pivoted and searched the crowd.

Wesley froze. His damn jaw dropped to the floor.

"What the fuck?" he gasped. "Lloyd!"

Caleb spoke into the microphone. "This is dedicated to a flirty Gem from a grumpy Cap. He knows who he is."

Lloyd found Wesley in the crowd and peered at him over the top of his sunglasses, just like the Elvis poster in his room. The leer, spot on. The lips, devastatingly fuckable.

The opening chords to Elvis's *A Little Less Conversation* pulsed around him, and Lloyd touch-stepped with a seductive swing of his hips. He smoothly triple-stepped, one hand leading Suzy into a turn.

Lloyd turned after, smack on the beat, and Wesley's heart fucking melted.

Almost without flaw, Lloyd and Suzy danced a fourteen-beat step. They rolled and tandem stepped, and Lloyd gave Suzy a spin with oomph, turning her and then turning her again. Holy shit. This was intermediate stuff, and Lloyd.

A couple of people either side of him jostled forward for a better view and Wesley thrust out an arm stopping them. "When Elvis is on the floor, you give him room."

Small push. Another tuck. Lloyd moved his hips.

Wesley's smile ate his face.

At the final verse, couples joined in the dancing. Wesley's gaze drank in every one of Lloyd's steps.

"Was that show for you?"

Wesley lurched around. His mom was right behind him, holding out a bulging napkin.

"You're back."

"I brought you the last rum balls. I saw how much you seemed to like them earlier."

He did like the rum balls. He took one. Before he could turn back to Lloyd, his mom blurted, "I think, I mean, I'm ready to watch the gaying."

"It's not something you watch." Wesley sidled around a dancing Randy to get a better view of Lloyd. His mom followed.

"I've thought long and hard about this," she said. "I am intent on understanding." Lloyd and Suzy danced toward him and did a reverse whip. The move made Wesley want to kiss the fuck out of his boyfriend. "You could talk to me about it, Wesley. The gaying. How it makes you feel."

Wesley glanced at his mom. "It's sort of, um, an internal emotion."

Elvis's *Blue Suede Shoes* started. A warm hand snapped Wesley's wrist and Lloyd pulled him onto the dance floor with such energy, his mom nearly toppled over.

Wesley found his footing, and Lloyd led him into a tuck turn. Wesley laughed, slipping into the role. "Holy shit, Lloyd. I about wet myself when you started dancing."

Lloyd whipped him close. "Seeing you floored like that was worth every minute of this secret."

Wesley subtly took over the lead, pulling Lloyd into a basket whip. Lloyd stumbled but caught the beat. "These were the meeting dates you went to? You and Suzy have been practicing the West Coast Swing?"

"Yes."

"Since when?"

"I called her the afternoon after we got back from Party Palace. I was a stumbling fool and I hated that I couldn't dance with you, because Wesley? I *needed* to dance with you."

Wesley's chest was overrun with butterflies. "I think it's about time we pick up our earlier conversation."

He overheard his mom talking to MacDonald. "We should cheer now, right?"

Wesley groaned. "I think Steve spiked the punch. She is not my mom."

Wesley spun Lloyd around, and Lloyd didn't miss a beat. The confidence he moved with had Wesley swooning. Literally. He was the one fudging his steps.

"Don't step on his shoes, Wesley!" his mom said with a giggle.

Wesley shot her a look as he narrowly avoided stumbling onto Lloyd's foot again. Lloyd's warm chest rumbled under Wesley as Lloyd caught him. They slowed their dance, Lloyd's hands sliding to his hips.

Putting his arms around Lloyd's neck, Wesley smiled up at him. "Elvis, eh?"

Lloyd dipped his head and spoke into his ear. "I know how much he does it for you."

Wesley murmured his agreement, touching the curl of Lloyd's wig.

"Wait a sec," his mom said at their side. Wesley yanked his hand back. "Now I know why this boy looked so familiar. He's Tabitha's nephew. She used to take him along to church."

Lloyd's flushed face. "You? At church?"

"I told you. She made me wait on her over the summer."

Mom's voice dropped, her shock palpable. "Oh, you can't do the gaying with him. He's a nice boy."

"Nice boys are gay too," Wesley called back to her. "Hold on. You don't think I'm a nice boy?"

Mom went quiet. "You are. Of course you are. I guess I thought of you as the exception."

The joy Lloyd had danced with drained from his face. "Maybe I should leave," Lloyd said, as his mom frowned.

"Stay," Wesley said to his mom while holding onto Lloyd. "You wanted to watch. This is what it looks like."

Wesley wanted Lloyd's smile back. "Please? Dance slow with me?" He gestured to Gavin, who was absorbed in a discussion with a resident's parent on the other side of the hall. "He won't notice."

Lloyd was already sliding his hands around his waist. "I'm in so much trouble," he whispered.

The song ended, and flutes whistled softly through the speakers. Wesley jerked, spinning in Lloyd's arms. He leaned back against his boyfriend's chest as Caleb played Randy Newman's *You've Got a Friend In Me*.

Wesley teased his twisted leather wristband and bit his lip. Caleb ended with a wink, and Lloyd coaxed Wesley around.

Wesley braced against Lloyd's forearms and looked up into his eyes. His voice sounded tight. "If I haven't said it enough, thank you for helping me with Hazelnut. For everything. But especially for that."

Lloyd tucked him in tight, holding him as the crowds danced around them.

As the song ended, he glimpsed his mom still standing at the edge of the room, a tiny frown on her face.

Their gazes connected, and she rocked back against her heels as if hit by an invisible force. Something glistened in her eye and it stunned Wesley. "Lloyd, I—"

"Go. I understand."

Wesley chased his mom, catching her in the parking lot. Puddles covered the ground and his breath fogged in the air.

"You're going home?"

She fumbled with her car keys, then looked at him over the roof of the car. "I saw you. You were just you."

Wesley stopped at the passenger door. "I was. I am."

Mom's face shattered as she fought to take it all in. She drew in a sharp breath, like she was choking. "How have I ever thought that was bad? You're happy."

She sniffed. Even dabbed the cuff of her sleeve under her nose.

Wesley's throat hurt watching his mom. He'd only ever seen her cry once, at Dad's funeral. "I don't want you to cry," he murmured. "But I'm glad you watched 'the gaying.'"

Mom hiccupped something between a sob and a laugh. "I should have more than listened to you, I should have heard you."

"Mom."

"I should have accepted you the way you are."

"You can still do that."

"And if I say I do, what happens?"

"I don't know," Wesley said.

"I can never make it right between us." Mom swiped at the tears leaking down her cheeks. "God. You have a fiancé."

Wesley rounded the car and cradled his mom in his arms. She smelled of jasmine and remorse, and he breathed it in. "Now's a good time to tell you I lied. Lloyd is not my fiancé. I wanted to force you to see that I'm not changing."

She pulled back. "I guess I deserve that."

"I'm sorry for the lie, but . . ."

She nodded. "I made you feel you had no choice." They stared at each other, and his mom did something she hadn't done since he was twelve. She pinched his nose. "What are you still doing standing in the cold with me when there is so much waiting for you inside?"

Let me French press you.

Chapter Twenty-One

It took Wesley five minutes to find Lloyd and drag him by the pompadour to his dorm room.

He shut the door and smirked at the idol plastered over his wall. Elvis watched him with hooded eyes. "I need . . . you touched me . . . I want . . ."

Wesley inched closer to Lloyd who stood at the end of his bed.

Wesley slid his fingers under the Elvis wig until it came off, revealing his closely shaven head. "I like you better like this." He tossed the wig onto his dresser.

Lloyd stepped forward, and Wesley backed up until he hit the door.

"You like rules," Wesley said. "You feel comfortable following them."

A frown. "What are you trying to tell me?"

"You love your job. You don't want to risk being fired. I accept that. I will wait for you."

Lloyd's eyes deepened as he absorbed Wesley's words. "You're not planning to drive me crazy with temptation anymore?"

Wesley threaded one of their hands together and kissed Lloyd's knuckles. He tasted of sweat and MacDonald's punch. "You're my Capricorn, and I'll keep you just the way you are."

Lloyd's voice came out thick and heavy. "No. I'm at the end, Wes. At the very, very end."

Wesley rocked on the balls of his heels as confusion rolled through him. "End of what?"

"My patience." Lloyd tugged Wesley against him and knotted his fingers in the back of Wesley's hair. Hot breath hit his throat and a shock of lust slammed into Wesley.

Lloyd kissed the crook of his neck. "You not wanting to break me? Broke me." He dragged his nose up the column of Wesley's to the base of his ear. Wesley gasped as Lloyd rocked his hard body against him.

His zip rippled open and Lloyd worked off his letterman jacket.

Wesley moaned. Then fought against the growing waves of lust. "I wasn't trying to trick you into anything."

"I know."

"Are you sure—"

Hands grabbed his ass firmly, hitching Wesley up off the floor. Lloyd dropped him to his bed and pinned his weight deliciously against him.

"The last four days since kissing you have been agony," Lloyd said in his ear. "I want to be inside you like I've wanted nothing else."

Wesley almost came from that confession alone. "In that case," he said, glancing toward the bedside table. "That stash of condoms and everything you need is in there. Make a dent."

"You loved teasing me, didn't you? Sneaking into my room for condoms once a week."

"Sometimes more than once. Oftentimes, actually." Wesley braced the back of Lloyd's shoulder and pulled him in. Their lips hovered, not quite kissing. Anticipation built in his body and electricity shot through him. His cock was so hard, yet Wesley held back from writhing, letting the ache grow, pleading with Lloyd to show him how not shy he could be. "Deep down I knew I'd be using them all with you."

Lloyd's tongue breached his lips with a drunk groan. He thrust against Wesley's crotch and dug his fingers into his ass cheek, tilting him for heavenly friction.

Lloyd kissed him, and it ravished Wesley's senses from tingling scalp to toes.

In perfect sync with Wesley's needs, Lloyd slipped his large warm hands under his T-shirt and worked it off.

Wesley scrabbled to shred Lloyd of his shirt, groaning in frustration when he couldn't pull the cuffs.

Lloyd straddled him, squeezing his thighs around Wesley's as he eased the shirtsleeves off his arms and whispered over Wesley's thighs.

Lloyd shifted over Wesley's hard cock and swiftly undid his pants.

"Always in control."

"Wesley?"

Wesley cocked a brow at him.

"I'm about to lose it." Lloyd curled his fingers at the waist of Wesley's jeans and shoved them to the top of his thighs. Lloyd's hot mouth cupped his balls through his boxers.

Wesley made an incoherent sound. His body screamed for more. "Need to feel your skin against mine."

Lloyd made quick work of their remaining clothes, tossed supplies between them on the bed, then lay next to Wesley, a fist around his straining shaft. His gaze stroked every inch of Wesley. "Pretty was never good enough to describe you."

Wesley bit his lip against the butterflies thrashing in his gut.

Lloyd pumped himself.

Wesley gasped. "Why aren't you inside me already?"

"So impatient."

"So Gemini."

Lloyd smirked. "You may have had some Capricorn facts right." Lloyd leaned over not touching him anywhere but their lips. "We like to make it last." He pulled back to look at Wesley gripping himself. "Touch yourself like you did in my bedroom. I want to know what you did."

Wesley showed him, and Lloyd's gaze dripped with lust. He watched as Wesley swiped some lube and wantonly fingered himself.

Lloyd's breathing stuttered, and he pushed Wesley's hands away, lifting them above his head as he sat astride Wesley's chest. The tip of his cock rubbed against Wesley's smooth chin. "Know what I was imagining?"

Wesley wriggled and captured the tip in his mouth.

Lloyd groaned and lifted onto his knees, one arm braced against the wall as he sank down Wesley's throat.

Fuck, he tasted good. Hot and salty. The hard ridges of his cock slid over his tongue and Wesley loved it. Their gazes connected, Lloyd watching his every reaction, just like he'd thought.

Like he'd wanted.

Lloyd slowly pushed in and out of his mouth, groaning deeply. The sound made Wesley's cock twitch. Lloyd pulled out and shifted down, dragging the wet tip of his cock over Wesley's torso. The damp line tickled.

Wesley arched against Lloyd as their cocks met and Lloyd locked their bodies together. Lloyd swallowed Wesley's pleading gasp, turning it into a wet, debauched kiss.

Against his ear: "There's so much I want to do to you."

"I should hope so after years of imagining us together."

Lloyd's lips curved into a soft smile, and Wesley's heart hammered between them. "Let me show you?"

Lloyd kissed him again, his thighs and stomach exploding

with goosebumps where they touched, their hard cocks gliding together with pre-come and lube.

Kisses peppered down his neck, over his collarbone to his pec.

"Wait. Do I have to lower my expectations due to your deficiency in creativity?"

"Wesley? Shut up."

Wesley grinned. "Make me—"

Lloyd grazed his nipple in time with a thrust that rubbed the sensitive tip of his cock along Lloyd's hard length.

Wesley grabbed a condom, tore it open, and slid it on Lloyd with an efficiency that had Lloyd raising a brow.

He added lube with a wink and a good couple of strokes. "Enough teasing."

Wesley locked his knees around Lloyd's hips and steered his mouth back to his. This kiss was frantic and demanding, their tongues twisted. Lloyd groaned against Wesley's lips and skated his prickly chin down Wesley's neck.

Wesley was so aroused he saw stars. He'd never needed to be fucked so badly in his life. Everything about Lloyd felt right. He was in control, firm. He was not shy. Wesley responded to each shift, comfortable and contentedly himself.

Wesley shifted until Lloyd's cock rubbed along the base of his balls and combed against his ass cheeks—

A door slammed. Voices sounded from the hall. Someone was upset.

Wesley's breath caught as Lloyd paused. He swore against Wesley's lips. He was the RA on duty.

Two more voices added to those outside, then came Gavin's distinct voice. Wesley threw his head back against the pillow in frustration. Of course, Lloyd would have to leave.

Wesley growled in disappointment, but Lloyd gripped Wesley's thigh, spreading his knee to the side. The tip of Lloyd's cock nudged the sensitive nerve-endings ringing his hole.

Wesley caught his breath, snapping his gaze to Lloyd.

Lloyd rubbed his lube-slick head over him again. He spoke, voice soft and clear. "Can you be quiet?"

Wesley nodded and bit his lip as Lloyd pushed inside him. They both struggled to resist groaning.

Lloyd smothered their lips together, drinking in Wesley's heavy breaths. "Oh, fuck. You feel good," Wesley whispered against raw lips.

Lloyd remained seated deep. He swiveled his hips and pumped Wesley's cock. Wesley clenched his ass and Lloyd's breath shuddered over his jaw.

In the background, Gavin was telling someone off. He bit out Lloyd's name in exasperation.

Lloyd pulled out—and slammed back into Wesley. The bed shifted with it and Wesley stretched his arms back to the wall, loving the bounce. Lloyd thrust in him repeatedly, stirring up an orgasm of epic proportion.

Lloyd watched him with hooded eyes, lips parted as he fucked Wesley. His cock rubbed deliciously inside him, at first slow and steady, and then faster. The chaos in the hall dissipated and Lloyd's fucking got messier. Needier. Their skin slapped together, and bursts of pleas bubbled over Wesley's lip. His cock throbbed.

"I take it back. Take it all back."

Their sexual chemistry was about to make him shatter.

Lloyd worked faster, shoving Wesley's knees to the side as he thrust his cock the way Wesley loved it most.

Wesley's whole body felt wrecked with teasing. He trembled on the edge of orgasm. "I love breaking rules with you."

Lloyd took Wesley's cock in hand and pumped him.

Wesley lost it. He wrung out a gasp, orgasm slamming into him in long rolling waves. Come hitting Lloyd over his stomach, that cleft . . .

Lloyd gave one final thrust and moaned Wesley's name as he came.

Pleasure continued to ripple through him. Lloyd pressed their sweat-laced bodies together and kissed Wesley hard.

Wesley massaged Lloyd's back and caught his breath against Lloyd's neck. He didn't want Lloyd to lift off him, but when Lloyd's cock slipped out, he reluctantly let go.

For the first time, Wesley was glad the bathroom was next door. Lloyd had barely snuck out of the room before he was back again, tenderly wiping a string of come off Wesley's stomach.

Wesley threw an arm over his face and swore into the crook. "I know I dragged you in here talking principles and how I was trying to have some. But."

Lloyd lifted Wesley's arm and kissed him.

"Now that I know it's like this?" Wesley said between Lloyd's kisses over his jaw. "Fuck me forever."

A knock came at the door, followed by his brother's voice. "Wes, I can hear you in there. Let me—"

Wesley whimpered. "No. Go home. Please."

"The busses don't run, and I don't want you driving me."

When Caleb jiggled the handle, Wesley groaned and rolled off his bed. He pulled on a pair of boxers and cracked open the door. "I'm busy."

"My things are in your room." Caleb forced his cowboy boot in the gap. A whoosh of air and hallway light punched over Wesley as the door lurched open.

"I said I'm busy."

Caleb stopped at the sight of Lloyd bunching a sheet at his waist. He slapped his hands over his eyes. "You said busy, not *getting* busy." He yelled frantically. "MacD?"

Steps approached his room. "What now, Hazelnut?"

"Can I sleep with you?"

MacDonald peered over Caleb's shoulder, her gaze quick and assessing. "Thank God," she said spiritedly. "Finally. Hallelujah."

Caleb removed his hands and glanced at her. "If you were that enthused, I'd have asked ages ago."

Wesley rolled his eyes, which was the kinder version of what MacDonald blasted at him.

"Keep this quiet, would you?" Wesley said, pushing the door until he was glaring at them from a two-inch gap. "Or I'll make my boyfriend go all Capricorn on your ass."

Caleb snorted. "It's hard to be afraid of your RA when he's naked. There's an idea. He should lounge around naked all the time."

Lloyd grunted. "Get out of here, Caleb!"

MacDonald grabbed him by his neck. Wesley winked at his brother. "I'll see to it."

You're the perfect Cap to my day.

Chapter Twenty-Two

Wesley returned from a morning shower refreshed and ready to get dirty with his boyfriend.

His boyfriend, who wasn't in Wesley's room where he had left him.

Wesley dropped his towel, yanked on his pants and a fresh T-shirt, and snuck to Lloyd's room. He wasn't there, either.

It was inhumanly early to be awake after last nights' bash, so finding a six-foot hunk shouldn't be this difficult.

Lloyd wasn't in the kitchen or the lounge, and he hadn't taken a random fancy to fixing the toilet again at four in the morning. Where had he gone?

A muffled "Idiot!" sounded from the stairwell.

Wesley approached the door and opened it.

Lloyd was dressed, his back to Wesley, addressing the stairs leading up to the fourth floor.

"I am aware I broke RA-resident rules, and I understand why these rules are in place. However, exceptional circumstances must be considered. I am in love with him."

The words reached deep into Wesley's chest, robbing him of

his next breath. Then he caught it sharply, unintentionally enlightening Lloyd to his presence.

Lloyd turned around.

Wesley tried to play it cool. He stepped up to the stair rail and lounged against it. He nodded to the stairs Lloyd had been talking to. "Stairs getting all up in your business, were they?"

Lloyd gave a self-deprecating laugh and rubbed a palm over his buzz of hair. "I was just . . ." With another laugh, Lloyd drew Wesley into him and brushed their lips together. "I love you, Wesley Hidaka."

Wesley kissed him, holding him tight as he poured all his feelings into his kiss. When they parted, catching their breaths, Wesley spoke to the stairs. "He means it. Give him whatever he asks for." He threaded their fingers. "Let's tell Gavin together."

They stared at the stairs, then with a squeeze of their hands, started up.

"By the way," Wesley said. "Why were you chastising yourself?"

Lloyd looked at him in confusion.

"You called yourself an idiot."

"Oh no," Lloyd said, pushing open the door to Gavin's floor. "That was my response to Gavin if he decides to rat on us."

"Good." Wesley halted him outside Gavin's room, lowering his voice. "We don't have to say anything. I can keep us a secret. It's only another three months."

∽

". . . AND IT'S ONLY ANOTHER THREE MONTHS," LLOYD SAID TO a sleepy Gavin who stood in his door wearing flannel button-up pajamas. "Then we're leaving Williamson. If you feel you need to report me, then do so. I don't want to get fired, but . . ." He looked at Wesley with adoration in his eyes. "I'd rather that than hide our relationship."

Wesley's heart felt as if it could burst. He linked their fingers.

"Let me get this straight," Gavin said tightly, drawing their attention back to his frowning face. "You guys just started a relationship?"

"Do you need us to kiss and prove it?" Wesley offered, already halfway to Lloyd's lips.

"No. I mean, you guys have *just started* a relationship?"

"Again. It's what we said." Lloyd pecked a kiss on Wesley's lips.

Wesley's eye caught movement behind Gavin. He eyed a suspiciously lumpy bed, and then a twitching hand dangling off the side of his bed.

Wesley bit his tongue, redirecting his attention to Gavin's frown.

"I thought you've been hiding it for months." Gavin looked at Wesley. "I thought your Cap-Gem bad-sex thing was a way to jokingly deny it." To Lloyd he said, "I was getting all up in your ass about this because I thought you were getting sloppy with your secret." He folded his arms, quite put out. "I didn't want you to be fired for it. I don't."

He stepped back into his room and picked up his leather binder. He pulled out a letter and handed it to Lloyd. "Our coordinator asked me to write a report, including one-sentence summaries on the current RAs."

Wesley read over Lloyd's arm, skipping to the part about his boyfriend.

"Woot! Lloyd does a serviceable job!"

"I'm not sure it warrants that much cheer," Lloyd grumbled, but he looked relieved.

"You're saying we could have been at it already an entire week?" Wesley said aghast. "Do you understand the torture I've endured?"

Lloyd winced. "I think he's saying we could have been at it the last two and a half years."

"I'm saying," Gavin enunciated. "My lips are sealed."

"Good," Lloyd said.

"Good," Wesley agreed.

"Good," Gavin finished.

Liberation jolting sparks between them, Wesley and Lloyd drifted toward the stairwell. They had almost reached it when Gavin barked after them. "I expect you'll help clean up. Some moron insisted on doubling-up the streamers."

∼

ONCE THEY WERE BACK ON THEIR FLOOR, WESLEY HAD A thought. Because it was morning. And certain traditions must be followed.

He slipped on footwear, grabbed a jacket, and dangled his work keys in front of the cubicle where Lloyd was fixing the toilet. "Want coffee?"

"Thought you'd never ask." Lloyd washed up and made a pit stop in his room.

He met Wesley in the hall with a messenger bag slung over his shoulder.

"I hope you're bringing that contraption with the misguided belief you'll need your wallet."

Lloyd raised his brow.

"All data-crunching fun can stay right there in your room."

Lloyd snorted. "Let's go."

Wesley let them into Me Gusta Robusta. It was two hours before it opened, so they had it to themselves.

Lloyd rested against the counter, his bag next to the till behind him. "It's different behind the counter."

Wesley left the coffee machine to wake up and slunk hot up against Lloyd, inching his feet between Lloyd's. "Boyfriend privilege."

Lloyd swept his hands through Wesley's hair and held the

back of his head as he delivered a shiver-inducing kiss. Wesley nuzzled closer and took a few more.

When they pulled back for breath, Lloyd rested his forehead against Wesley's. "Have I mentioned how much I like being your boyfriend?"

Wesley grinned. He felt so fucking light and fluttery. He stepped back to the coffee machine.

"Did you notice the moving lump in Gavin's bed?"

"I can't say I was paying attention to his bed."

"Oh. It was moving."

"And why does this interest me?"

"I'm ninety-nine percent sure that moving lump was Suzy. On account of the flower tattoo on her wrist."

That sparked Lloyd's interest. "No."

"I was this close to whipping out the term 'leverage' but remembered the last time I tried that and stopped myself. Growth."

Lloyd slipped his arms around Wesley's waist and kissed the curve of his neck.

The coffee machine stopped dripping its first throwaway run. Wesley pulled a cup off the stack and Lloyd stopped him. "Use this instead?"

From his messenger bag, he pulled out the stainless-steel cup Wesley had bought him for Christmas.

A laugh filling his entire body, Wesley used the cup and made Lloyd his favorite roast. When his boyfriend was busy sipping it, he climbed up the stepladder and removed the blackboard with *No RA business allowed on premises*. He wiped it clean and grabbed a piece of chalk.

"What are you writing?"

Wesley licked his lips that still tingled with Lloyd's kisses. "Best Cap in the world. Found right here, if you get what I'm talking about."

Lloyd let out a charmed snicker. "I don't know, you might have to explain that one to me."

Wesley dropped the chalk and yanked his boyfriend into a kiss. "Or I could show you."

"Repeatedly, I hope."

Wesley slid his fingers into Lloyd's belt, and Lloyd halted him. Wesley laughed. "You really do want to do it in a bed, don't you?"

Wesley pulled him toward the door, and Lloyd was right on his heels. "In sixty years, you'll thank me."

Love is a Brewtiful thing.

Epilogue

"How about he goes next to the bed?"

"How about the attic?"

Wesley glared at Lloyd. "The attic? No."

Lloyd side-eyed him as if to ask why the hell Wesley had to bring this one home.

Time for a toothy I-couldn't-help-it-and-you-love-me grin.

His boyfriend didn't budge. "I don't want him in the same room we fool around in."

"How about no fooling around at all?"

Lloyd paused mid-argument. "There's no way you could go a day without action."

That was true. Dammit. Wesley narrowed his eyes. "Why do you have to be so gifted with all your appendages?" Lloyd's lopsided grin had him wrapping his arms around his boyfriend and struggling to maintain a scowl. "How about we put him in the dining room?"

A chuckle danced over Wesley's cheekbone. "Laundry room."

Wesley growled in outrage against Lloyd's shoulder, nipping him at the collar of his shirt. "The entryway. Beside the cabinet your mom bought for us."

"The garden-slash-coffee-roasting shed."

"And have him catch Caleb and MacDonald at it?"

They both winced, remembering when that happened last summer after Caleb's first successful year at Treble. Wesley still maintained he needed therapy. He would never look at MacDonald's silver pendant the same way again.

"Okay," Lloyd relented, glancing at the bed, "even I wouldn't bestow that on him."

Wesley nuzzled against his boyfriend, nibbling small kisses up his throat. "I'm hungry. You want to cook us dinner tonight, Cap?"

"You're going to nail him against the wall when I leave, aren't you?"

"You can stay and watch if you like," Wesley said, rubbing his cheek over Lloyd's short stubble. "Or better, you can nail him while I watch."

Lloyd sighed, but there was an amused hitch in it. "You and watching."

"It really turns me on."

"How about we take him to the basement and you watch me there?"

Wesley pulled back an inch. "Can't. I spent the day filling it with all the equipment and furniture for my very own café."

Lloyd's laugh rumbled against Wesley's chest. "Your very own café. You love saying that every chance you get."

Wesley grinned. Thanks to MacDonald investing her thirty grand in his dream, he was two months out from opening his own place. "I still can't believe she believes in me."

"Why not?" Lloyd said between kisses. "You're a good investment. I venture to say the best."

"The best?" Wesley was totally fishing for more compliments.

Lloyd knew him well. He threaded his fingers into Wesley's hair and kissed him hard. "The flirtiest, the most fun, the—"

"Prettiest guy in the world?"

"Cutest guy in the world, and most creative."

Wesley melted into another kiss. "You're not so bad yourself."

Lloyd laughed. "Thank you, Wesley. You live up to the definition of romantic."

"I meant creatively. Like, the things you do to me on this bed." Wesley thrust against Lloyd.

"You want me to throw you onto the mattress, don't you?"

"And take me hard. After"—Wesley pointed to the bed and then across the room—"nailing him on that wall."

Lloyd still didn't budge.

Which meant it was time for Wesley to bring out the big guns.

He stripped and hunted down a suit in the closet. The one his mom had given him after he'd graduated. The only clothing Lloyd had never seen him wear.

He jiggled the coat hanger. "Nail him now and I'll put this on."

Lloyd picked up the nail and hammer.

As he nailed the black-and-white, half-naked print of Elvis against the wall, Wesley slipped into his suit. Quick and efficient, just like he had a thousand times before going to high school. He caught his reflection in the full-length mirror behind the door as he pushed up the tie. Ridiculous.

Lloyd finished and turned around. His gaze swept over Wesley. "I've been curious to see you dressed in a suit a long time."

Wesley glanced from Lloyd to Elvis behind him. The print looked out of place in this room. Lloyd pinched Wesley's navy tie, slid his fingers to the knot, and pried it open.

"Getting kinky, are we?" Wesley asked.

"No," Lloyd said softly, breath flittering over his lips. "I don't like it. It's not you."

Piece by piece, Lloyd stripped him until he was down to his tented boxers.

Wesley attacked Lloyd, shoving him to the wall next to Elvis. "I don't like it, either," he said and pulled down the poster. "I only want one person against this wall."

Wesley kissed his boyfriend deep and hard, then pulled back. "The one is you, by the way. You are the only one I want against this wall. And any wall."

Lloyd laughed.

"On any surface," Wesley continued. "The bed. The floor with the spongy carpet. The couch. The grass on my birthday showed how creative you're getting."

Tender hands cupped the sides of his face and a soft kiss touched his bottom lip. "I have another creative idea."

"Oh yeah?"

"Stop laughing. I haven't even suggested it yet."

"Okay. All serious here," Wesley said, grinning. "Give it to me."

"Role-playing."

Wesley swallowed a burst of laughter and waggled his brows. "I'm up for it. What do you want us to be? Nurse and patient? Rizzo and Kenickie? I still have that skirt."

Lloyd pulled Wesley tight against him and whispered in his ear. "How about fiancés?"

Wesley's stomach dropped and didn't stop. A nervous flutter leaked into his voice. "Fiancés?"

"What do you think?"

"Let's start now."

Lloyd touched his bottom lip, slowly leaning in. "As long as we only end at peak lavender season."

"Wait, what? End? Why would you want to end?"

At Lloyd's rumbling laugh, Wesley stopped. "Oh. You mean because then we'll have tied the knot. We'll be married. We'll be—"

Lloyd kissed him.

~ THE END ~

Acknowledgments

As always, thank you first to my wonderful husband for getting up at four in the morning to walk our baby around Berlin. Those walks were wonderful for chatting through scene ideas and for ducking into the bakery to write when the baby finally gave in to sleep.

Another crazy big thanks to Teresa Crawford, who helped me through my plot holes while vacationing in the States.
Cheers so much to Devil In The Details for working through a development edit with me.
Thanks to HJS Editing for copyediting. Your edits were amazing, as always. You have magic fingers!
Thanks to Labyrinth Bound Edits for catching all those pesky UKisms - no more dressing gowns in this one LOL!

Big thanks to Melanie Ting for sensitivity reading. I appreciate it!

Cheers to Natasha Snow for the cover art! Seriously, I know it was hard getting the right model this time—but I think you got the best Wesley we could!

For beautiful chapter graphics of Gemini and Capricorn, thanks go out to Maria Gandolfo.

Another thanks to Vicki and Todd for reading and offering valuable feedback, and to Sunne for always being the best at catching those inconsistencies. And, finally, a special thank you to Vir for your encouragement and for our mutual love of Buffy.

Anyta Sunday

HEART-STOPPING SLOW BURN

A bit about me: I'm a big, BIG fan of slow-burn romances. I love to read and write stories with characters who slowly fall in love.

Some of my favorite tropes to read and write are: Enemies to Lovers, Friends to Lovers, Clueless Guys, Bisexual, Pansexual, Demisexual, Oblivious MCs, Everyone (Else) Can See It, Slow Burn, Love Has No Boundaries.

I write a variety of stories, Contemporary MM Romances with a good dollop of angst, Contemporary lighthearted MM Romances, and even a splash of fantasy.
My books have been translated into German, Italian and French.

Contact: http://www.anytasunday.com/about-anyta/
Sign up for Anyta's newsletter and receive a free e-book:
http://www.anytasunday.com/newsletter-free-e-book/